FORTUNE HUNTER

JANA DELEON

Jana DeLeon

❀ Created with Vellum

MISS FORTUNE SERIES INFORMATION

If you've never read a Miss Fortune mystery, you can start with LOUISIANA LONGSHOT, the first book in the series. If you prefer to start with this book, here are a few things you need to know.

Fortune Redding – a CIA assassin with a price on her head from one of the world's most deadly arms dealers. Because her boss suspects that a leak at the CIA blew her cover, he sends her to hide out in Sinful, Louisiana, posing as his niece, a librarian and ex-beauty queen named Sandy-Sue Morrow.

Ida Belle and Gertie – served in the military in Vietnam as spies, but no one in the town is aware of that fact except Fortune and Deputy LeBlanc.

Sinful Ladies Society – local group founded by Ida Belle, Gertie, and deceased member Marge. In order to gain membership, women must never have married or if widowed, their husband must have been deceased for at least ten years.

Sinful Ladies Cough Syrup – sold as an herbal medicine in Sinful, which is dry, but it's actually moonshine manufactured by the Sinful Ladies Society.

FOREWORD

A catfish is a person who creates a false identity on social media and uses it to deceive others into online romances. The term was popularized by an MTV show by the same name, created by Yaniv "Nev" Schulman, who with his brother's assistance, made a documentary of the search for the true identity of his online girlfriend.

CHAPTER ONE

I OPENED my eyes long enough to glare at Ida Belle from my prone position on the couch, then shut them again and flopped over, turning my back to her. I heard her sigh.

"You can't stay on this couch forever," Ida Belle said. "The EPA is going to condemn it unless you get up and shower, at least. You've been wearing the same clothes for two days."

"Three," I mumbled, "but who's counting?"

"Gertie and me, for starters."

If I tried really hard, I knew I could force myself back to sleep, but I also knew that Ida Belle would still be there when I woke up. After the big showdown where Ahmad escaped again, and my breakup with Carter, Ida Belle and Gertie had alternated between checking in and giving me space, but now that five days had lapsed and I had yet to leave my house, they were starting to get bossy. I imagined it was only going to get worse from here, and there was a lot of summer left. I really didn't want to spend it pretending to sleep.

Adding to my general malaise was the fact that Ally's kitchen remodel was finally completed three days before and she'd moved back into her own home. I'd always known I would miss her cooking when she left, but I hadn't realized how much I'd grown to enjoy just having someone around for general complaining or to watch a late-night movie and have a beer. Unless Ida Belle and Gertie were there, the house sounded eerily quiet. Even Merlin had taken to spending more time sleeping outside and less time hounding me for cat treats.

"Fine," I said as I rolled over and sat upright.

Ida Belle sat on the end of the coffee table and gave me a critical eye. "You look like hell. When was the last time you ate?"

"When Gertie made me."

"That was yesterday afternoon. It's almost lunchtime. Aren't you hungry?"

I shrugged. "Maybe. I don't know."

Ida Belle's expression shifted from the slightly aggravated parental look to sympathetic. "I know this has been hard for you—dealing with things you're not used to. But as much as we both wish it weren't the case, the reality is you can't lie here on the couch and wish it all away."

I knew she was right, but somehow it didn't seem fair. I'd never experienced this kind of angst before, even when my mother died. I was devastated at losing her, of course, but I think both the finality of the situation and my young age factored into my ability to move forward. Although looking back, I wasn't completely sure I'd moved forward so much as I had stepped onto the path my father had carved and never once looked outside the lines to form my own thoughts about my life and future.

Now all those lines were blurred, and my future was a big dark blob of uncertainty.

I looked at Ida Belle, trying to decide whether I should say what I was thinking, especially as I thought it sounded weak. Before I could change my mind, I rushed into it. "As strange as this is going to sound to someone who knows the real me, falling for Carter is the riskiest thing I've ever done."

And it was something I knew I should have avoided. Getting involved with a local deputy when you're undercover and can't even reveal your true identity is always a bad idea. It becomes a disaster when you blow your cover and he realizes you've been lying the entire time.

I felt the tears well up in my eyes and struggled to keep them from falling. "I cried at a coffee commercial yesterday. Coffee! Do you have any idea how mortifying that is?"

"Oh, Fortune." Ida Belle reached over and put her hand on mine. "You know if I could fix this, I would."

I nodded. "Like my mother used to."

Ida Belle smiled. "You're the daughter I never had, but if you tell anyone I was that sentimental, I'll kill you. And you know I'm capable—at least, I'm capable if I shoot you from a distance. Hand to hand, you'd probably take me."

Because I knew she wanted me to, I forced a smile. "Under normal circumstances, I'm pretty hard to kill, but I suppose I'm at a disadvantage lying on the couch all day."

"Not to mention that a predator on four legs could probably smell you a mile away."

"It's not that bad, but I get your point."

Ida Belle rose from the coffee table. "Let's get you something to eat, then I'll root around in the laundry room and find you a pair of those yoga pants you like so much. A good meal and a shower will do you a world of good. You'll see."

I followed Ida Belle into the kitchen and plopped down at the table as she pulled leftover pot roast and potatoes from the refrigerator. She set a plate of it heating in the microwave and poured us both a glass of sweet tea. As the food heated, she wandered into the laundry room and came back out with yoga pants and a T-shirt and laid them across an empty chair. The microwave dinged and she pulled the plate out and shoved it in front of me, along with a hunk of French bread and a container of butter. She grabbed some cookies from the jar before taking a seat across from me.

Now that the food was in front of me and I could smell the enticing aroma of one of Gertie's signature dishes, I was starving. I picked up the fork and attacked the plate of food with more gusto than I would have thought possible when I was entrenched on the couch. Ida Belle gave me a pleased nod and bit into one of the cookies.

"These are great," she said. "One of Ally's new creations?"

"Toffee, chocolate, something or other," I said in between bites. "I predict she'll make a million."

Ida Belle took another bite. "I wouldn't bet against you. These are incredible. What a talent she has."

"She's awesome. Not just the food, but her, too, you know? She'll be great with customers when she opens her bakery."

"She will. I know she had to get back to her own house, but I almost wish she could have stayed here longer."

I shrugged. "It's probably easier this way, given the circumstances."

The circumstances being that Ally didn't know the real me and therefore couldn't know the truth behind why Carter and I had split. She was firmly committed to the idea that Carter was a stubborn man and would come to his senses. It had been tough coming up with a reason for our breakup, but I'd finally decided on a combination of two things—the first being my constant involvement in things I ought not to be involved in and the second, the biggie, being that I had no intention of remaining in Sinful when the summer was over. I pitched it as the smart thing to do before we got more attached. Ally, being the good friend and romantic that she was, still held out hope that Carter would get unstubborn and I would change my mind about staying.

"You're right," Ida Belle said. "Gertie or I would be happy to move in for a bit, or both of us, if you'd like."

I felt a tingling of warmth run across my skin and smiled for real this time. Having friends was also new to me, but I was not only getting used to people caring about me as a person, I was starting to like it. It brought back feelings I hadn't had since my mother was alive. Feelings I'd almost forgotten and never thought I'd have again.

"You know I appreciate the thought," I said, "but people would talk, and we don't have a decent cover story. You guys staying here after the hurricane was one thing, but if you set up residence here without some sort of emergency situation, everyone will take a closer look."

Ida Belle took another bite of her cookie. She knew everything I'd said was true, so there was no effort to argue. "People are already talking, you know," she said. "Carter's doing the honorable man thing and refuses to say anything to anyone, including his own mother, much to her dismay. But unless someone spreads a rumor, people will keep speculating until there's something more interesting to focus their attention on."

"Well, Sinful has had quite a crime wave since I arrived. Maybe someone will get murdered or blow something up."

"That's quite possible. And if we're lucky, it won't be someone we like."

I smiled. Ida Belle was nothing if not practical.

I was just about to suggest we start a list of potential casualties when the back door flew open and Gertie hurried inside, her face flushed. She flung her enormously large handbag onto the kitchen table and, I swear, the table dipped slightly to one side. I didn't even want to think about what she might have inside. She pulled out a chair and slumped into it, then panted for a bit. Ida Belle studied her old friend for several seconds, probably trying to figure out if Gertie needed CPR or a defibrillator. Finally, Gertie sucked in a big breath and let it out with a whoosh, then appeared to return to normal. The Gertie sort of normal, that is.

"What the heck is wrong with you?" Ida Belle asked.

"I was running," Gertie said.

"Was something chasing you?" Ida Belle asked.

"Not this time," Gertie said.

"What about last time?" I asked, curiosity overriding my general crappy mood.

Gertie waved a hand in dismissal. "Long story, ending with the destruction of a perfectly good pair of polyester pants, and a potential lawsuit. Anyway, that's not interesting, but what I have to tell you is."

"Well, get it out before you relapse," Ida Belle said.

Gertie sat up straight in her chair, her cheeks flushed with excitement...or exertion. Either way, her energy was somewhat infectious and I found myself leaning forward, waiting for her to spit out the news. A distraction was just what I needed.

"Remember when Beulah Latour dyed her hair black and started wearing a bra again, and I told you something was up?" Gertie asked.

"What you told me," Ida Belle said, "was that she must have a man somewhere, and given that I have known Beulah my entire life, I still contend no man worth his salt would come within fifty yards of her unless he was armed."

"I don't think I've met her," I said. "Is she scary?"

"If you'd met her, we would have heard about it, I'm sure," Ida Belle said. "Beulah is six foot two and looks like Arnold Schwarzenegger in drag. When she opens her mouth, you realize her looks are the pleasant part of her."

I cringed.

Gertie nodded. "I heard the nail salon uses a sander on her feet, and one time a toenail clipping hit the technician in the eye and scratched her cornea."

"So what did this bigfoot woman do?" I asked. "Pull the roof off a car? Eat a small child?"

"She got catfished!" Gertie gave us both a triumphant look.

I looked over at Ida Belle, but she didn't appear any more informed than I was. "Someone hit her with a catfish?" I ventured.

"No," Gertie said. "She got catfished...you know, like that TV show."

"Ah," Ida Belle said, "the one where silly people fall in love with strangers on the Internet, all of whom claim to be a prince or a model, but instead turn out to be some guy in cell-block four, scamming them out of cigarette money."

"You made me watch an episode of that," I said. "Those had to be the most obtuse people ever created. Who actually believes that Al Pacino is dating them online?"

Ida Belle raised an eyebrow. "Apparently Beulah Latour."

"Exactly," Gertie said. "This hot young stud claiming to be a marine stationed in the Middle East friended her on Facebook. Apparently, he sent her long letters and poetry and even a nude photo."

"Doesn't sound like anything worth putting a bra on for," Ida Belle said.

"Well," Gertie said, "in all fairness, that photo is probably the closest Beulah will ever get to male plumbing."

"Are you kidding?" I said. "The Internet is full of male plumbing. It's like the Walmart of man parts."

Ida Belle and Gertie both stared at me.

"Don't tell me you haven't clicked on a search result and gotten a surprise," I said.

Gertie's eyes widened. "Just the other day, I was thinking I would bake some pecan pies. I looked up my pecan supplier, Dee's Nuts, but forgot the apostrophe, and I got the most inappropriate image of a squirrel with oversized...er—"

"Yes, yes." Ida Belle waved a hand at her. "Enough about squirrel privates. Tell us about Beulah."

"According to the local gossip," Gertie said, "Beulah was over the moon for this guy. She even mailed him a pair of her underwear."

"If he was really a marine," Ida Belle said, "he could have used them as a parachute."

"Oh, even if I didn't know the rest of the story," Gertie said, "I'd know for sure he wasn't a marine, at least not one stationed overseas. You see, he had her send the underwear to a PO box in New Orleans."

"So he catfished her out of underwear," Ida Belle said, "which, given certain factors, could serve as a reason for life-long embarrassment—especially if the underwear is still around for Mardi Gras—but what in the world about that story had you running yourself into a heart attack?"

"If you'd stop interrupting," Gertie said, "I'd get to the part where he scammed her out of twenty thousand dollars."

"Holy crap!" I said. "It's a big jump from underwear to that kind of cash."

"How'd he do it?" Ida Belle asked.

"He told her he had leave coming and wanted to meet her in Italy and have a romantic week away. Then he gave her some story about wanting to book the perfect getaway but not being able to access his bank account where he was stationed."

"So she sent him the money." I shook my head. "I would say I can't believe it, but I stopped saying that my second day in Sinful."

"Well, I'll say it," Ida Belle said. "Beulah is no rocket scientist, but I never pegged her for an utter fool."

"Love makes you do strange things," Gertie said.

"It might some people," Ida Belle said. "But plenty of us have the good sense to know when we're being fed a line of bull from a man."

I frowned. Carter hadn't fed me a line of bull, but I'd definitely fed myself one, even if I wasn't aware I was doing it at the time. "Maybe she wanted to believe it so badly, she refused to see the truth," I said quietly.

Ida Belle and Gertie looked at each other, then Gertie nodded. "I'm afraid that's just the kind of emotion these people prey on."

"It's unfortunate," Ida Belle said, "but I imagine her money is long gone to some foreign bank account never to be seen again. How did she send it?"

"PayPal," Gertie said. "But that's not the only thing."

"What else did she have to send?" I asked. "Her left leg? A kidney?"

"No," Gertie said. "I mean, Beulah's not the only one. Myrtle said Bessy Thompson and Willa Maples were down at the sheriff's department this morning, demanding Carter find the scoundrel and get their money back."

"They all got taken by the same guy?" I asked.

Gertie shrugged. "The profiles were different, but really, it could be anyone, so that doesn't mean much."

"And all of them sent money?" Ida Belle asked, already shaking her head in anticipation of the answer she knew was forthcoming.

"Yep," Gertie said. "I don't know how much. Myrtle got interrupted for a bit because Old Man Marcantel's goat ate the lock on the jail cell they were keeping him in and started eating his way through a filing cabinet."

"Why was a goat in jail?" I asked.

Gertie waved a hand in dismissal. "The usual offenses. Anyway, my point is someone is scamming lonely Sinful women out of money." She clapped her hands. "We have a crime to investigate."

My automatic protest quivered on my lips, but for the first time since I'd arrived, I actually paused. In the past, I'd attempted, although somewhat halfheartedly, to avoid involvement in anything that law enforcement would be addressing because I had to be careful not to blow my cover. Since that cat had burst out of the bag, I had no reason to continue pretending to be a law-abiding librarian, at least as far as Carter was concerned. Which left me options I didn't have before.

Ida Belle and Gertie looked at me, expectant expressions on their faces. I knew they wanted me to toss my hat in the investigative ring—mostly to help bring me out of my current funk, but also because the two of them were physically and mentally incapable of not poking their nose into things.

"Why the hell not," I said.

CHAPTER TWO

"YAY!" Gertie cheered as Ida Belle broke into a grin.

Apparently, my pronouncement had scored big.

I held up one hand. "But...I have no idea where to even start. I've barely looked at Facebook and only have vague exposure to this whole catfish thing. You two are going to have to get all this going."

"Don't worry about that," Gertie said. "I've got it all figured out."

"Uh-oh," Ida Belle said.

Gertie shot her a dirty look then looked back at me. "I'm going to go fishing."

I frowned. "This is another metaphor, right?"

"I'm going fishing for a catfish," Gertie said triumphantly. "Get it?"

"And just what are you proposing to use as bait?" Ida Belle asked.

"Me, of course. That should be enough for any man," Gertie said.

Ida Belle snorted. "More than."

Gertie ignored her. "But since this isn't a regular romance

sort of situation, I'm going to need more than my natural beauty and charm, so I figured I'd use money to make it an even better deal."

"What money?" Ida Belle asked. "It's not like you're the Caesar of Sinful or something."

"I'm not going to actually send him money," Gertie said. "I just need to reel him in enough that he asks for money. Then maybe we can track him down."

"But how are you going to get him to notice you in the first place?" Ida Belle asked. "We don't know for sure that it's the same guy scamming all the women, and even if it is, we don't know how he's choosing them."

"He must live here," I said, "or be very familiar with the area. Enough to know the people. I mean, think about it, he's picked the perfect victims—lonely women with available cash. How could he do that if he didn't have insider knowledge?"

"Which makes it worse, not better," Ida Belle said. "Everyone in Sinful knows Gertie is a confirmed bachelorette, not to mention the fact that she has a decent retirement, but she's not rolling in it."

She had a point. Gertie already had a Facebook account. Assuming that whoever was catfishing Sinful women had prior knowledge of his victims, then chances were he already knew all about Gertie's lifestyle and her pocketbook.

"I can fix the money thing," Gertie said.

Ida Belle snorted. "If you know how to make money materialize, I wish you'd have let me know before now."

"I don't have to actually have the money," Gertie said. "He just has to think I have it. For instance, what if I put out a rumor that my great-aunt died and left me a fortune?"

"If you had a great-aunt who was still alive," Ida Belle said, "she'd be rich because of that alone, *and* in that Ripley's Believe It or Not thing."

"That could work," I said.

They both looked at me.

"Seriously," I said. "Louisiana is full of distant relatives and people with cash buried in their backyards, right? No one has questioned me being here and inheriting my supposed great-aunt's stuff. Why would they question Gertie if she said she had money coming?"

"They wouldn't," Ida Belle said. "The money is not the real problem. It's the part where Gertie all of a sudden decides to start man-hunting."

"I could pull it off," Gertie said. "I could do that whole thing where my spinster aunt's death made me look at my own life and rethink my choices. And one of those choices is men. So now I want to have a great romance before I die."

I sighed. It wasn't voluntary, but I may as well have screamed. Gertie and Ida Belle both went silent, staring at me with those concerned looks I'd seen so much lately. "I'm sorry," I said. "I don't want to derail the festivities."

"You can't keep holding everything in," Gertie said. "It's not healthy."

"She cried at a coffee commercial," Ida Belle said. "It's not all in."

"Oh, honey!" Gertie reached over and squeezed my hand. "It's going to be okay. You'll see. And something to take your mind off things is just what you need."

"I know you're right," I said. "It just doesn't feel like it at the moment."

That's what I said, but I wasn't sure if the words were to convince Ida Belle and Gertie that I would be fine or to convince myself.

I POPPED another cookie in my mouth and watched as Ida Belle stalked to the stairs and yelled up at Gertie for the fifth time in the past thirty minutes.

"If you don't hurry up," Ida Belle said, "all of us and the catfish are going to be dead and it's going to be a moot point."

"Hold your horses!" Gertie yelled back. "It takes time to look this sexy."

"Unless that time is the time-machine sort, you're wasting it."

I grinned. We'd been parked in Gertie's house for two hours now, first creating the perfect backdrops for her new Facebook profile picture and then settings for some casual shots that she wanted to post different days. The last hour, Ida Belle and I had been mooning around the kitchen while Gertie was upstairs, rendering herself into catfish bait. I couldn't wait to see what she came up with because I already knew it wouldn't be normal or even remotely age-appropriate.

Ida Belle stalked back into the kitchen and poured herself a glass of wine. "If she comes down in lingerie, I'm leaving. There are limits to what you should ask a best friend to help with."

I was just about to pop another cookie in my mouth, but I paused. Lingerie was something that hadn't crossed my mind, and now I was silently cursing Ida Belle for putting the image there.

"I thought she was supposed to look lonely, not desperate," I said, praying that if nightwear was involved, it was fuzzy pj's with cats on them.

Ida Belle sighed. "I'm convinced she has a funhouse mirror up there—you know, the kind where you see something completely different than everyone else unless they're standing behind you."

"It could be worse," I said. "She could be wearing flowered

dresses with lace trim like Celia. Nothing could be less character-appropriate."

Ida Belle and Gertie's archenemy was a particularly loathsome woman who had taken an instant disliking to me and was constantly trying to get me arrested for whatever crime had just transpired in Sinful. Any minute, I expected a knock on my door and Carter to be standing there accusing me of being the catfish. Unfortunately, as Celia was currently the mayor—although contested—she had the ability to wreak more havoc than before. We were praying the election audit overturned the results and she would be ousted soon, replaced by the other candidate, Ida Belle and Gertie's friend, Marie. Until then, however, Celia would continue her campaign to make life difficult for all three of us.

"There are no clothes that are character-appropriate for Celia," Ida Belle said, "unless you count those demon costumes at Halloween."

"We could get her some T-shirts made. They could say something like 'Butthole' and have an arrow pointing up."

Ida Belle stared at me for a couple seconds. "That's not a bad idea."

"We'd have to drug her to wear it, but it might be worth sacrificing an Ambien for."

Ida Belle glanced back at the stairs. "Not so loud. If you-know-who overhears, she'll be plotting a way to make it happen. Celia is enough trouble when we're not poking at her. I'd prefer to keep her at arm's length, at least until the election recount is over."

"If that recount doesn't come out in Marie's favor, you're in for four years of hell."

"If that happens, I predict an exodus bigger than the one Katrina caused," Ida Belle said. "People are very unhappy, including people who voted for her."

"Serves them right, but then as you always say, 'you can't fix stupid.'"

Ida Belle nodded. "If I could, I'd be the richest woman in the world."

"Ta-da!" Gertie sounded off behind us, and we both turned to look.

As Gertie's costumes went, it wasn't the worst I'd seen, but then I'd seen a lot. Her pants were fake black leather, fitted tight on the legs and low-slung on the hips. The hot-pink tank with gold-glittered skull and crossbones on it cut off just below her rib cage, leaving a strip of soft, undesirable white flesh in between. Her hair was teased out like an eighties stripper and her makeup was more suited to a heavy metal music video or Goth party than a senior lady supposedly lounging around her house. Red cowboy boots completed the look...because nothing says relaxing at home like footwear you need help taking off.

Ida Belle stared silently at her, and I wasn't sure if she didn't know what to say or was afraid that if she started, she wouldn't run out of things to say.

"What happened to the rest of your shirt?" she finally asked, apparently deciding to tackle one problem at a time.

"Nothing. This is how it's supposed to fit," Gertie said.

"Maybe if you're eighteen and built like an athlete," Ida Belle said.

"If I put on a longer shirt, then I won't be able to show off my tattoo," Gertie explained.

"Oh God," I mumbled. I *had* been locked up in my house for several days. Gertie could have gotten up to most anything in that amount of time.

Gertie spun around and pointed to a crooked set of swirling disk things on her lower back. "It's one of those temporary jobs—like Fortune and I used that time at the Swamp Bar."

Ida Belle stared in dismay. "Lord help. A tramp stamp."

"Don't worry," Gertie said. "It will wash off."

I grimaced. The tattoo that Gertie had provided me for our Swamp Bar excursion hadn't been nearly as temporary as she'd claimed it would be. At least this one wasn't on my body, and under normal circumstances, it would be covered up on Gertie's. That was, of course, assuming that the lovely town of Sinful got back around to normal any time soon.

"Let's get this over with," Ida Belle said. "I've got some work on my motorcycle to do. And some drinking. Definitely some drinking."

"Okay," Gertie said. "For the first shots, I want to be lounging in the living room. I'll put on some mood music."

She headed out of the kitchen, the tramp stamp tilting and swaying on her backside. A couple seconds later, the stereo fired up Metallica. Ida Belle shook her head and grabbed the camera then we both trailed into the living room. Ida Belle drew up short at the entry and I almost ran into her. I started to ask what was wrong, but then I peered around her and saw what had caused the quick stop. Gertie was in the recliner, but she wasn't sitting normally. She was cocked to one side, with one leg slung over the armrest and one arm thrown back over her head.

It was *Gone with the Wind*—the inappropriate senior version. I was just waiting for the "woe is me."

"I'm not taking a picture with you sitting like that," Ida Belle said, practically yelling to be heard over the music. "You look ridiculous."

"I do not," Gertie protested.

"This is supposed to be casual," Ida Belle said. "No one watches television that way except in the movies. Sit up right or slouch like a normal person, but this whole sex-kitten thing is not going to fly. Not only that, the outfit already goes against that lonely-old-woman thing. That pose might get your Facebook account banned for soliciting."

Gertie looked over at me, apparently wanting me to weigh in. Damn.

"I agree with most of what Ida Belle said," I said. I happened to watch television with my legs hanging over the side of the recliner, but I didn't see a good reason to mention that now.

Gertie slung her leg off the recliner and moved into a normal sitting position. "Party poopers."

Ida Belle lifted the camera and took a picture.

"I wasn't ready!" Gertie protested.

"I know," Ida Belle said. "That's why I took it. I don't want you posing."

Ida Belle took a couple more shots of Gertie sitting in the chair, some with her holding the remote and making an attempt to look forlorn. Then Gertie popped up from the chair.

"Now, let's take some girlfriend shots," Gertie said.

"What?" Ida Belle said. "No."

Panic coursed through me. "I can't." And then my automatic out hit me. "I can't risk having an image of me online. Ahmad's facial recognition software is as good as the CIA's. Maybe even better."

"Then it's me and you," Gertie said to Ida Belle. "Hand Fortune the camera."

Ida Belle glared at both of us and I motioned to the camera. "Come on. It's for a good cause."

Finally, Ida Belle relented and sat on the couch. I passed her the bowl of popcorn that we'd made for a prop earlier and popped the top on two beers.

"Let's see some smiles, ladies," I said and started snapping some shots.

Gertie gave me a big grin and held up her beer as if giving a toast. Ida Belle managed to almost not grimace, then downed half of her beer in a single swig. I took about ten shots, then Gertie called it done and declared we were moving into the kitchen for the next round.

"I thought we were done," Ida Belle groused to me on the way back to the kitchen.

I handed her the camera. "Apparently not."

"I heard that," Gertie said. "These pictures are that final hook that will snag the catfish. Everyone knows men love to eat, so pictures of me preparing baked goods should seal the deal."

As I was fond of Gertie's baked goods, I couldn't really argue with her in theory. The problem was the practice end of the equation. Gertie put on mittens, grabbed a pie off the counter and opened the oven.

"Wait," Gertie said. "I'm not in position yet." She bent over holding the pie. "Get one from behind. I want the tattoo in the shot."

"I'm not taking a picture of your butt," Ida Belle said. "And that is final."

I could see her point, but I also knew Gertie wasn't coming up from that oven or out of those clothes until we finished with the pictures. "Give me that," I said to Ida Belle.

She passed me the camera and leaned back against the kitchen counter, shaking her head. I moved behind Gertie at an angle where I could get both the tattoo and the pie and took some shots.

"Get a close-up of the tattoo," Gertie said.

It wasn't even worth arguing over, so I stepped closer and focused the camera on Gertie's back end.

"I knocked, but no one answered. The door was unlocked." Carter's voice sounded from the kitchen doorway.

I took a startled step backward, almost dropping the camera. Gertie jerked upright, but between the too-tight pants and her being bent over for longer than usual, she lost her balance and stumbled backward. I couldn't catch her or I'd drop the camera, so I did what any smart person would do and moved out of the way. She threw her hands up, trying to regain her balance, and the pie went soaring across the kitchen and directly at Carter.

Reflex made him try to catch it, but pies and Frisbees don't exactly perform in the same way. He managed to grab hold of the pie with one hand, but the pie tray bent in half and most of the pie continued its forward journey and smacked right into Carter's chest, scattering pieces of crust, filling, and meringue all over him.

Never one to miss a golden opportunity, I lifted the camera and took a picture.

"Nice," Ida Belle said and gave me an approving nod.

Carter stared at the three of us, and for the first time since I'd known him, his expression was impossible to read. If he had laughed, yelled, or arrested us, I wouldn't have been surprised by any of them. He stared for a bit longer, his hand and most of his shirt covered in pie, then finally he lifted his hand and ate a piece off his thumb.

"I'm going to use your bathroom," he said, "and then I need to talk to Fortune."

He whirled around and stalked out of the kitchen, bits of pie trailing behind him.

"He's going to arrest me for taking that picture, isn't he?" I asked.

"If he's going to arrest anyone," Ida Belle said, "it would be Gertie for assaulting him with a pie."

Gertie cast a sad gaze at the remnants of the dessert. "I was really looking forward to having that tonight with dinner."

"Stop worrying about dinner," Ida Belle said and elbowed her, then inclined her head toward me. Gertie looked momentarily confused, then her eyes widened as she put the "then I need to talk to Fortune" part of Carter's statement into perspective.

"I told you he'd come to his senses," Gertie said. "They always have to take a macho stance, but men are pushovers when it comes to the right woman."

Ida Belle frowned. "I don't think that's what this is about."

"I don't either," I said. "If he wanted to talk about something personal, he would have waited until I was at home alone."

Ida Belle nodded. "It's something else."

"But what?" Gertie asked. "Oh no! What if Ahmad didn't leave? What if Fortune is still in danger?"

"Harrison would have called me," I said. I pulled out my cell phone and groaned. Three missed calls from Harrison. No messages. "I forgot I put it on silent."

My CIA partner was my only contact with my old life, for my own protection. But his path had intersected with Carter's when we tried to take down Ahmad a week ago, and now that Carter knew my secret, Harrison knew he could contact Carter if it was an emergency. Not answering three phone calls over the span of two days probably counted as an emergency on Harrison's part.

"Harrison?" Ida Belle asked.

I nodded.

"Maybe he was checking in on you and is worried that you didn't answer," Gertie said. "It might not be anything serious."

I could hear the hope in Gertie's voice as she spoke and said a quick prayer that she was right. I heard the bathroom door open and braced myself. Whatever was going on, I was about to find out. Carter walked back into the kitchen and glanced at Ida Belle and Gertie.

"Let's give them some privacy," Ida Belle said.

"What?" Gertie asked. "Oh, yeah, of course."

"That's not necessary," Carter said. "She'll tell you everything as soon as I leave anyway, and that would only be necessary if she doesn't start yelling. Given what I'm about to say, yelling is a good possibility."

I stared at him. What the hell was going on? Was he going to tell me off for being a liar right here in front of Ida Belle and Gertie? Surely not. I knew my actions had hurt Carter, and my fooling him had probably caused him more than a little personal embarrassment, but I couldn't imagine him being so tactless.

He sighed. "I don't know if you've heard, but there's a guy on the Internet who's swindled some local ladies out of money."

Huh? This conversation had just gone a direction I'd never anticipated.

"You mean the catfish?" I asked.

"I don't follow," he said.

"The television show," Gertie said.

"Oh," Carter said. "I've seen an advertisement for that. Is that what they call the perpetrators? Catfish? I don't get the connection but yes, that's what this is about."

"Well," I said, "no one has swindled me out of money, so I don't see how I could help you on this one."

Carter shuffled his feet and stared at the floor for a moment, then looked back up at me. "Certain parties have suggested that you are the, uh, catfish."

I let out a string of curse words that ended with "Celia Arceneaux."

Carter's annoyed expression let me know I was right.

"Unbelievable," I said. "I was just thinking earlier that I was surprised you hadn't shown up at my door to accuse me of being the catfish, and here you are."

"For Christ's sake," Ida Belle said, "you can't possibly believe that Fortune is taking money from old women. What is wrong with you?"

Carter looked at Ida Belle and I could tell he was exhausted. "Of course I don't believe it, but unless Celia's election as mayor is overturned, I don't have a choice but to question Fortune when Celia makes an accusation. Not if I want to keep my job."

"This is bull and you know it," Ida Belle said, clearly not having any of it.

Ida Belle's face was flushed red. She was more than a little aggravated with Carter and wasn't about to cut him any slack, wounded ego and broken heart or no. Ida Belle was a soldier first and always. She would always side with protecting the mission and the agent. Collateral damage was an accepted part of the job, even if it was someone you liked.

Still, I couldn't blame him for his anger. Certainly, I had every reason to keep my cover a secret and if I had it to do all over again, I still wouldn't reveal my true identity to Carter. But if I had a do-over, I wouldn't get involved with him, either. That was 100 percent on me. I had let overwhelming, unfamiliar feelings lead me to choices I would never have made before I came to Sinful, and I was paying for them now. Unfortunately, so was Carter.

"It's not his fault," I said. "If he gives Celia a reason to fire him, then she wins. And that's exactly what she's hoping for. She doesn't think for a minute that I'm behind this."

"I just need something for my report," Carter said.

"Then I'll make this easy," I said. "Did any of these victims chat with this money-grubbing Romeo while I was in New Orleans handling that situation?"

He nodded. "Two of them had contact during that time frame."

"Then it's simple. Put in your report that I was in the custody of the police in New Orleans. It's not exactly a lie—the FBI and CIA are sort of police—and that should shut her up. Someone in police custody couldn't possibly have been chatting online."

"And what exactly should I say you were in custody for?"

"Jaywalking? Public intoxication? Walking naked down Bourbon Street?"

Gertie shook her head. "None of those would even get you a second look in New Orleans, much less arrested."

"Fine, then I picked a fight with two guys in a club and lit the bar on fire."

Gertie gave me an approving nod. "That sounds like a good time. I'm glad we were there with you."

Ida Belle, who had gone oddly quiet during our exchange and had been studying Carter, crossed her arms and cocked her head to one side. "I wonder why it is that Celia is the one making the accusation. Surely only a victim could accuse someone of a crime."

Carter stared at her for a moment, and that hesitation was all we needed to know the truth.

"I knew it!" Ida Belle said. "That stupid woman got taken by this guy."

"I never said that," Carter said.

"You didn't have to," Ida Belle said. "It all makes perfect sense now, and I have to say, pleases me to no end. In fact, it tickles me so much I can almost forgive you for coming here and questioning Fortune. Almost."

Carter's dismay was so apparent that I felt a little sorry for him. If Celia found out he'd let the cat out of the bag, she'd make his life miserable. And secrets in Sinful always seemed to find a way to surface.

"Don't worry," Gertie said, trying to reassure him. "We're not going to tell anyone. We're just going to have a bit of champagne with dinner is all."

I could tell he didn't buy that for a minute.

"Is that all you need from me?" I asked.

I knew I sounded terse. Based on the way Carter's eyes widened ever so slightly, I knew he thought so too. And while I could appreciate Ida Belle's delight at finding out their nemesis had been foolish enough to fall for the catfish, being in the same space with Carter was so uncomfortable that I was starting to feel my chest contract. I wasn't ready to see him, much less be this close. And I certainly wasn't ready to be accused of criminal activity simply because I was an outsider and a Yankee.

"Yeah, that's it," he said, then narrowed his eyes at us. "In case you've got any ideas, I'm telling the three of you right now, don't get in the middle of this."

"I'm sure we don't know what you're talking about," Gertie said.

"We're not interested in helping Celia," Ida Belle added.

"I mean it," he said. "If I even think that you're interfering with this case, I will arrest you and you'll all spend two weeks in jail while I take my time processing the paperwork."

He whirled around and stormed out of the house, slamming the front door shut behind him.

"What the hell was that about?" Gertie asked. "Carter has always been annoyed with us, but I've never seen him that angry."

"He's frustrated," Ida Belle said. "And hurt. When he was enamored with Fortune and they were doing the dance of romance, he intentionally glossed over things we did that he felt were harmless. My guess is that most of his anger back then was because he was afraid for our safety."

"And now that he knows we're not a bunch of helpless females, he feels played all over again," I said.

"Just because we've had the occasion to kill a person or two doesn't mean he has to get all belligerent," Gertie huffed.

"No," Ida Belle agreed. "He doesn't have to, but I suppose it makes him feel better."

"To hell with him," I said.

They both stared at me.

"Seriously," I said. "To hell with him. If he wants to stalk around all pissy because I was protecting my cover—something I'm sure he did himself while he was a marine—then he's welcome to it, but I don't have to watch. I'm sorry I had to lie to him and even sorrier that I hurt him in the process, but I'm not sorry *for* lying and if I had to do it all over, I'd do the same thing again."

"Of course," Ida Belle said. "We would expect nothing less."

Gertie nodded.

"Because I'm a professional," I said quietly.

A professional killer.

CHAPTER THREE

I WASN'T sure whether it was anger or heartache that had me refusing a ride home with Ida Belle, but suddenly, I felt like jogging. It was as though five days of pent-up energy needed to get out of my body before I exploded. So I set out of Gertie's house at a fast clip and jogged around the block twice before heading for Main Street. With Ally back in her own house, I needed to stock my kitchen with things I could handle. Basically, things that went in the microwave.

Gertie was good for a couple meals a week and Ally was always dropping by a dessert, but I couldn't depend on either of them to be my personal caterer. I was fairly certain Ida Belle lived on bread and cans of beans. She preferred simple and efficient to elaborate and time-consuming. I had spent my share of time living on only one or two items, but as long as Walter stocked a decent supply of microwave dinners at the General Store, I saw no reason to resort to peanut butter sandwiches every day.

The General Store was busy. A couple of the men I recognized as regulars from the café. They both nodded on their way out. Two of the women sang in the choir at church. There was a young woman with a baby in a stroller at the checkout counter that I didn't know and a woman with a man in a wheelchair picking out potato chips.

I gave the woman with the stroller another look.

Twenty-ish, five foot four, thin but poor muscle tone. The baby was a much bigger threat to someone like me.

I gave the couple in front of the potato chips a once-over.

Man in his late forties, hard to determine height in the chair but not tall, decent upper body, signaling he'd probably been in the chair for a while. No threat at all.

Woman in her midforties, five foot six, good muscle tone, no discernable threat.

I waved at Walter, who was in his usual spot behind the register, and grabbed a plastic shopping bin.

I'd selected a week's worth of frozen entrées and was just about to move on to snacks when I heard the bells jangle on the front door. A couple seconds later, Celia's voice sounded behind me.

"It should be a crime for you to stroll around loose in this town," she said.

The store went quiet, and I sighed before turning around. There wasn't a chance in hell she was talking to someone else. The last thing I was in the mood for was a stupid argument with Celia, but short of going the coward route and walking out of the store, it didn't appear I had a way out. She stood there in the center of the store, hands on her ample hips, her flowered dress hiked up unevenly on the right side. Her face was contorted in the usual scowl she wore when I came into her view.

"I see Deputy LeBlanc is shirking his responsibilities again," Celia said.

"Carter can't arrest someone without evidence," I said, "no matter how badly you want him to."

"I don't need evidence to know you're a lying, scheming outsider. Nothing bad ever happened in this town until you arrived."

"Same argument, different day," I said. "And I refuse to waste my time on logic with you. Here's the bottom line—I can't be the perpetrator because while the Internet Romeo was working his magic last week, I was in police custody in New Orleans."

"So you claim."

"So Carter *verified.* And trust me when I say, if I were going to pretend to be a secret online lover or whatever, the absolute last person in the world I would do that to is you. I don't have the imagination or the stomach to even look at you without wincing. If I said something nice to you, much less romantic, I'd cut my own tongue out with a butter knife."

The woman with the baby choked back a laugh and Walter grinned. Celia sucked in a breath and her face flushed with anger. She shot a dirty look toward the cash register, then glared at me. "You are a lying, thieving tramp, and if it's the last thing I ever do, I will see you run out of this town."

She whirled around, clearly intending to make her dramatic exit, but as she took one step forward, her shin connected with the footrest on the man's wheelchair and she went sprawling into a rack that held toiletries. The rack tipped over, sending a shower of shampoo and lotion down on top of her. One of the shampoo bottles tipped to the side on the rack, and a stream of shampoo trickled over the side and on top of Celia's head.

"Cleanup on aisle four," I said.

Celia scrambled around in the mess and finally managed to get to her feet. She gave the man in the wheelchair a dirty look, then stalked out the door.

"Nolan!" the woman with him said. "You did that on purpose."

The man in the wheelchair smiled. "Can't stand that woman. Simply odious."

The woman put her hand over her mouth, clearly torn between propriety and hilarity. Universal dislike for Celia must have won out because she lowered her hand, exposing the smile.

Walter hurried over. "Are you all right?" he asked Nolan. "You didn't get hit, did you?"

Nolan waved a hand in dismissal. "Perfectly fine. I'm afraid my little stunt made a bit of a mess, though. Put anything that was damaged on my bill."

"Nonsense," Walter said. "I'd have paid you to do it."

The woman stepped forward and stretched out her hand. "I'm Gail Bishop and this scoundrel is my husband, Nolan."

I shook her hand, then extended mine to her husband, who gave me a hearty shake with a firm grip. He grinned up at me. "I hope I didn't create more trouble for you. No doubt, she'll see it all as your fault."

"Don't worry about it," I said. "Blaming me for everything has become Celia's new pastime. Reality has never entered into her accusations."

Gail shook her head. "I think it's just shameful the way that woman treats people. What in the world were people thinking when they voted for her?"

"They weren't thinking," the woman with the stroller said. She extended her hand. "I'm Penelope Dugas, but everyone calls me Peaches."

Gail smiled. "On account of her sweet disposition."

Peaches grinned. "I've just got everyone fooled. Well, I better get home and make Brandon some dinner." She gave us a wave and headed out of the store.

"Let me help you clean this up," Gail said.

"Don't worry about it," Walter said. "I was planning on moving that shelf to the back wall anyway. Always figured someone would eventually knock it over. It was just good fortune that it was Celia."

"Then I guess we're ready to check out," Gail said. "I need to get this man some dinner as well."

They headed to the cash register, and I made my way around the mess and picked up a box of crackers and a bag of potato chips. I knew Ally would keep me supplied with sweets, but a box of cookies seemed to be calling to me, so I tossed those in as well. Gail and Nolan were just finishing checking out as I made my way back to the register.

"It was nice meeting you," she said. "I've heard a lot about you. Maybe one day we can have tea and chat."

"That would be nice," I managed, even though it sounded reasonably horrible.

Nolan winked at me and smiled. I couldn't help but smile back. His stunt with the wheelchair had seriously improved my afternoon.

I put my basket on the counter. "I also need two cases of diet Coke and one case of those flavored waters, blackberry if you have it."

Walter nodded. "Got a shipment in. You in your Jeep?"

"No. I was jogging, and shopping was an afterthought. I'll pick it up later."

"Don't worry about it. I can have Scooter run it over."

Scooter was Walter's right-hand man. He mostly took care of automobile maintenance and small repairs, but since that didn't keep him busy full time, he was always doing whatever odd job Walter needed done. He also had a crush on me, but it was the harmless sort, and I'd been careful to never encourage him.

Walter tallied up the items and put them on my account. Then he looked up at me and narrowed his eyes. "How are you doing?"

"Fine," I said, putting forth my best attempt at sounding perky.

He didn't buy it for a minute.

"Uh-huh. Well, if you need anything, you let me know. I mean it."

Because I knew he did, I smiled. If I were thirty or so years older or Walter were younger, I'd totally fall for him. Heck, I was a little in love with him already. He and Carter shared the same strong facial features that seemed to run in their family, and Walter's quiet way of looking after those he cared about was so endearing it was impossible not to love him. When I'd first arrived in Sinful, I wondered why he wasn't taken, but I'd soon found out that Walter had been helplessly and hopelessly in love with Ida Belle since they were kids.

"I appreciate it," I said.

He nodded and I headed out of the store, shaking my head. Ida Belle was one of the smartest women I'd ever met, but I couldn't help wondering if she'd missed the boat on this one. Surely, if there was ever a man that was a catch, it was Walter.

Like uncle, like nephew.

I frowned and pushed that thought out of my mind.

It had no place there.

I WAS HALFWAY home when I remembered Harrison's calls. I immediately stopped jogging and pulled out my cell phone. With all the Celia drama, I'd completely forgotten about the missed calls. My mind was seriously going to crap. I hoped it improved before I needed it for something important. I dialed

Harrison's number and started slowly walking toward my house.

"What the hell, Redding!" Harrison answered on the first ring. "I was about to send out the cavalry, or at least call that deputy of yours."

I couldn't help feeling guilty. Harrison was a great partner and a good person. He was also the only contact I had with my real life, and he was carrying a lot of weight around on his shoulders trying to get me back to normal status. He didn't need me unnecessarily adding to his worry.

"I'm sorry. I, uh...sorta took a break from everything."

The line went quiet and I knew he was processing not only my words but also my tone. One didn't become a CIA operative without excellent perception, and your partner usually knew you better than anyone.

"I take it things didn't go well once you returned to Sinful?" he asked quietly.

"No."

"I'm sorry to hear that."

I felt my chest constrict. He should be chastising me for getting involved with Carter in the first place, for blowing my cover, and for a million other things I'd done since I'd been here that I shouldn't have been involved in. But he hadn't said a word about any of it, and his simple and genuine expression of sympathy had almost undone me.

"Thanks. Is anything wrong?"

"No. I mean, nothing other than what you already know. An agent spotted Ahmad in Brazil, but he took a private charter out. We tracked it to Iraq, but our people there haven't picked up the trail yet."

"No more movement from his organization in New Orleans?"

"Not even a peep. Looks like they've all cleared out."

"How's Morrow doing?"

Director Morrow was my boss and had been injured in an intentional hit-and-run. We figured it was all part of an attempt to get to me.

"He's grouchy as hell, so that must mean he's better."

"I didn't think he could be any other way."

"Ha. Yeah, well, when you're around, that seems to be the case."

I knew I was a constant trial to Morrow, both professionally and personally. In his younger years, he'd worked with my father, one of the most respected assassins that the CIA had ever employed. After my father's death, Morrow had watched out for me as best as he could. I wasn't exactly the easy-to-watch type, nor was my job conducive to playing the protective role. And I didn't make it any simpler by breaking policy and risking my cover when I shouldn't have. But that was all water under the bridge. When I'd first come to Sinful, I was pretending to be someone I wasn't. Now I wasn't even sure I ever knew who I was.

"I have something to tell you," Harrison said.

I frowned. His tone was serious, but he'd just gotten through updating me on Ahmad and Morrow. "Okay. What is it?"

"When this situation with Ahmad is resolved, I'm transferring out."

I stopped in my tracks and clenched my phone. Never in a million years would I have guessed I'd hear those words coming out of Harrison's mouth. Something must be wrong. Harrison had wanted to be a CIA agent his entire life. He was completely devoted to his job, and he was great at it.

"Are you sick?" I asked, suddenly worried.

"No. I'm perfectly healthy, and I aim to stay that way."

"I don't understand..."

"You remember Cassidy?"

"The girl who lives in the apartment across from yours?"

I'd met her once when I was returning a scope I'd borrowed to Harrison. She was young, pretty, and friendly and was an emergency room nurse.

"Yeah, that's her," Harrison said. "The thing is, we've been hanging out some and I never thought I'd say this, but I really like her."

"That's great. Right?"

"It's great except for the part about what I do for a living. Look, the truth is, I never thought I was the settling-down kind of guy, but being with Cassidy feels right. I don't know how to explain it. It just is."

"But?"

"But then I went down to New Orleans. I saw how much you cared for that deputy, and how much he cared for you. But I also saw the strain between the two of you and I started thinking about the realities of our work. I don't think it's fair to get involved with someone and do the job we do. They would constantly be worried about us, and we'd constantly be worried about them. This situation with Ahmad shows how quickly everything can get personal. If you had family..."

He didn't have to finish his statement, because I knew exactly where he was going with it. If I'd had any living relatives, Ahmad would have gotten to them a long time ago trying to find me.

"We put those we love at risk," I said quietly.

"I can't do that to her. At first, I thought I could pull back and leave it alone...let whatever it was die out, but it's not that easy."

"No. It's not."

"I've been thinking about it for a long time, and seeing you and Carter in New Orleans made it all clear. I can have one life or the other, but not both. And as much as I love what I do, I can't love it and Cassidy both. It wouldn't be right."

"So what are you going to do?"

"Transfer to a different department. I don't want to leave the agency. Counterintelligence is what I know, but I want to start doing my part from an office in DC. But not until it's safe for you to return. I'm not about to leave you hanging. We've been through a lot together, and we're going to finish this together, too."

"I'm happy for you, Harrison. I mean that."

"Thanks." He was silent a few seconds, then said, "I know you're not in a good place right now, but I also know you'll come out of it all right. You always do."

I slipped my phone back into my pocket, overwhelmed and confused. Harrison's news had caught me by surprise, but then, it had probably caught him by surprise as well. He'd never been the romantic sort.

But he was normal.

I sighed. That was true enough. Harrison had two loving parents, a regular childhood with Little League and a Labrador retriever. He had college buddies he played poker with and was a regular at a pool bar down the street from his apartment. Even though he was dedicated to the job, he'd managed to have a life beyond it. Something I was just learning how to do.

And failing miserably.

CHAPTER FOUR

I'D JUST STEPPED into my driveway when I heard a car screech to a stop behind me. I turned around and saw Ida Belle gesturing from the passenger seat of Gertie's ancient Cadillac. "Hurry up," she said.

I had no idea what I was hurrying for, but since it didn't involve sitting alone in my quiet house, I figured what the hell. I climbed into the car and Gertie set off down the street. Two casserole dishes sat on the backseat next to me, so I figured we were on some sort of charitable mission.

"Who's the food for?" I asked, hoping one for was whoever was ill and the other might be for me. I loved Gertie's casseroles.

"We've had a bit of luck," Ida Belle said. "Beulah has agreed to talk to us about the catfish."

"Did you bribe her with a casserole?" I asked. As far as bribes went, it was a fairly decent one.

"We didn't have to," Gertie said. "She said if we could prevent this from happening to another woman, then she was willing to tell her story, however embarrassing it might be. The casserole is because I feel sorry for her and Beulah likes to eat."

"And the second casserole?" I asked, still hoping.

"Backup plan," Gertie said. "Just in case."

"In case of what?"

Ida Belle shook her head. "No need to worry about that unless it happens. Let's just concentrate on learning everything we can from Beulah."

I didn't much like the sound of that, but once Ida Belle's lips were sealed, I knew there was no getting information out of her. I watched as we headed out of the subdivision and down one of the farm roads about half a mile. Gertie turned onto a long gravel drive with a small white farmhouse at the end and pulled slowly down the bumpy path. The house had blue shutters and huge rosebushes out front. It looked fresh and pleasant.

"This is pretty," I said, admiring how the giant oak trees behind the house created a backdrop of green.

Gertie nodded. "Beulah's daddy built the house. He was an excellent carpenter. He built the Baptist church as well. If those silly Catholics had allowed him to build their church, the place wouldn't have so many issues."

"I take it he was Baptist?" I asked.

"Worse," Ida Belle said. "Atheist. Said he'd believe in a higher being when one stepped down from a cloud and had a beer and a chat with him."

"That must have endeared him to the local population," I said.

"It was practically scandalous at the time," Ida Belle continued, "but that didn't stop Donald Sr. from hiring him to build the new church. That's Pastor Don's father."

Pastor Don was the current preacher. He was an earnest but boring man who managed to make even an interesting topic sound as if he were reciting from a law journal. I did a lot of dozing in church.

Gertie nodded. "Pastor Don Sr. said the congregation deserved the best, and if the Lord saw fit to change a soul or two while the church was being built, then that would be a fine thing."

"So he thought building a church would make Beulah's father have a conversion?" I asked.

"Oh, I don't think he thought anything of the sort," Gertie said as she pulled to a stop in front of the house. "But that's the way he sold it to the building committee. Don Sr. knew Beulah's father was the best carpenter in the parish. He didn't care what the man believed in as long as he built a church that would last."

"And last it has," Ida Belle said. "Made it through every hurricane with only minimal damage."

Since I'd recently spent time holed up in the church during a hurricane, I could personally attest to the strength of the building. Don Sr. had made a good choice in carpenters. I climbed out of the car, snagging one of the casseroles as I went. "So did Beulah's father ever end up converting?"

"Not exactly," Gertie said. "He never stepped foot in church again once it was built, but he starting dropping Beulah off every Sunday for children's church."

"You said Beulah never married, right?" I asked. "So how come she's not a Sinful Lady?"

"When she turned forty and still hadn't attached herself to a man," Ida Belle said, "we extended an invitation, but she never accepted."

"Why not?"

Gertie lowered her voice as we stepped onto the porch. "I think she was still hoping. Beulah was a sad little girl. Her mother died when she was eight; her father was a good man but one of those strong, silent types. She was a large child and not a pretty one, so the other children made fun of her. She didn't have friends, and there was no family nearby. I think she's been lonely most of her life."

"Making her the perfect target for the catfish," I said.

"I'm afraid so," Ida Belle agreed as she opened the screen door and knocked on the blue wooden entry door.

I heard rustling inside and a couple seconds later, the door opened and an enormous woman peered out.

Midfifties, six foot two, three hundred twenty pounds, could probably bench-press a car. If she could catch you, she'd snap you in two like a twig.

I glanced over at Ida Belle. She hadn't been joking. If Beulah put on some men's clothes, cut her hair short, and took off the makeup, she could pass for Schwarzenegger's younger brother. It wasn't the best look on a man. It was even worse on a woman.

"Hello, Beulah," Gertie said. "We've brought our friend Fortune with us. She's younger and more up-to-date on certain things. I hope you don't mind."

Beulah barely glanced at me before pulling the door open and motioning for us to come inside. Her eyes and nose were red from crying, and she shuffled into the living room as though all the energy had been sapped out of her. She plopped down on a recliner that had seen its better days and I heard it creak in protest. Ida Belle and Gertie took seats on the couch next to the recliner, and I sat on an ugly antique-looking chair that turned out to be just as uncomfortable as it appeared.

I looked over at Gertie and Ida Belle, who were both studying Beulah, and waited for Gertie to get things going. She was the more emotional of the two. Ida Belle would perk up when we got down to business, but Gertie would get the lonely hearts ball rolling.

"I brought you a chicken casserole," Gertie said as I put the dish on the coffee table. "I remember it's your favorite."

Good job, leading with food.

"Thank you," Beulah said. "I haven't felt much like cooking. Haven't felt like doing anything, if I'm being truthful."

"Perfectly understandable," Gertie said. "You're having a bad time of it, not to mention a nasty shock."

Beulah nodded. "Yes. It all came as such a huge surprise to me...I still can hardly believe that people do this sort of thing. And for what? I suppose they have their bit of fun at others' expense."

"Oh, I wouldn't think it was fun," Ida Belle said. "I'd say some of the unscrupulous and lazy have made it their profession. A lot easier than learning a trade and working eight hours a day."

"It's evil is what it is," Beulah said. "Playing with people's feelings. Making them promises and getting them to believe that their life is going to be that dream they always had."

I held in a sigh. Ida Belle and Gertie had been right. Beulah had been carrying the torch for a big romance. Unfortunately, the torch had burned her badly.

"It's a despicable thing for one person to do to another," Gertie agreed. "I'm so very sorry that you got caught up in this."

Beulah flushed. "I should have known better. No man has ever been interested in me. Why in the world did I believe that someone younger and so very handsome would want anything to do with someone like me? I'm a fool."

"You're not a fool," Gertie said. "You just come from different stock than other people. In Sinful, we tend to take things at face value. It's speaks to your character that you didn't suspect the man of nefarious business. It's simply not in your makeup to do such things, so you don't expect others to do them, either."

I was impressed that Gertie managed to deliver that nice little speech with a straight face. Anyone taking things at face value in Sinful was just asking for trouble. Since I'd arrived in town, I'd had the hardest time trying to figure out which end was up, and that was saying a lot given my profession.

Beulah must have bought it, because she gave Gertie a grateful look. "I appreciate your kindness. I know I'm not always the most pleasant person to deal with. You and Ida Belle are saints for offering to help."

"Are you going to be all right?" Ida Belle asked. "Financially, I mean?"

"Yes," Beulah said. "Things will be a bit tight for a while, and I'm praying that the air-conditioning and the roof hold out for another year, but I won't have to sell the house or anything like that."

"That's good," Ida Belle said. "Are you ready to talk about what happened?"

Beulah nodded. "Might as well get it over with. I don't know that I can be more embarrassed than I already am, and I haven't died from it so far."

"Then start at the beginning," Ida Belle said.

Beulah took a deep breath in and blew it out, then began. "It all started with Facebook. Maryanne said as how I should make an account so that I could see what was going on with my friends and family and such. I couldn't see the point at first. I only have extended family left and haven't had dealings with them for years. I probably wouldn't know most of them if they knocked on my door. My friends are right here in Sinful, and I already know what their lives consist of because I see it firsthand. And quite frankly, no one's life is so interesting that

I think they ought to be taking the time to write it up and post it online."

From Beulah's perspective, I could see her point. My minimal exposure to Facebook had been random pictures of people's meals, a lot of ranting, and odd pictures of people with their lips stuck out and cheeks pulled in like they'd eaten something sour. On the other hand, if Ida Belle and Gertie wrote up their daily lives and posted it online, they'd either be arrested or carted away to the loony bin. I was voting on the latter. No one would buy the truth.

"But Maryanne kept insisting," Beulah continued, "saying as how I could meet people in groups online...groups for growing roses and cooking and the like. I do enjoy a good discussion on hybridization, and I'm always looking for a new take on an old recipe, so I finally gave in and set up an account."

"And was it everything Maryanne said it would be?" I asked.

Beulah stared at me for a moment and blinked, like she was trying to remember who I was and why I was there. "Just curious," I explained. "Gertie keeps trying to convince me to set up an account, but I'm more or less in the same position you are with family and friends."

"I suppose what Maryanne said was true," Beulah said. "I found a few groups of flower gardeners, one in particular that had a horticulturalist in it that was very knowledgeable. She provided me with several tips that worked well."

Beulah frowned. "And then Thorne joined the group."

"Thorne?" I asked.

Beulah's expression shifted from frown to disgust. "Thorne Thompson. The man who stole my heart and my money."

"His name was Thorne?" I asked. What the heck kind of name was that?

Beulah nodded. “He said his mother was a fan of some soap opera that had a character by that name. I thought it ironic, him being in a rose gardening group and being named Thorne. He even made a joke about it.”

“How old is Thorne?” Gertie asked. “Or I guess I should say, how old did he claim to be?”

“He said he was thirty-eight,” Beulah said.

“And that didn’t seem strange?” Ida Belle asked. “A relatively young man, stationed overseas with the military, showing up in a group that I can only imagine was predominantly composed of older women?”

“It did at first,” Beulah said, “but he had an explanation for everything. He said his mother was a big gardener and had lovely roses. But her eyesight was failing and she couldn’t see the computer screen well anymore. So he said he’d find her the information she needed and relay it to her during his weekly phone call.”

I glanced over at Ida Belle, who looked completely disgusted. I agreed with her. The catfish had created the perfect man—younger, presumably good-looking, and dedicated to his aging mother. It would be a hard combination for an any older single woman to resist, much less someone like Beulah, who’d been alone most of her life. It was insidious and cruel, and suddenly, more than anything, I wanted to see whoever had done this pay.

“I won’t go into all the details,” Beulah said. “I can’t stomach it right now. Maybe not ever. Thorne chatted with the group a bit most days, asking questions about hybridization. Then one day he sent me a private message, complimenting me on a picture I’d posted of my purple-and-white hybrids, and asking me how I’d managed the color combination.”

Beulah sniffed and rubbed her nose with her finger.

"That's how it all started. The message turned into a conversation and pretty soon we were talking for hours every day. Roses gave way to discussions of our personal lives. He told me about being stationed in Iraq and the hardships our soldiers had to face every day. It was disheartening to hear how bad things were. I felt sorry for Thorne, living that way."

"Of course you did," Gertie said. "Any decent person would."

"I suppose that's what he wanted," Beulah said. "Just to get my money."

"When did he ask for the money?" I asked.

"Not right away, of course," Beulah said. "We'd been talking every day for six months or so before he even hinted at marriage. Of course, I didn't take him seriously, but he kept insisting and finally, I believed him. Or maybe I didn't. But I wanted to bad enough to send the money."

"Then what happened?" Ida Belle asked.

"I went online the next morning, as usual, and tried to send Thorne a message but his account was gone. I thought at first it was a mistake...that Facebook had accidentally removed his account. So I sent an email to the address he'd given me for PayPal."

Ida Belle shook her head. "But he never answered."

"No. That was two weeks ago. At first, I didn't want to report it. I thought what if he'd died in combat? But then who would have deleted his account? Once I finally faced the fact that I'd been snookered, I knew I should go to the police, but I was so ashamed. It took me another week to work up the courage to report it."

"There is nothing for you to be ashamed about," Gertie said. "That criminal is the one who should be ashamed. There's a hotter place in hell for people like him."

"I certainly hope you're right," Beulah agreed, "but if it's all the same to God, I'd like to see him pay here on earth first."

"I don't blame you," I said. "Do you have any pictures of Thorne?"

Beulah nodded. "I downloaded them to my desktop. I'd made this montage with one of those picture softwares." She sighed. "More things to be embarrassed about."

"Any information you have will be helpful," Ida Belle said, "even if you think it might not be true. Mailing address, email, Facebook account name."

"And any proper names he mentioned," I said. "Like cities, people, schools, churches."

I was in Sinful pretending to be someone else, but I'd still asked people to call me by the name I usually responded to. I claimed it was a nickname, and so far no one had questioned it. Even when people were lying, sometimes the truth slipped into their conversations.

"I typed it all up after I talked to Ida Belle," Beulah said. "I know it's a lot to ask, getting you involved with such things, but I can't help but think you'll have a better go at it than Carter. He's a great deputy, but he's a man. This is women sort of business."

What she meant was that ferreting out the catfish was better done by conniving, sneaky females than an average male. I had to agree with her on that one. Not just because Ida Belle and Gertie could get the truth out of a death row inmate, but because the victims were exclusively women, and they were far more likely to give details to other women. They would probably skimp on specifics when talking to Carter.

Beulah rose from her chair and came back a couple minutes later with her laptop. "I have everything in one folder. Who do you want me to send it to?"

"Email it to me," Ida Belle said. "We'll take a look at it tonight and let you know what we figure out."

Beulah tapped on the keyboard, then closed the laptop. "I can't tell you how much I appreciate this. I'm okay without the money, but it's not right. He already broke my heart. I don't see any good reason why he should cripple my savings account, too."

"He shouldn't," Ida Belle said. "And if there's anything we can do about it, rest assured, we will."

We all rose from our chairs and Gertie gave Beulah an awkward hug. Awkward, mostly because with the height difference, Gertie's face was pressed right in the middle of Beulah's breasts. I opted for a handshake and we headed out the front door.

And right into Carter.

CHAPTER FIVE

When he locked in on the three of us exiting Beulah's house, Carter's expression registered surprise at first, then quickly shifted to aggravation. He marched up the front steps and glared at us.

"I told you to stay out of this," he chided.

"And we are," Ida Belle said.

"Then what are you doing here?" he asked. "You're not friends with Beulah."

Gertie put her hands on her hips. "You have become downright insufferable. Since when do I have to be bosom buddies with an ill person in order to bring them a casserole? I have another in the car for Herbert Myer who had his hemorrhoids out. Anything you want to accuse us of with him?"

He raised an eyebrow. "I'm supposed to believe Beulah is ill?"

"She's heartsick and depressed," Gertie said. "In my book, that counts as much as having something yanked out of your butt."

"Not in mine," Carter said.

"Well, I don't really care about your book." Beulah's voice

sounded behind us. "These women brought me a casserole and chatted with me about roses to help take my mind off things. Shame on you for giving them grief over it. I thought your mother raised you with a better sense of charity than that."

Carter's dismay was apparent. Nothing was worse for a Southern man than being accused of not living up to the standard his mother raised him by, especially when his mother was well-respected and liked by everyone in town. "I apologize, Ms. Latour, but these ladies have been known to meddle in police business, and that's against the law."

"There's no lawbreaking going on here," Beulah said. "If you need something from me, I suggest you get inside and get to it. I'm going to pop that casserole in the oven, and when it's done, I'll expect you to be gone so I can sit in my recliner and watch *Justified*...unless that's against the law now."

Beulah turned around and went back inside, the screen door slamming shut behind her. We headed down the steps and jumped in Gertie's car. Carter turned around and frowned at us before he stepped inside Beulah's house.

"He didn't buy a word of that," I said as Gertie pulled away from the house.

"Doesn't matter what he thinks," Ida Belle said. "Only what he can prove, and Beulah's not telling."

"So what's the plan?" I asked.

"Well, now that Gertie shot off her mouth about that extra casserole," Ida Belle said, "we're going to have to take it to Herbert because Carter is sure to check."

"Ah," I said. "Backup plan."

Ida Belle nodded. "I figure you don't much care to hear about the old coot's butt, so we'll drop you off and you can get started on the Internet part of the investigation. I'll forward Beulah's email to you."

"Sounds good," I said, relieved that I was going to be left out of the hind end part of the afternoon.

Gertie dropped me off at my house, and I headed into the kitchen and fired up my laptop. Ida Belle had forwarded the files from Beulah, so I downloaded the information and got up to grab something to drink and a snack. All this activity had made me hungry, or maybe it was so much talk about casseroles and knowing I wasn't getting one.

I had just finished making up a sandwich when I heard a knock on my door. I stiffened for a moment, then relaxed. It wasn't loud, angry rapping, so it probably wasn't Carter. I opened the front door to find Walter standing there with a big box.

"My delivery," I said. "I'd completely forgotten."

I stood back to let him in, then grabbed the case of water that was next to the front door and followed Walter to the kitchen. He sat the box on the kitchen counter, then went back for the soda that had been sitting next to the water.

"How come Scooter isn't delivering?" I asked.

"He's working the cash register," Walter said. "I needed to get out for a bit. Sometimes sitting there behind that counter, listening to all the locals squawk about their ailments and family problems, can wear on you."

"It would wear on me after about five minutes."

Walter laughed. "Yeah, you're not exactly what I'd consider a people person."

"Especially by Southern standards, since I don't cook."

He nodded. "Hard to bring food to the ailing when all you have is microwave dinners. Still, some of them aren't too bad. I like to grill some, but I'm not a fan of cooking for the sake of the activity. More for the sake of eating."

"I can drink to that. Speaking of which, would you like a

beer? I brought some back from New Orleans. I'm fully stocked."

"Can't say as I would turn one down."

I grabbed a couple of beers from the refrigerator and passed one to Walter, who took a seat at the kitchen table. I uncovered the plate of cookies and sat it in the middle. "Bet you can't stop at one," I said, and pointed at the plate.

Walter picked up a cookie and took a bite. "Good Lord! That's one of the best things I've ever eaten."

"Ally."

"The girl's got a gift. If she packaged these, I would sell out in a matter of minutes."

I nodded and took a bite of a cookie. The sandwich could wait.

Walter took a sip of his beer and studied me with a pensive look. A look that said he wanted to say something but wasn't sure that he should. Because I liked Walter and respected him, I actually didn't mind hearing anything he had to say, so I decided to make it easy on him.

"Any other reason you made the delivery?" I asked. "You look like a man who has something on his mind."

"Yeah, I guess I do. You're a sharp one, Fortune. I knew it from the first moment I met you. When you took up with Ida Belle and Gertie, I thought, Lord help that poor pretty thing. She has no idea what she's getting into." He narrowed his eyes at me. "But nothing they dragged you into seemed to faze you, so then I thought, maybe the girl's made of tougher stuff than her mother alluded to."

"My mother?" I felt a bit of panic rise in me. The real Sandy-Sue's mother had never lived in Sinful and had only visited a handful of times decades ago, and never after Sandy-Sue was born. That was one of the reasons Director Morrow had thought this plan would work. No one knew Sandy-Sue, therefore no one could insist I wasn't her.

"Yep. Ophelia was a pushy woman, but then I don't suppose I'm telling you anything you don't already know."

He stared at me, and once again, the huge feeling of unease spread throughout my body. "No. I guess not," I said.

"Came here to visit Marge when she was twenty or so... before she met your father. I was the young local catch back then, much like my nephew is now."

I smiled. "I can see that."

"Yes, well, Ophelia took a liking to me and I took to avoiding her. I had no interest in the woman. She was pleasant, but we both know pleasant isn't exactly what does it for me."

He winked at me and I laughed. "No. The last word I'd use to describe Ida Belle is pleasant."

"It's that fire that gets me. Strength and intelligence. Those are the sexiest things a woman can wear, so to speak."

He blushed when delivering the "sexiest" part of the statement and I was charmed by him all over again. What the hell was Ida Belle thinking not marrying him? One of these days, I was going to pin her down and make her explain it to me.

"Anyway," Walter continued, "summer finally ended, and Ophelia headed back north to finish college and met the man she would marry."

"So you were off the hook."

"On paper, it would seem that way, but that wedding band didn't stop her from trying a bit more. She'd send me a letter now and then, talking about how unhappy she was and how her husband wasn't at all the person she'd thought he would be."

"That's sorta mean," I said.

Walter nodded. "I figure she married him because he was

going to be a good provider. Her parents had insisted on college, but I don't think Ophelia was interested in being a career woman. I think she wanted to sit inside all day and figure out ways to control other people's lives. Like her only child's."

"Sounds right," I said. It was a logical guess that Sandy-Sue had been overrun by her domineering mother just as I had been overshadowed by my hyper-successful father.

"She used to send pictures," Walter said. "Pictures of her at the beach or sitting on the back porch next to her rosebushes. Then you came along. She stopped sending pictures of herself and started sending pictures of you...I got the last one ten years ago."

I felt the blood rush out of my face. "Oh."

"The thing is, I hadn't thought much about it, but when I saw how you reacted to the messes you got into with Ida Belle and Gertie, it just didn't gel with Ophelia's complaining about having to push her daughter to do things. I think the phrase she used was 'shrinking violet.' So a couple weeks ago, I dug up those old letters and took out the photos."

I looked down at the table, unable to look him in the eyes. I knew what was coming, and I had no earthly idea what I was supposed to say.

"I know you're not Sandy-Sue," Walter said. "Known it for a while."

I sighed and looked up at him.

"I'm not looking for confirmation," he said, "and I damned sure don't want an explanation."

I frowned. "Why not?"

"Because I figure it's better on both of us if I'm left in the dark with my own suspicions. If I thought you were some sort of con woman, I'd have handled things differently, but that doesn't fit. And if you were in witness protection, you would have done a better job of lying low. My best guess is some sort of law enforcement or military. I don't know why you're here or why you're pretending to be someone you're not, and I don't want to know. I'm just going to assume that there's a good reason and hope everything works out for the best for you."

"There's a good reason," I said quietly.

Walter studied me for several seconds, then nodded. "I like you, Fortune. Have from the first time I met you—roped into going to Number Two with the meddling twosome. It was clear then that you weren't a people person, but your sense of justice had been outraged and it wouldn't let you hide out like you were supposed to."

"My desire for fair and equitable has always been a problem."

"I bet it has." Walter took a drink of his beer and set it down on the table. "I'm also figuring that whatever secret you're hiding, Carter finally figured it out, and that's why the two of you aren't an item anymore."

I opened my mouth to speak, but didn't know what to say. Walter might like me, but Carter was family. I'd lied to his nephew the same way I'd lied to everyone else, but Carter had feelings for me that no one else did, which made it far worse.

"You don't have to say anything," Walter said. "I can see it in that stricken look on your face. I'm sorry it worked itself out that way, but I can't say that I'm surprised. If I'd thought Carter was going to get hung up on you that quickly, I might have said something. Or maybe I wouldn't have. A young man rarely listens to what an old man has to say. Likely anything I said would have only caused friction between the two of us, and besides, I didn't want to give away whatever secret you were hiding. I figured that was for you to say."

"I appreciate you keeping quiet," I said, "and I'm sorry I put you in that position."

"I know you are. If you weren't, we'd be having a totally different conversation." Walter downed the rest of his beer and rose from the table. "I best get back to the store. It's been busy today and Scooter's bound to make a mess of things. But I couldn't let any more time go by without saying something."

I nodded and he put his hand on my shoulder. "Carter's a stubborn man. Always has been. And I'm sure he has his reasons for the decision he made. But I still have hope that whatever this mess is, it will untangle sooner or later and leave you two considering your options."

"Me too," I said, surprising myself because I actually meant it.

Walter smiled. "You hang in there, honey. And if there's anything I can do, you let me know."

He started out of the kitchen and I turned around in my chair. "Walter?"

He stopped and looked back. "Yeah?"

"Ida Belle's crazy not to marry you."

He gave me a sad smile. "I know."

IDA BELLE SCOOTED her chair closer to mine and Gertie leaned over my shoulder and looked at my laptop screen. "That's the same picture," Gertie said.

"So are the others," I said. "See?"

I started flipping through the photos Beulah had provided and then back to the Facebook page I'd found for Austin Jennings, a young man from Waco, Texas, who had just finished up his last tour in Iraq and was now back home with his wife, two kids, three cats, and a Labrador retriever.

"It can't be him, right?" Ida Belle said.

"I'm sure it's not," I said. "The catfish lifted this guy's

photos because he's good-looking and several of them are in military dress and clearly in the desert."

"Should we check?" Gertie asked.

"Check how?" Ida Belle said. "We can't exactly drive to Austin and accuse the poor man of bilking old ladies out of their retirement. He's got a wife and kids. Imagine all the trouble that would stir up."

"It's not him," I said. "Everything he's done has been carefully planned. There's no way he'd use real photos of himself. The women he's targeting don't know what catfishing is, but clearly, he's well informed."

Gertie nodded. "What about the mailing address?"

"It's a post office box in New Orleans," I said.

Gertie shook her head in disappointment. "Beulah should have known better. She's sent charity boxes overseas. She knows the military has special addresses for such things."

I pulled up the Word document with Beulah's notes and pointed. "She says here that he claimed the box belonged to a friend who collected stuff for several of the men he served with and got it to them through other channels."

"Other channels?" Gertie said.

"She probably took that to mean the friend had a way of getting them contraband," Ida Belle said. "Girlie magazines, maybe some drugs."

"So Beulah mailed a pair of underwear to this post office box," Gertie said. "I still can't wrap my mind around the lengths he went to in order to convince her that their relationship was real."

"It's wicked," Ida Belle said. "I know it's an old term—one my mother was fond of—but it fits."

Gertie nodded. "We have to find him."

"Do you think any of his other victims will talk to us?" I asked.

"Bessy and Willa won't," Ida Belle said. "They're both friends of Celia. Myrtle was supposed to let us know if there were any more complaints, but I haven't heard a peep out of her."

"I'm afraid most will keep quiet," Gertie said.

"Probably true," Ida Belle agreed.

"Okay," I said, "then let's approach it a different way. The Sinful Ladies are all single and older. Do you think any of them was a victim?"

"No," Ida Belle said. "I sent out an email to all members earlier today, and they've all responded that none were victims."

I frowned. "And you think they're all telling the truth?"

"I'm certain of it," Ida Belle said. "I stressed the importance of information. They all understand what's at stake. They wouldn't hold anything back, especially when I'm outright asking."

"But isn't that strange?" I asked.

"Well," Ida Belle said, "the Sinful Ladies wouldn't be the best target. Our members are single because they chose to be, not because of a lack of options, and several were widowed young. It's not the cat lady group."

"Exactly," I agreed, "but how would anyone know that simply by looking at profiles on Facebook? Why would Beulah look any different, from a potential target standpoint, than one of your members?"

Ida Belle scrunched her brow. "I don't suppose anyone could know simply by looking online."

"Right," I said, "which goes right back to my saying that whoever is doing this has a lot of information on the people of Sinful, a lot more than I initially thought."

"You think he's intentionally avoiding the Sinful Ladies?" Gertie asked. "But why? Why not give it a try?"

"I think he wanted to avoid the two of you finding out what was going on," I said. "Think about it. If he pulled this scam on one of the Sinful Ladies, she would have reported it to you guys, right?"

"Almost certainly," Ida Belle agreed.

"And you two would have encouraged her to file the appropriate police reports, then you'd have gone on a manhunt, just like we are now."

Ida Belle nodded. "So he picked women he thought would keep quiet. But he made a mistake with Beulah."

"Yes," I said, "and I bet that piece of information has made it around to him by now."

"Oh no!" Gertie said. "He'll shut up shop and we'll never find out who he is."

"That would be the smart thing to do," I agreed.

"Maybe he's not that smart," Ida Belle said. "Or maybe he's addicted to the rush and won't be able to quit."

"I hope that's the case," I said, "because otherwise, he'll be harder to find."

"He's not going to hit on me, is he?" Gertie looked disappointed. "All that time spent on sexy pictures and the tattoo."

"It's a huge long shot," I agreed. "But maybe we can figure out who he did move in on. You guys know all the older single women in town. Let's start a list of everyone who's not in the Sinful Ladies."

"And then what?" Gertie asked. "We can't go knocking on doors and demanding they tell us if they were swindled."

"Why not?" Ida Belle asked. "The worst they can do is shut the door in our face."

"The more of them that we can get information from," I said, "the more likely that we can find some sort of pattern."

"There is one other victim we're aware of," Gertie said.

I shook my head. "Celia will never talk to us."

"She doesn't have to," Gertie said. "I happen to know that the election auditors confiscated her laptop as part of their investigation. They're using a conference room at the Southern Inn just off the highway on the way to New Orleans."

"Oh no," I said. "If we get caught, it could compromise the audit."

"So we won't get caught," Gertie said. "One of my cousins works in housekeeping at the hotel. I bet she could get us in."

"And why would she do something like that?" I asked.

"Shirleen has always been a bit of a troublemaker," Gertie said. "She'd do it just because she's not supposed to."

I looked over at Ida Belle. "Well?"

She shrugged. "It would give us more to go on, and it's certainly not the worst thing we've done, or the most dangerous."

"So now the decision bar comes down to the percentage chance that we'll be killed?" I asked.

"Seems reasonable," Ida Belle said.

I stared at her for a moment, trying to formulate an argument, then suddenly realized that I didn't even want to argue. "To hell with it. I haven't done anything illegal in days. Let's do it."

Gertie clapped her hands. "Nothing says a night with girlfriends like a little B&E."

CHAPTER SIX

AT 10:00 P.M., I hopped in the backseat of Gertie's Cadillac and we set off down the highway toward New Orleans. I'd suggested taking my Jeep—one, because it was the more reliable vehicle, and two, because I was the more reliable driver—but Ida Belle had insisted that Gertie's car blended while mine was more easily remembered. As every fifth car on the road seemed to be an old Cadillac driven by an even older woman, I couldn't really argue the point.

"Shirleen is meeting us in the parking lot," Gertie said. "She'll slip in the back door and get the key from the housekeeping drawer at the front desk, then bring it to us."

"Won't the person working the front desk notice?" I asked.

"Apparently, the night clerk works a day job as well and sleeps most of his shift," Gertie said. "As long as Shirleen hears snoring, she's in the clear."

"Sounds perfect," I said.

Gertie shot Ida Belle and me a guilty look. "There's just one little thing."

"Uh-oh," I said.

Ida Belle narrowed her eyes. "What thing?"

"Well, Shirleen has been dating the night maintenance guy and she thinks he's seeing someone else on the side."

"And what does that have to do with us?" Ida Belle asked.

"She thinks he's doing it during his shift," Gertie said. "You know, getting a free room and having a little fun on the clock. So I told her we'd see if we could catch him in the act."

"Why doesn't Shirleen catch him herself?" I asked.

"Everyone at the hotel knows her," Gertie explained. "She can't just stroll in during the middle of the night and roam around the hotel without someone asking her why she's there. And she definitely couldn't follow Winky around without him noticing."

"Winky?" I asked.

"On account of the eye tic he has," Gertie said. "Or maybe he's just a big flirt. I never really figured it out."

"So in exchange for the ability to break and enter," I said, "we also have to follow around Winky the cheating maintenance man. This sounds like a bad sitcom."

"I couldn't tell her no," Gertie said. "She wouldn't get the key otherwise."

"I don't see this ending well," Ida Belle said.

"It usually doesn't," I concurred.

The drive to the hotel went quickly, and Gertie pulled into the parking lot and spotted Shirleen's car in the back of the lot behind a row of SUVs. She pulled in beside it and a woman jumped out. I got out of the car, eager to get a look at the troublemaking Shirleen.

Early fifties but looked older, five foot three and a hundred and twenty pounds of what Ida Belle would call piss and vinegar. I could take her, but she would fight dirty.

I could see the piss and vinegar part in her stance. And her facial expression. And her tattoos, one of which said "Trouble" and another that said "I did it." I couldn't help but appreciate both her honesty and her self-awareness.

Shirleen eyed Ida Belle and me, and I wondered if I was going to have to arm wrestle to get the key. Gertie pointed to us. "These are my accomplices, Ida Belle and Fortune."

Shirleen must have appreciated the word "accomplices" because she nodded and handed Gertie a key. "This is a master key. It will get you into any room in the hotel. Why do you want in that conference room anyway? Just a bunch of men in suits with stacks of paper everywhere. The manager said they was some sort of accountants."

"They're auditors," Gertie explained. "They're investigating the mayoral election in Sinful. It's being contested."

"That mean bitch that won did something sneaky, didn't she?" asked Shirleen. "Momma said she don't know how that woman steps inside of church without it exploding. You going to fix it where she's not the mayor anymore?"

"Not exactly," Gertie said.

Shirleen nodded. "Smart. Don't give me the details, then I can't testify against you or nothing. All right. You guys do your thing. Drop the key off at Jerry's Pool Hall when you're done."

"We might be a while," Gertie warned.

Shirleen grinned. "So will I."

She gave us a wave and jumped in her car. We studied the front of the hotel, trying to decide the best way to enter.

"All the rooms are accessed through the front lobby," Gertie said.

"Which means walking by the front desk," I said. "Is the conference room on the first floor?"

Gertie nodded. "Shirleen said it's at the end of the hall past the elevators."

"Not optimum," Ida Belle said, "but if the night clerk is

really a sleeper then we might be able to sneak by without him noticing."

"I'm more concerned about security cameras than the clerk," I said.

"Why would someone look at the security footage?" Gertie asked.

"They wouldn't," I said, "unless something goes wrong, and something always seems to go wrong."

"That's why I brought disguises," Gertie said. She went to the trunk of her car. "I ordered some last week. I figured they might come in handy sometime and sure enough..."

I looked over at Ida Belle, but she looked as nervous as I felt. Clearly, she hadn't been consulted on the disguise purchase. Gertie pulled three boxes out of the trunk of her car and tossed one each at Ida Belle and me. I took one look at the picture on the box and shook my head.

"No way," I said. "I'm not dressing like a hooker. I always have to dress like a hooker."

"I wanted the hooker costume for myself," Gertie said, pouting, "but the spandex put my thighs in a bind."

"What the hell is this supposed to be?" Ida Belle asked, holding up a flannel shirt and giant black ball cap.

"It's a truck driver costume," Gertie said. "If you pull the hat down and keep your chin tucked in, no one will be able to see your face."

"I could have used my own wardrobe for this," Ida Belle said. "Am I supposed to be the guy who hired the hooker?"

Gertie frowned. "Hmmmm. I was concentrating on costumes that would prevent us from being recognized. I guess I hadn't thought about how they'd look together."

"What's your costume?" I asked.

She held up her box and Ida Belle sighed.

"A hooker, a truck driver, and a nun walk into a hotel," Ida Belle said. "There's the start of a bad joke."

"A nun?" I asked. "Really?"

"It's the perfect disguise," Gertie said. "Who would suspect a nun of doing something illegal?"

"The police?" I said. "They suspect everyone. Besides, you're Baptist. Won't you burst into flames or something if you do this?"

"I don't think so," Gertie said. "We're doing charity work, after all."

I supposed if one used skewed logic, it made sense. As much sense as a trucker, a hooker, and a nun walking into a hotel together, anyway.

"Maybe one of us should go in first and see if the clerk is asleep," I said.

Gertie nodded. "Which one of us would draw the least amount of attention?"

Ida Belle pointed at me. "Hooker girl, here."

"Why am I always first choice?" I asked.

"This place doesn't rent by the hour," Gertie said, "but I agree that a hooker probably wouldn't stick out as much."

I stared at the two of them. "A truck driver would be more glaring than a hooker? Really?"

Ida Belle nodded. "In a hotel, sure. This isn't seedy, but it's not the Ritz, either. Most truck drivers sleep in their cabs."

"Fine," I said. "I'll go check it out."

"Let's suit up," Gertie said.

"I'm not changing in the parking lot," I said. "Especially into that. I'm pretty sure I can't have undergarments."

"Oh, stop whining," Gertie said and grabbed my costume bag from me. She pulled out the dress and handed it to me. "Take off your T-shirt and slip that over, then take off your jeans. A bra is no different than a bathing suit."

"Except that people can't usually drive by and see a bra in the parking lot of a hotel," I said.

"Mardi Gras." Ida Belle and Gertie both spoke at once.

I shook my head and shrugged off my T-shirt. Next year, assuming I wasn't on assignment, I was coming back to Louisiana to see this Mardi Gras spectacle. I pulled the dress over my head and yanked and tugged until it was at my hips. I shrugged off my jeans and pulled some more until it was down over my previously exposed rear.

"It would look better with a push-up bra," Gertie said.

"I doubt there's one in the vending machine." I held out my hand. "Give me those ridiculous shoes and that wig. This dress itches. I don't want to be in it any longer than I have to be."

Gertie passed me the shoes—a ridiculous combination of clear plastic and pink glitter—and I climbed up onto them.

"Can you walk in those?" Ida Belle asked.

I pulled the wig comprising wavy, flaming-red locks over my head. "We're about to find out."

I took one step and my ankle wobbled. Gertie grabbed my arm and steadied me. "I'm going to start walking," I said. "You guys get changed and meet me at the front door. Hide in those potted plants. I'll signal if it's safe."

"I need to take the license plates off the car, too," Gertie said. "Just in case."

I didn't want to think about just in case. I set out at a slow clip, concentrating on one footstep at a time. I'd had to wear girlie clothes for some of my undercover work, but I'd never worn anything this high or this pointy. I felt like I was walking on my toes. Thank God for superior balance, because it only took me ten steps or so to get into a rhythm that at least didn't make it appear as if I was going to fall on my face at any minute. By the time I reached the lobby door, Ida Belle and

Gertie stepped up beside me, then slipped behind the fake plants under the entry overhang. One look at Gertie in the nun's costume, hiding behind a fake ficus, had me struggling not to laugh. The irony was simply too good. Ida Belle, on the other hand, looked perfectly comfortable in a flannel shirt, enormously wide ball cap, and work boots, but then now that I thought about it, Ida Belle almost always got to opt out of the ridiculous dress part of things.

I took two steps toward the sliding doors and they opened. No other sounds indicated my passage, which made me happy. I stepped inside the lobby and looked over at the front desk, but no one was there. I frowned and stepped closer. That's when I saw a sign on the desk indicating that the clerk would return at ten fifteen. I checked my watch. Ten forty. Maybe he'd fallen asleep somewhere. There was a button on the counter with a sign that read "Press for Emergency Service." He was probably taking advantage of that fact and was crashed in one of the nearby offices.

I went back to the front door and waved at Ida Belle and Gertie, who hurried inside. I pointed at the empty desk and the sign and they nodded as we slid by and headed down the hallway past the desk. At the end of the hall, we found a sign for the conference room and Gertie pulled out the key to unlock the door. We slipped inside and locked the door behind us before turning on the lights.

Under the bright fluorescent lights, Gertie looked even more ridiculous than she had in the dim light outside. For starters, the habit was too big for her head and the front of it kept slipping over her eyes. The collar appeared to be strangling her, and she kept coughing. The cross she wore was so large that the top started at the base of her neck and continued almost to her midsection.

"Why is that cross so huge?" I asked.

"I got the costume from one of those vampire-hunter stores," Gertie said.

"Are you supposed to use the cross to knock the vampire out?" I asked. "And what are you holding?"

"A Bible," Gertie said. "No nun is complete without her Bible."

I stared down at the black book. "Uh-huh. Why do you need both hands to hold it?"

"I might have hidden a couple things in it," Gertie said.

"What things?" Ida Belle asked.

"Nothing you need to know about," Gertie said. "If everything goes as planned, we won't need any of them."

Ida Belle didn't looked convinced, but short of wresting the fake Bible from Gertie's two-handed grasp, we weren't going to find out what she was hauling. She'd had her purse in the car, so the answer was "potentially anything."

"Let's get moving," Ida Belle said. "If we can get out of here before the clerk comes back, that would be optimum."

We headed to the table that was piled high with boxes and stacks of paper and started shuffling stuff around.

"Here it is," Gertie said.

"You sure it's hers?" I asked.

"Pretty sure." Gertie held the laptop up where we could see the "Celia the Great" sticker on the side.

"She had stickers made," I said. "Wow."

"The great *what* is the question," Ida Belle said, "and there are so many options."

Gertie nodded. "Great pain in the butt."

"Great liar," Ida Belle said.

I took the laptop from Gertie and opened it before they got too carried away. *Words that described Celia* was a long and unpleasant list. I opened the laptop and the password box popped up.

"Of course she has a password," Gertie said.

"No worries," I said, and typed in *celiathegreat*. The password box disappeared and the operating system started powering up. I looked over at Ida Belle, who rolled her eyes.

"Okay," I said, and clicked on Facebook. "Let's go see who the great idiot has been messaging with."

It didn't take long to find what we were looking for. Mainly because there was only one message, from a corporal named Jimmy Barlass. Either Celia deleted messages once the conversation was over or people avoided messaging her at all. I was going with option number two.

I opened the message thread and we all leaned over to look at the exchange.

I hope you got that photo I sent of me in my new green dress.

Yes. The shade of green brings out the sparkle in your eyes. I have never seen you look so beautiful. You should always wear that dress.

I looked up. "Is that the baby-shit-green dress?"

"Probably," Gertie said. "It's the only new one she has."

I grimaced and looked back at the screen.

I promise to wear it whenever we meet. Unless, of course, I'm not wearing anything.

"I'm going to be sick," I said.

"Me too," Ida Belle agreed. "I shouldn't have had Italian for dinner."

"I'm thinking we all should have skipped dinner," I said.

"Look," Gertie said. "He's talking about money."

I have leave coming up soon. I would love to see you, but funds are tight right now. I send everything I make back home for Mother's care.

You are such a wonderful son. Your mother raised you well. If money is all that is keeping you from visiting, I can send you the amount you need to get home.

You are very kind. The military will get me home to my mother. I just wouldn't have the funds to see you once in the States. Perhaps you could visit me in Virginia.

I'm afraid my duties as mayor prevent me from leaving Sinful right now. How about I send you the money to visit me here? I could get away for a couple of days to New Orleans. You'd love the city.

"And here we go," I said.

Ida Belle shook her head. "This is ridiculous. How can she be so silly?"

If you wouldn't mind, that would be incredible. Five thousand should cover everything.

I blew out a breath. "Five thousand dollars? To get him from Virginia to New Orleans? Is Richard Branson personally picking him up?"

"He's got an angle," Gertie said, pointing at the screen.

Five thousand seems an awful lot.

It's not the trip that would cost so much. I can drive there, and gas would be very little. It's Mother. She needs a treatment for her cancer that Medicare won't cover. The doctor said it would relieve eighty percent of her pain. The cost is $4,500 and I don't have that kind of money. But I couldn't go to New Orleans with you, knowing she was there suffering. I will probably try to pick up some construction work while I'm home to see if I can make the money.

"The man has no conscience," I said.

"I hope his mother's already dead," Gertie said. "I always figure this sort of thing comes back to haunt you if you're doing wrong."

"Karma does have a great sense of irony," Ida Belle said.

"Well, that's it," I said after I'd scanned the last of the messages. He gave her a PayPal address and she said she'd send the money the next day. After that, nothing. She sent him five messages with no response.

"Same MO with the 'taking care of Mother' plea," Ida Belle

said. "The only difference is this time the profile hasn't been deleted. Click over and let's take a look."

I clicked on Jimmy's name and it took me to a profile page with a picture of a group of military men standing in front of a tank. It was clearly overseas.

"Jimmy is the one on the end," Ida Belle said.

I saved his bio picture to the desktop, then opened a search page and did a reverse-image search. Immediately, a Facebook page for Corporal Eddie Spencer popped up. I clicked on the profile and checked out the photos.

"That's Jimmy," Ida Belle said.

I nodded. "Except Eddie is legit. Six hundred friends. Facebook history that goes back three years."

"And a wife," Ida Belle said, and pointed to the relationship status.

"I think we can safely assume that Eddie Spencer is not the catfish. He was just another good-looking guy in uniform."

Gertie frowned. "How many of these people do you think there are? I don't mean good-looking guys in uniforms. I mean these scammers?"

"Thousands?" I said. "Tens of thousands. I have no idea."

"Well, there's only one in Sinful," said Ida Belle, "best we can tell, anyway. So that's the one we concentrate on."

"We still don't have anything to go on," I said. "All this did was confirm Beulah's story and our suspicion that it's the same man working all the women."

"Check her email just to be sure there's nothing else," Ida Belle said.

I clicked over to her email and saw an outgoing email to "eddietheman" at a Gmail address.

"Eddie the man?" Ida Belle said. "When we find this guy, I'm going to shoot him. I'm just letting you know up front."

"You're not hurting my feelings," I said.

"Mine either," Gertie said. "In fact, I'll load the gun."

Eddie,

I'm attaching the pictures I mentioned last week. I hope you find them to your liking.

Love always,

Celia

I clicked on the attached folder and the screen came alive with images. Two selfies of Celia in the horrible green dress and one with Celia mostly out of the green dress.

"My eyes!" Gertie cried.

I looked over at Ida Belle, who'd closed her eyes and had an expression as if she'd smelled something rotten.

"I never thought I'd say this," Gertie said, "but the dress was better. Close those down before one of us needs therapy."

"Too late," Ida Belle moaned.

I turned my head sideways a little and squinted so that I wouldn't have to take in the photos with perfect vision, then closed the Internet browser and shut the laptop.

"Maybe," Gertie said, "we should keep a copy of those pictures. For security purposes."

"What security purposes?" I asked.

"The kind where she stops bothering us," Ida Belle said.

I considered this for a moment. Getting Celia off our butts would be awesome, and I had no problem with a little blackmail, especially if Celia was the target, but it wasn't worth the other risks. "No," I said finally. "I can't email them because it could easily be traced."

Gertie opened her Bible and pulled out a USB drive. "I thought just in case."

I looked over at Ida Belle, who shrugged. "It's a lot less risky than shooting her," she said.

I took the USB drive from Gertie, opened the laptop, and squinted again. Once the pictures were saved, I handed her back the drive, shut everything down on the computer, and stuck it back in the box where Gertie found it.

"Since we're here," Gertie said, "why don't we check on the audit?"

"Check how?" I waved a hand at the table. "This place is a mess. We wouldn't even know where to start."

"She's right," Ida Belle said. "Besides, Celia's laptop is the only one in the room, but I'm willing to bet they're not using an abacus to tally this stuff up. I bet the auditors take their laptops with them when they head up to their rooms at night."

Gertie looked disappointed but didn't disagree. "Then I guess all that's left to do is find Winky and make sure he's not carrying on with another woman."

"I'm not following him around all night," Ida Belle said. "We locate him once, and if he's sleeping or drinking or dancing with chickens, I don't care. As long as we see him alone, our job is done."

"Shirleen doesn't expect us to follow him all night," Gertie said. "We just need to watch him long enough to report back about something that he did, and I think Shirleen will be all right with that."

"Great," I said. "So where do we find Winky?"

"Shirleen said the entrance to the maintenance room is at the back of the lobby behind a screen," Gertie said.

"Let's hope the desk clerk is still sleeping," Ida Belle said.

I nodded. "And not with Winky."

CHAPTER SEVEN

I CREPT down the hall and peered around the wall at the desk. The clerk was nowhere to be seen and the sign still read "Back at 10:15." I waved to Ida Belle and Gertie and we all hurried across the lobby to the back, where a worn set of panels with Chinese dragons on them stood. On the other side of the panels was a door stamped with the word "Maintenance." This was the place.

I tried the handle, but it was locked. I gestured to Gertie, who handed me the key. I unlocked the door and pushed it open an inch, peering inside. The room was about fifteen by twenty with tables on each side that held appliances in various states of repair. A desk on the back wall contained stacks of paperwork and a lamp, which was the sole source of light in the room.

I slipped inside, Ida Belle and Gertie close behind, and pointed to another door in the back corner.

"Probably the storeroom," Ida Belle whispered.

"Let's see if he's in there," I said.

"And if he is?" Gertie asked. "What do we say if he catches us?"

"We could start with we're looking for the desk clerk," I said.

"That's a valid point," Gertie said. "I hope he's not dead somewhere."

"So do I," I said. "Especially since there's a security camera in the lobby. If someone dies here, the police will look at everything."

"Let's get this over with and get out of here," Ida Belle said. "Aside from some good blackmail pictures, this has been a total bust."

I headed for the door but when I got within a foot of it, I heard a noise. I drew up short and turned around to face Gertie and Ida Belle, one finger over my lips. I pointed to the door and inched closer, pressing my ear against it.

Either the hotel had the cheapest doors money could buy or the couple on the other side of the door was fairly loud. I was betting on both. Either way, I had no doubt what was going on inside. Gertie and Ida Belle listened for a couple of seconds, then stepped back.

"Looks like Shirleen was right," Gertie said. "I suppose we can sit in the lobby until they come out, then snap a picture."

I shook my head. "We look ridiculous and the clerk can't sleep forever. Besides, there's probably a back door for maintenance to use so they're not carting a bunch of dirty parts through the hotel."

"I don't want to sit around here half the night, either," Ida Belle said. "The longer we're here, the more likely we'll run into trouble. The last thing we want to do is get accused of fiddling with the audit, and that's exactly what people will think if someone sees us here."

"Okay," I said, "then here's what we do. Ida Belle, since you've got better night vision, you go out to the parking lot and pull the car up to the front door. I'll throw open the door and use that spotlight on the table to light up the room. Gertie will take a picture and then we'll get the hell out of here."

"What if he chases us?" Gertie asked.

"Naked?" I asked.

"Good point." Gertie handed Ida Belle the car keys and she hurried off.

I grabbed the spotlight and Gertie got her phone ready to snap a picture. I gave Ida Belle a minute to get in position, then grabbed the door knob with my left hand and the spotlight with my right.

"On three," I whispered. "One, two, three!"

I flung open the door and shone the spotlight at the ceiling, lighting up the entire room.

Winky and his friend were on a workbench in the middle of the room, but the only parts they were working on were each other's. They both bolted up from the bench, and Gertie held her finger on the camera button and took about a hundred pictures in a second.

"What the hell!" Winky yelled, signaling our moment to retreat.

I spun around and ran out of the room, Gertie close behind. I could still hear Winky yelling behind us, and then behind the yelling, running.

I burst out of the maintenance room, knocking over the screens, and sprinted over the top of them. I was halfway across the lobby when I turned around and saw Gertie run through the doorway, habit over her eyes, then trip on the screens and slide ten feet across the lobby floor. Winky, who'd been right behind, followed suit and fell on top of her.

I heard a gasp and looked over to see that the missing desk clerk had chosen that moment to return to his job. I ran back to Gertie and grabbed her shoulder, trying to pull her out from under the sagging mass of maintenance man who had her pinned to the ground.

"You're going to give me that phone, you bitch," Winky yelled, his hands clutching Gertie's collar.

I dropped Gertie's shoulder and started pulling on Winky's hands, trying to pry them off her robe, then I heard an electrical charge. Winky screamed and fell backward off Gertie, clutching his right butt cheek. I yanked Gertie up from the ground and we ran past the startled clerk and out the door.

Ida Belle stomped on the gas before we even got the car doors shut. The car lurched forward, tires squealing as we sped out of the parking lot.

"He was chasing you butt naked," Ida Belle said, somewhat incredulous. "I've seen it all."

"We've all seen it all," I said. "That desk clerk is probably going to need counseling. A naked Winky on top of a nun is not for the faint of heart."

Ida Belle grinned. "Yeah, without having all the facts, that probably looked way worse than it was. What made him jump off? I was afraid Gertie pulled a gun out of that Bible of hers and shot him, but I didn't hear anything but the shouting."

"I Tased him," Gertie said and held up the Taser for Ida Belle to see. "The Bible was underneath me and I could barely get the Taser out and reach around, but just managed. I have no idea where I hit him, but it worked."

"Right in the butt cheek," I said. "If you'd been over just a bit more, Winky might have developed more than an eye twitch."

"Did you get a picture, I hope?" Ida Belle said.

"Oh yes," Gertie said and lifted the phone. "I held the button down and got a bunch."

"Oh, goodie," Ida Belle said. "Now you have a hundred naked Winkys on your phone to cull through."

Gertie grimaced and accessed the photos. "Oh no."

"Please tell me you didn't take a hundred pictures of the ceiling or the floor," I said.

"No," Gertie said. "It's definitely Winky and his pinky. It's the woman that's a problem."

"You know her?" Ida Belle asked.

"Uh-huh. It's Shirleen's sister."

"Oops," I said.

Ida Belle shook her head. "I'm still trying to wrap my mind around one woman wanting that man, much less two, but whatever. We did what she wanted and she has her answer. I'm sure it's not the one she wants, but our job here is done. Now we just have to hope that clerk doesn't call the police."

"Unfortunately," I said, "I think that's probably a given. If anyone looks at the security footage and sees the clerk standing right there in front of the fray, the first question will be why didn't you call the police. Liability and all."

Ida Belle sighed. "Then let's hope these costumes covered enough to keep anyone from recognizing us. Did everyone keep their heads down?"

"I did," I said. "I was practically staring at my chest the entire time, even when I was running. I think Gertie's safe with that habit on, so we're probably in the clear."

I said it to reassure the two of them, but I couldn't be certain, at least not about the being recognized part. My other assumption was confirmed a couple miles down the highway when a police cruiser sped by in the opposite direction, lights flashing.

"Maybe there's something else going on," Gertie said.

"I seriously doubt it," Ida Belle said. "The hotel is the only thing out here for a good stretch except the bar, and he passed that. Let's get this key back to Shirleen and get out of here before we're spotted by someone we know."

"First things first," I said. "I'm getting out of this nonsense."

I yanked off the wig, then lifted and raised and pulled and tugged until I got the hooker dress over my head. I pulled on my T-shirt and jeans, then slipped on my socks and tennis shoes and breathed a sigh of relief. "That wig was hot. My head's all sweaty."

"So is this flannel," Ida Belle said. "As soon as we get to the bar, it and these boots are coming off." The hat was already long gone and sitting on the floorboard in the back of the car.

Gertie pulled and tugged on the collar but didn't seem to be making progress. "This is stuck," she said.

"Lights please," I said to Ida Belle, then leaned forward, trying to see what was keeping the collar in place. "How is it attached?" I asked.

"There's a string that ties it," Gertie said, "but I can't get it undone."

I flipped the rear of the habit over Gertie's head and tugged at the knot. "It's pulled too tight from when Winky was choking you. This isn't coming off without a knife. I don't suppose you have one in your Bible?"

"Crap," Gertie said. "It's probably the only thing I didn't bring."

"We'll take it off when we get to Fortune's house," Ida Belle said.

"Easy for you to say," Gertie complained. "You're not being choked by your outfit."

"I'm going to point out that *you* picked the outfit you're in," Ida Belle said.

Gertie gave her a dirty look, but there wasn't much else she could do. Five minutes later, Ida Belle pulled into the bar parking lot. It was an old run-down building made of red brick with wooden eaves that were rotted on the corners. Country music blared from inside, and slivers of light streamed out of the narrow slits between the window coverings and the walls. We hopped out of the car and Ida Belle shrugged off the flannel shirt and work boots and pulled on her tennis shoes. Then we headed for the entrance.

The noise level on the inside was ten times worse than in the parking lot, but as soon as we stepped through the front door, all talking ceased, decreasing the sound level to an eerie sort of quiet. A big beefy guy behind the bar looked over at us and shook his head.

"We don't want any weird stuff in here. Take that nonsense to New Orleans."

Shirleen jumped off a barstool and hurried over. "I'll give them directions to a club I know," she said. The bartender frowned at her, then went back to pouring beer. We hurried outside and across the parking lot, where it was easier to hear.

"Why are you dressed like a nun?" Shirleen asked Gertie.

"It's a disguise," Gertie explained. "So if things got hairy, no one would recognize us. I was going to take it off, but the knot in the collar is too tight."

Shirleen pulled a knife out of her pocket, grabbed the collar, and cut it in two. "There. Now you can talk without sounding like you're choking. Did you get something?"

Gertie nodded and handed her the key. "You probably don't want to put that back tonight. There was a bit of a, uh...fray. We're pretty sure the police are there now."

Shirleen's eyes widened. "What the hell did you do?"

"What you asked us to do," Gertie said. "We got a picture of Winky with another woman."

Shirleen flushed. "That lying cheating bastard! But why are the cops there?"

"He chased us naked through the lobby," I said, "and

landed on Gertie, who fell flat on the lobby floor. Right in front of the desk clerk, I might add."

Shirleen looked back and forth between us, clearly waiting for the punch line, but when none was forthcoming, she blew out a breath. "So Winky attacked a nun? Naked?"

I nodded. "All he was wearing was a frown."

Shirleen still didn't seem completely convinced, but she also couldn't think of any reason we'd make up such a story. "Let me see the picture," she said.

Gertie lifted the phone and turned it around. "You're not going to like it."

"That bitch!" Shirleen screamed and grabbed Gertie's phone from her. "I knew she was up to something when she wouldn't come out with me tonight even though I offered to pay. Said she wasn't feeling well. Amber has never once passed up a chance for a free beer because she wasn't feeling well. When she had surgery, I sneaked her beer into the hospital."

"I'll text you the picture," Gertie said, "but you have to save the picture and delete the text. I don't want it traced back to me. I'll delete the pictures off my phone as soon as you receive it."

"I'm no rat," Shirleen said. "Besides, you got me the answer I needed. I ain't going to say it's the one I wanted, 'cause that would be a lie. But at least now I know what I'm working with."

Shirleen pulled her phone out of her pocket and checked the text messages. She saved the photo, then deleted the message and showed us the log. "You're in the clear."

"Unless someone recognizes us on the security tapes," I said.

Shirleen waved a hand in dismissal. "Those cameras haven't worked in years. The manager keeps them up there to make the staff think they work. Keeps people from stealing if they think someone's watching."

"But if you know they don't work, how does that stop anyone from stealing?" I asked.

"Oh, not everyone knows," Shirleen said. "Just me and the day clerk. We both had a go at the guy from the security company that installed them. He told us the manager wouldn't pay to repair them. But we don't tell the others because that would leave less for us to pilfer."

"Of course," I said. I suppose it made perfectly good sense, assuming you weren't burdened with morals.

"I appreciate you gals," Shirleen said. "I best get back inside. I need to win some money at pool. I'm going to need cash for a new apartment and probably bail."

"You live with your sister?" I asked.

"Not for long," Shirleen said. "Of course, I might have to refill the shampoo bottle with Nair before I go. Things happen." She gave us a big grin and headed back for the bar.

"Let's get out of here," I said.

By the time Ida Belle dropped me off at my house, the neighborhood was dark and silent. I invited them in for drinks and cookies, but they both begged off, saying they needed a shower and bed. Gertie promised to burn the costumes in her fireplace, just in case. I was pretty sure I needed the shower part, too. After all, I'd touched Winky's hands and I knew where they'd been. But I'd spent so much time sleeping lately that I didn't think bed would look inviting any time soon.

I took a long, hot shower, then headed downstairs for the kitchen. I still had some leftovers, but I grabbed one of the frozen dinners instead and popped it in the microwave. While that was cooking, I checked the refrigerator and reached for a beer, then changed my mind and pulled out a bottle of wine. By the time I'd gotten the cork out and poured a big glass for myself, the microwave dinged and I pulled my Salisbury steak and mac-and-cheese dinner out. It needed a bit of salt and pepper and could never be confused for Gertie's or Ally's home-baked offerings, but there was something comforting about sitting alone at the kitchen table and eating a frozen dinner like I had so many late nights in DC.

I pulled my laptop over and opened it up to check my email. Nothing from Harrison, which could be seen as either good or bad, depending on which side of the half a glass I wanted to be on. I flipped over to Facebook and pulled up Gertie's account, shaking my head at the picture that was 80 percent butt and tattoo and 20 percent pie and oven. She'd gotten a couple of comments on it, including one from Celia who'd told her she ought to be ashamed. Like Celia was one to talk. She'd been sending someone young enough to be her son pictures of her half out of her best dress.

I scrolled down to the next post. It was fairly lengthy and didn't include a picture. Usually Gertie wasn't long-winded online, but as I started reading, I understood. This was her "I'm questioning my life" post. The one where she talked about the death of her fictitious aunt and money was nice but it couldn't make up for all the things she hadn't done. Then she went on to talk about how her aunt had never married or had children and had died alone, and while Gertie had friends that loved her, it wasn't the same as sharing your life with someone day in and day out. I had to give her props for delivery. It was a fine snow job, and if I hadn't known that's what she was up to, I might have wondered if it was real.

Maybe some of it is real.

The thought flashed through my mind like a bullet and I

paused, fork right in front of my lips. No. That couldn't be the case. Gertie was perfectly happy with her life. She'd never once intimated that she had any regrets for the choices she'd made or the way she lived right now. And while her age slowed her down physically, that bit of news hadn't reached her mind yet. It was still convinced she was twenty.

Was it possible, I wondered, to choose a single path at a young age and be so certain it was right for you that you never questioned it at all? At one time, I would have said absolutely, but I would have been answering with no exposure to anything else but my narrow existence. And that wasn't an answer that came from a place of truly knowing. It was an answer that came from a place of ignorance. Now that I'd been exposed to a different type of life, I couldn't seem to stop questioning every choice I'd ever made or ever would.

And just when I'd started to convince myself that I was overthinking everything and that my true place in life was back in DC, busting the bad guys with Harrison and generally being unsung heroes, Harrison had to go and tell me he was chucking everything over a woman. Of all the things he'd told me since I'd arrived in Sinful, that was actually the most shocking.

Not once had I ever thought about Harrison as a husband or father. I couldn't wrap my mind around him washing a car in the driveway in front of a pretty clapboard house, or spending his Friday night at a children's choir recital instead of the gun range. It didn't fit.

Or maybe it did.

Before Sinful, I wouldn't have pictured myself with even one friend that I confided in and trusted, much less several. Granted, some knew more about me than others, but I'd let all of them become part of my life. I shook my head. The problem with the future was there was so much unknown. If only someone could look past today and tell me what to do.

My feelings for Carter had taken me completely by surprise. And that surprise had led me to make foolish decisions that had only resulted in hurting both of us. I regretted hurting him, but not what I felt for him. Never that.

Without warning, my thoughts shifted to my mother. It was amazing to me how after so many years, I could still picture her as if she were standing right in front of me. I could still smell the coconut body lotion she always wore. I could feel her fingers gently pushing my bangs out of my eyes.

Did she love my father? I guess she must have. She married him and had me. I was young when she died, but I couldn't remember them arguing or even disagreeing.

I frowned.

Maybe that was the most telling thing of all. My feelings for Carter were real and I believed his were as well, but that hadn't stopped either of us from arguing. Two intelligent people couldn't be expected to agree on everything, but yet, no matter how hard I tried, I couldn't recall a single instance of disagreement between my parents. Were they careful to make sure I never heard? I doubted it. Kids tended to hear everything eventually. Or were they just pretending to be the perfect couple?

I stretched my mind, trying to remember what daily life had been like when my mother was alive. My father was gone often for work, sometimes weeks or a month at a time, so it was just my mom and me most of the time. But when I thought about the times I remembered my father at home, I couldn't recall him doing anything with us or anything with my mother. I remembered having a sitter once when they attended a funeral, but otherwise, I was never far from my mother's reach.

I slumped back in my chair and blew out a breath. Why hadn't I ever thought about my parents' marriage before? My father was cold and uninterested in raising his own child. I had never stopped to consider that his disinterest might have also included my mother, but thinking about it now, it must have.

Dwight Redding could be charming when he wanted to be, and likely that charm is what sucked my mother in. And maybe in the beginning, he'd really wanted her or thought he did. But at some point, his narcissism took over and everything became about him. Or maybe it always had been and he'd simply been able to hide it for a while. Playing the role of the devoted husband and father. He played roles every day in his work. The only difference was this role didn't have an expiration date. Until my mother died.

I reached for the wine and downed half the glass. This was too much to think about. There was no way I'd ever know the truth, and dwelling on it would only depress me even more. I remembered my mother as a kind and happy person. I didn't want anyone or anything to alter that memory.

CHAPTER EIGHT

"Fortune, wake up."

Ida Belle's voice was in my dream but I couldn't see her. The room was black. Then I felt someone touch my shoulder and I bolted upright. Ida Belle stood next to my bed, wearing a worried expression.

"Is something wrong?" I asked. "Where's Gertie?"

"She must have been in the shower when I called," Ida Belle said. "I left a message for her to meet us here."

I looked over at the clock. Seven a.m. Not the crack of dawn, but considerably earlier than an accepted time for house calls. "Did someone at the hotel recognize us?"

"Not that I'm aware of. Get dressed and come downstairs. Gertie should be here any minute. I want to wait for her before I tell you what's happened."

She headed out of the room and I heard her footsteps on the stairs. I hopped out of bed and pulled on yoga pants and a T-shirt before hurrying behind her. Ida Belle was in the kitchen putting on a pot of coffee. I grabbed some bagels from the refrigerator.

"You want one?" I asked.

She shook her head. "I had eggs and toast." She pointed at the empty wine bottle on the table. "Party for one?"

"What else?"

She put the bottle in the trash can and the glass in the dishwasher. "You sleeping all right?" she asked.

"Let's see. Running for my life from a naked man, hot shower, half a plate of cookies, and a bottle of wine. After all of that, you should worry if I *didn't* sleep."

She started to respond when I heard the front door bang shut. A couple seconds later, Gertie stepped into the kitchen, her hair still in rollers. "How come nothing ever happens after I'm done with my hair?" she asked.

"Because that would be convenient," Ida Belle said. "Grab some coffee. I have news."

I fixed my bagel, poured some coffee, and sat at the table across from Ida Belle. I glanced over at Gertie but she appeared to be as much in the dark as I was.

"Myrtle called me early this morning," Ida Belle said. "Gail Bishop was murdered last night."

Gertie dropped her coffee cup and it crashed onto the floor, sending coffee and bits of porcelain all over the kitchen floor.

"Don't worry about it," I said and hopped up to grab Gertie another cup.

Gertie took the cup, her hands shaking. "I can't believe it. Myrtle is sure it was murder?"

"Shot in the forehead while sleeping."

I frowned, trying to recall anything about the woman I'd met in the General Store that would explain why someone would want to murder her. "She's in her forties and pleasant-looking, right? Husband in a wheelchair?"

"That's right," Ida Belle said. "You met them at the General Store."

"Yes. When her husband tripped Celia with his wheelchair."

"What about Nolan?" Gertie asked.

"He's got some bruises but is otherwise all right," Ida Belle said. "Physically, anyway. Myrtle said he fell apart when the paramedics told him Gail was dead."

"Did he see anything?" I asked. "Do you have any details?"

Ida Belle nodded. "The story as I heard it was that Gail had a headache and turned in before Nolan. Their bedroom is upstairs. They have one of those rail things that lifts Nolan's wheelchair up the stairs. Nolan was watching television downstairs in the living room when the power went out. He heard a scream, then a pop, but he said it didn't register at first what it was."

"That makes sense," Gertie said. "No one expects to hear a gun being fired upstairs in their house. He could have thought it was a lightbulb bursting or something of the sort given the power outage."

"Except for the scream part," I pointed out.

"Exactly," Ida Belle said. "He wheeled over to the bottom of the stairs and called for Gail, but she didn't answer. Then someone with a flashlight ran down the stairs straight for him. He shoved Nolan's wheelchair over and ran out the front door."

"How did he get in the house?" Gertie asked.

"The window in the master bedroom was open. The latch on it doesn't work properly. Apparently all you have to do is jiggle it some and it will work its way loose. There's a trellis on the back wall of the house that leads right up to it."

"No alarm?" I asked.

"No security system," Ida Belle said, "but Nolan has one of those buttons on a necklace that he can press to call the paramedics. They responded quickly, thinking it was for Nolan, of course, but he sent them upstairs and they promptly called for the police."

Gertie shook her head and sniffed. "That's awful. Gail was such a nice woman, and I actually mean that. I'm not just saying it because she's dead."

Ida Belle nodded. "She was nice for real. No put-on."

"Do the police think it was a robbery?" I asked.

"I don't know what they think," Ida Belle said. "Carter was there, of course, but he hasn't typed up any reports yet. If he's got any ideas, they're all in his head. Myrtle got most of the story from the paramedics, and then she overheard Carter telling some of it to Deputy Breaux."

"I don't think Gail owned any valuable jewelry," Gertie said. "At least, I never saw her wearing anything valuable. Even her wedding ring is a plain gold band. And no one is foolish enough to keep cash in their house these days. Not enough cash worth killing over, anyway."

I frowned. "Well, there has to be something. Genuinely nice women don't get murdered over nothing."

"That's what worries me the most," Ida Belle said.

"We need more information," Gertie said.

"We should have some later on today," Ida Belle said. "Marie is a large donor to the charity that Gail administered. Gail helped her find the home Charlie is in. She's been friends with them for years and knows Nolan's personality and his disability as well as anyone in Sinful. She went over first thing this morning to help Nolan. He's going to need someone to lean on, both physically and emotionally."

Marie was one of Ida Belle and Gertie's best friends and Charlie was her autistic brother. She was perpetually nice and always worried about things being right and fair. She was also the candidate who called for the audit of the mayoral election. If the vote was found to be fraudulent, then Marie would be the new mayor of Sinful. The city probably couldn't do any better, at least in my opinion.

"I'm glad he's got Marie," I said.

"I'm glad we've got Marie," Gertie said. "I know we have this catfish thing going on, but I think murder trumps it."

"The police might solve it before we even get all the facts," I said, hoping it was true more than actually believing that would be the case. Facts tended to make their way to Ida Belle and Gertie on the express train, and no way were they going to leave this one alone.

"It would be nice," Ida Belle said, "but I'm not counting on it. I expect Carter will be by here any minute now, reminding us to mind our own business."

I held in a sigh. She was probably right.

I rose from the table to pour myself another cup of coffee. I'd barely gotten two sugar packs poured in when I heard the rap on the door. I knew that knock. I looked over at Ida Belle and Gertie and the sigh I'd held in earlier escaped.

"I'll get it," Ida Belle said. "You sit back down and drink your coffee."

She headed out of the kitchen and I sat down again. The expression on my face must have reflected exactly what I felt because Gertie reached across the table and squeezed my arm. "Don't let him get to you," she said. "At the very least, don't let him see that he is."

I smiled and nodded. Gertie was right. No way was I letting on to Carter how bad I felt about our breakup. My life and my feelings were no longer his concern.

A second later, he walked into the kitchen behind Ida Belle and I felt my smile slip for just a second, then I forced it back on. Not a big toothy grin sort of smile, but a small pleasant one. The kind reserved for when you're trying to be polite and don't really want to be.

"I see you're all up early," Carter said. "No surprise there. I suppose you've already heard about Gail Bishop."

We all nodded.

"So tragic," Gertie said. "Gail was such a nice woman and now, poor Nolan on his own again."

"Yes, it's all extremely unfortunate and unpleasant," Carter agreed. "It's also a police matter and a serious one, so I expect you to stay out of it. I mean it. This was a callous crime. Whoever did it wouldn't think twice about popping off any of you three to cover his own ass."

All of a sudden, my forced pleasantness vanished and I just felt tired and angry.

"We're not stupid, you know?" I said. "In fact, I'm certain you know we're not stupid because you know more about us than anyone in this town. Are you stopping by anyone else's house to tell them not to butt their nose into your investigation, or just the people who might figure it out before you do?"

Gertie sucked in a breath.

Carter's eyes widened and his jaw dropped a bit. Of all the things he'd expected me to say, that apparently wasn't on the list.

"I'm tired of this entire song and dance," I said, unable to stop now that I'd gotten the rant started. "Before you knew my true identity, I had to pretend to be some helpless, ignorant female, as Gertie and Ida Belle have done for years. Well, now you know the truth and I'll be damned if I'm going to continue acting like something I'm not. At least not in front of you. You can arrest me if you'd like, or handcuff me to my couch, but what you cannot do anymore is condescend to me. Or them."

I rose from the table and stomped out of the back door and onto the lawn. I didn't stop stomping until I reached the edge of the bayou that ran behind my house. I could feel the heat on my face and struggled to get control of my emotions. I stared out at the moving water. It seemed so peaceful. The entire town did, really. Yet so many bad things had happened. So many secrets exposed. So many lives ruined.

I was tired of it all. Tired of pretending to be something I wasn't. Tired of being who I thought I was. Tired of not knowing what I wanted. Tired of caring what other people thought. And most of all, tired of being judged for the things I'd done.

"Are you all right?" Ida Belle's voice sounded behind me.

I started to say "yes" but then decided there was no point in lying. "No."

"I don't blame you," she said, and stepped up beside me. "I wasn't either."

I looked over at her. "What do you mean?"

She looked out over the water for a while and I could tell her mind was somewhere else. At first, I thought she wasn't going to answer, then finally she spoke.

"When I first came back from Vietnam, I thought I was going to live happily ever after, so to speak, but I was never able to slip into it. Oh, everyone thought I should be thrilled to be back from that hellhole and grateful that I'd returned alive and in one piece. I was, and I wasn't. You see, the young woman who came back from the war was a lot different from the young woman who went to war."

I nodded. That was always the case.

"I went," Ida Belle continued, "because I wanted to make a difference. I wanted to save our American soldiers, and I knew I had the intelligence to do more than wrap wounds or clean bedpans. And I was right. I was very good at what I did, just like you, and with that knowledge comes a feeling of strength and...I don't know how to describe it exactly, so I'll just say purpose."

"That's a good way to describe it."

"I thought you might agree. I believe that women like us are not made like other people. Gertie, for all her common domestic pursuits like knitting and baking, still doesn't have that average manner of thinking that drives most women to normal lives. Even successful career women mostly go on to have husbands and children and barbecues with family. But women like us can't ever wrap our minds around such a life of simplicity."

"We can't let go of that part of us that wants to do something bigger than we are. That thing that makes us who we are."

Ida Belle nodded. "It's our nature that makes us so good at what we do. It saves the lives of many and improves the lives of so many others, and most will never know. It's like a drug, almost, the knowledge that you make a difference to so many just because you're the best at what you do. You feel as if you were born for this thing and this one thing only."

"Yes! That's it exactly."

"Then one day, we're faced with not doing it any longer. Not being who we inherently are. And that's the worst day of our lives because it makes us question every choice we've ever made and will ever make. Because we start to wonder if we're real or simply a well-oiled machine."

I felt the tears well up and I nodded. "How do I know the answer?"

"It will come. I promise you that, and I wouldn't say it if I didn't believe it to be true. It takes time, and that part is like death to people of action. But one day, you'll know the truth, and it will be so obvious that you'll wonder why you didn't see it to begin with."

She put her hand on my shoulder.

"You're a person born with purpose, Fortune Redding."

I SPENT a long time standing there staring at the bayou. The answers Ida Belle told me would come never materialized, but then I hadn't figured they would. They weren't simple questions, so I couldn't expect simple answers. I finally headed back inside and found a note from Gertie saying they would be back at lunch to talk things out. Gertie was bringing a chicken casserole.

I smiled. As they would say in the South, Gertie was such a "dear." She knew I coveted those casseroles we'd delivered the day before and now she was going to go home and boil chicken, mash eggs, or whatever else was required, just to perk up my mood. I'd never met people like them before and I was fairly certain I never would again. They understood me like no one else ever would, and that made for strong bonds. I'd never imagined having friends like this, but now that I did, I couldn't imagine not having them.

I put on my tennis shoes and a ball cap and headed out to run. The exercise yesterday had done me good. My muscles complained a bit because I'd lain off exercise for so long, but once put in motion, they settled back into normal performance. I set out at a good pace around the neighborhood. I could have jogged down one of the farm roads that led into the swamps, but I liked seeing what was going on.

Mr. Hartwell waved at me from atop his new riding mower. Mrs. Hartwell stood on the front porch yelling as he lost control and ran over a patch of her gerbera daisies. Mrs. Boudreaux of Perkins Street—I had to label them by street since Louisiana produced Boudreaux like it did mosquitoes—was painting the rocking chairs on her front porch a bright blue. They looked good against the bright white siding on her house.

"Looks great!" I called out as I ran by.

She looked up and waved. "Come by and sit in a couple days."

It was the sort of invitation people in Sinful made every day. It didn't matter to Mrs. Boudreaux that I'd only spoken to her once and that was at church when I'd accidentally stepped on her foot. I'd complimented her, and that required an invitation to chat. Some days, I found it charming. Other days, I found it intrusive.

Today, I didn't think about it at all. My mind kept going back to Gail Bishop. Who would want to murder someone like Gail? By all accounts, she was a nice woman, and nice women rarely had enemies. Sometimes people were jealous, but it took a lot more than a little envy to resort to murder. And poor Nolan. He'd been so irritated with Celia and so pleased with himself for tripping her. It probably wasn't something Gail would have done, but despite her niceness, I don't think she minded overly much.

What would Nolan do now? Was he dependent on Gail to manage day to day or was he capable of doing it alone? Ida Belle and Gertie should be able to fill me in on all of that at lunch. I didn't think Nolan's disability had anything to do with Gail's murder, but in order to work on theories, I needed to know the entire picture. So many things that had happened in Sinful had roots in the past. I'd learned quickly that the more you knew about someone, the more likely you were to figure out what was going on. The less you knew, the more likely you were to step right in it.

"Fortune?" I heard a woman's voice call out.

I slowed to a walk and looked at the park in the direction of the call.

The young woman I'd met in the General Store the day before waved at me from a swing set. Penelope, but she'd called herself something else. A fruit. Apple. Pear. Peaches! That was it.

I started to wave and continue on, but then changed direction and headed into the park. Peaches and I were probably two of the last people to see Gail alive. She would want to talk about it, and in doing so, might give me a lead. You never knew what gossip was making it through Sinful, and the younger crowd probably had different tidbits to share than Ida Belle's older contacts.

"Nice day for the park," I said as I stepped up.

Peaches' baby was in a swing made for infants and she was pushing her gently. The baby let out a happy scream every time the swing went forward.

"She loves it outside," Peaches said. "I have a hard time with her when it's raining."

"Ought to be even more fun when she starts school." I could remember being cooped up inside every day when I wanted nothing more but to be outside in the sunlight. I usually turned my frustration and boredom into causing trouble.

"I don't even want to think about it," Peaches said. She was silent for several seconds. "Did you hear about Gail Bishop?"

I nodded. "It's hard to believe."

"I said the same thing! I was telling Brandon—he's my husband—that I just saw her yesterday at the General Store. I never thought..."

"Of course not. How could you?"

"Yes. I suppose that sounds silly. You can't just look at a person and know they're going to be murdered. Still, if it had been someone like Celia Arceneaux, I would have been shocked but not surprised. I don't know if that makes sense."

"It does to me. I only just met Gail yesterday, but she didn't strike me as the type of person who incited people to violence."

"Not at all! She's one of the nicest people in Sinful. I've worked with her a couple of times on charity events. Between her job in New Orleans and Nolan, she didn't have a lot of time to spare, but she always helped when we had something going on in town, even if it was only for an hour or two. She spent all her time taking care of other people. Why in the world would someone want to harm a person like that?"

"It doesn't seem to make sense," I said. "Does anyone have ideas?"

Peaches shifted her gaze to the ground. "Oh, well, I couldn't say."

Another thing I'd learned is that in the South, "I couldn't say" often meant "I've heard things I shouldn't repeat because it's crass."

"I don't mean evidence," I said. "That's for the police to handle. I just wondered if anyone had been talking. I know it sounds rude of me to ask, but I know so little about Gail and about Sinful as a whole." I paused for a moment for dramatic effect. "It makes me a bit...uneasy, I guess you'd call it. Living alone and not knowing what happened."

"Oh, of course! I understand that completely. When my dad passed, my mom decided to sell her house and move to one of those retirement condos in Florida. I was seeing Brandon and working at the café. We were starting to get serious and I didn't want to leave, so I stayed in the house until it was sold. It took some getting used to. Things you never heard when another person was around seemed to materialize as soon as the sun went down. Nothing ever happened, but I knew if someone wanted to do something, I'd be an easy target."

I nodded. "That's it exactly. If only I knew that it was for a specific reason, that couldn't apply to me. It sounds so selfish, but fear isn't always rational, is it?"

"No. I have the most horrid fear of spiders. Hate them really. Most of what we have here can't really hurt you, but there's something about them that just creeps me out. Every time I see one, I yell for Brandon and he comes with the flyswatter."

She stared at me for several seconds and I could see she was trying to decide whether or not to share the gossip she'd heard. The whole "girlfriends have to stick together" must have won out because finally she let out a breath.

"I wouldn't want you to repeat this, of course," she said.

"Of course. It's for my own peace of mind and that's it."

She looked around—I assumed to make sure no one was in hearing distance—then leaned closer to me. "The rumor was she was having an affair."

Of all the things I'd expected to hear, that one wasn't even on the list. "You're kidding me."

"I know. It sounds ridiculous. I mean, Gail? She wasn't unattractive, but she would hardly stand out in a crowd."

"Pleasant but unmemorable."

"Yes. I mean, I know average-looking people have affairs too, but I just can't see it, you know? She just didn't strike me as the type."

"It does sound rather unbelievable. Did you hear it from a reliable source? And what was their source?"

"I heard it from a friend, and I think she said she heard it from Florence Thompson. My friend cleans house for her."

Florence Thompson was a name that was vaguely familiar. The image that came to mind was that of a very tall, thin woman with a dour expression. Like her underwear was too tight.

"I wonder who Florence heard it from," I said.

"My friend didn't say. For all I know, neither did Florence."

"Probably not. Well, if that's true, then this may turn out to be a crime of passion. I guess that lets me out of the victim pool."

"Really? Because I heard you were seeing the yummy Carter LeBlanc." She grinned.

Yummy? I tried not to cringe.

"We spent some time together," I said, "but ultimately, it didn't work out."

Her expression fell. "Oh, I'm so sorry. I thought you would have made a cute couple. Girls have been throwing themselves at Carter ever since he got back to Sinful, but you're the first he seemed interested in."

"It's probably for the best. After all, I'm only here for the summer."

"I guess so."

The baby started to scream and this time, it was an unhappy scream. Peaches checked her watch, then removed her from the swing. "She's hungry. I best get her home before she yells down the neighborhood. It was nice talking to you. If you hear anything being in that big house alone, give me a call. I'll send Brandon over with a shotgun."

"Or a flyswatter?"

She laughed. "That too. See you later."

I watched as she secured the baby in a stroller and headed up the sidewalk.

Gail was having an affair.

It didn't sound right, but I supposed one never really knew about another person unless you were standing on top of them twenty-four hours a day.

Still, it was a workable angle. One I would offer up to Ida Belle and Gertie.

They'd know if it was a possibility.

CHAPTER NINE

My chat with Peaches put me behind, so by the time I'd showered and made it downstairs, Gertie had already put the casserole in the oven to heat it up a bit, and Ida Belle had retrieved whiskey glasses and was pouring us all a round of Coke and the hard stuff.

Gertie looked at Ida Belle and shook her head. "Our mothers are rolling over in their graves. Whiskey at lunchtime."

Ida Belle raised one eyebrow. "If our mothers are rolling over every time we do something on their list of things a lady shouldn't do, they've been flopping like flounder since they were buried."

Gertie perked up. "That's true enough. Make mine a double."

"I'll make it a single until you've eaten and we've talked turkey. If you want to spend the afternoon sloshing around in whiskey, you can do it after the business portion of the day."

"Fine, a single then, but I'm chasing it with a beer."

"Sounds like a great idea," I said and opened the refrigerator. "Ida Belle?"

"Make it three," she said.

I grabbed the beers and sat them on the table. Gertie pulled the casserole out of the oven and put it in the middle of the table next to a basket of French bread. I grabbed plates and we all dug in.

"Okay," I said after downing a big bite of the incredibly awesome casserole. "I think the first thing we need to do is cover everything we know about the Bishops. Every time we get into something, their personal lives matter. So give me the skinny."

"Gail is a local girl," Gertie said. "Her parents retired and moved to Arizona. It's supposed to be better for arthritis, I think. Gail bought their house from them and still lives there today. She runs a charity in New Orleans that helps the homeless and the disabled acquire jobs and housing. I've made donations but never been to their office. My understanding is that it's a fairly decent-sized outfit."

Ida Belle nodded. "Twenty full-time employees, is what I heard. They get grant money from the federal government and the state, and of course, there's the usual list of private donors and events to raise money. Gail is—was very clever with money and the paperwork for grants and such. I worry that they'll have a hard time finding someone to run the organization as well as she did."

"What about her and Nolan?" I asked. "High school sweethearts?"

"Gail and Nolan met two years ago at one of the charity events she hosted," Gertie said.

"Was she married before?" I asked.

"Yes. That one *was* her high school sweetheart," Gertie said. "And a big mistake. That boy was always trouble, but Gail thought she could save him. You know how some teen girls can be."

I didn't have any idea how teen girls could be, but I figured I'd take Gertie's word for it. She had years of teaching experience to back up her opinion.

"It was just when she was a teen," Ida Belle said. "She had a few more unfortunate attempted rescues later on before she finally threw in the towel. We figured she'd decided to give it up until she met Nolan."

"Was Nolan born unable to walk or was that some sort of accident?" I asked.

"Nolan was already in the wheelchair when Gail met him," Gertie said. "I believe it was the result of a car accident a few years before."

"Drunk driver," Ida Belle said. "Not Nolan. The other guy."

"Yes, that's it," Gertie said. "Anyway, Nolan volunteered to speak at group meetings about learning to live in the wheelchair and the transitions one had to make both professionally and personally."

"So he wasn't dependent on Gail?" I asked.

"Not completely," Ida Belle said. "He's an editor or proofer...business papers, I think, or maybe law briefs. He's told me about it before, but I confess that the topic bored me completely so I tuned him out. Anyway, I think before the accident, he worked in corporate America in some similar capacity. But the editing or whatever, he could do at home, so it was a better option than commuting each day, although it's probably considerably less money. I think the work is contract, so not always available."

"What about physically?" I asked. "I assume he was living alone before he married Gail?"

"He was living in an apartment in New Orleans," Gertie said. "I think he had some sort of aide that came to help him with things several times a week. But I remember him saying that he had tried to become independent quickly because there hadn't been much insurance money and he couldn't afford to continue the service once it was gone."

"So he got a settlement from the wreck, but medical bills and the health aide probably ate it up quickly," I said.

"Probably so," Gertie said. "It does seem that everything to do with health care is so expensive these days. Anyway, Gail told me once that he was quite capable in most areas. They modified her home to accommodate the wheelchair and that helped tremendously. The only problem was his strength. Ever since the accident, he had bouts of fatigue and she said he couldn't lift himself when those happened."

"So he can't live completely independently, at least not all of the time," I said, and sighed. "That sucks."

Ida Belle nodded. "Just when his life had reached a new normal, another tragedy throws him back into a tailspin. He's more capable now, of course, since more time has passed, but it's still a huge blow."

"Did Gail have money?" I asked.

"Not to speak of," Ida Belle said. "Her parents are still alive and live on a small retirement. Gail spent most of her savings buying their home. She was a frugal woman but I don't think she drew a large salary."

"Well," I said, "when a woman dies, the first suspect is usually the husband, but I don't see the point in this case. No money, so no motive. In fact, Nolan is worse off now than before."

Gertie nodded. "Not to mention that unless he developed wings and flew upstairs and through that window, he couldn't have managed it physically."

"So we have this notoriously nice woman," I said, "who helps the disabled and homeless and marries a man in a wheelchair, and yet someone killed her."

"It doesn't make much sense, does it?" Gertie asked.

"Not at the moment," I agreed, "but clearly there's a reason, because she's dead. When I went jogging this morning, I ran into Peaches Dugas at the park. I assume you know her?"

"Of course," Gertie said. "Peaches was such a pleasant baby, and she turned into such a nice young woman."

"She was in the General Store yesterday when Nolan tripped Celia," I said.

"So of course she wanted to talk about Gail," Ida Belle said.

I nodded. "She said the same thing you did—that Gail was super nice and she had no idea why someone would want to kill her. But I could tell there was something she wasn't saying."

Gertie stopped eating and leaned forward. "Did you get it out of her?"

"Of course," I said. "I'm trained to get information out of people."

"Ha," Ida Belle said. "Well, military methods..."

"I could hardly torture her on the playground," I said. "Besides, you get much better information if people offer it up themselves."

"So what was the offering?" Gertie asked.

"She said she'd heard Gail was having an affair."

Ida Belle and Gertie both stared, neither one saying a word. Finally, Gertie shook her head. "I don't think so," Gertie said.

"But you can't be sure," I pointed out.

"No one can be sure," Gertie said, "unless they're speaking of themselves, but it doesn't fit her at all. Who told Peaches that story?"

"A friend of hers who cleans house for Florence Thompson. I didn't get the friend's name. Peaches said Florence told her friend."

"The friend is Valerie Guidry," Ida Belle said. "She cleans for several widowed women."

"Is she reliable?" I asked.

"Oh, I wouldn't let her organize my closet or trust her to remember too many things without writing them down," Gertie said, "but I'd say she's reliable as far as repeating simple gossip, and I've never known her to make things up."

"What about Florence?" I asked.

"Florence is an old gasbag," Ida Belle said.

Gertie frowned. "That's not polite. Florence has had a rough time of it since her husband died."

"Not as rough as her husband had while he was alive," Ida Belle said. "Admit it. The woman is an old sourpuss and quite happy being that way."

"She does tend to dwell on the negative side of things," Gertie said.

"I could have guessed that based on that slightly annoyed and consummately bored expression she's always wearing," I said. "But is she reliable when it comes to gossip?"

"Oh, I should think so," Ida Belle said, "especially the negative kind. That would be right up her alley."

"So you don't think any of the three people I mentioned would make up that story and all of them have probably relayed it correctly, but neither of you buys it."

"I wonder where Florence heard it," Gertie said.

"Probably at that knitting group she has," Ida Belle said. "Five impossibly depressing old biddies, knitting the most horrible baby blankets and always shoving them at some young mother, expecting them to fawn over cheap, scratchy yarn in whatever color was on clearance."

"I'm afraid that's true," Gertie said. "I always use the finest yarn for babies. Their skin is so sensitive, but the pretty colors aren't cheap."

"Well, it's not much to go on, and will probably amount to nothing," I said, "but it's the only thing we've got to pursue right now. Unless you guys have heard anything else?"

"Not yet," Ida Belle said. "Myrtle is still trying to get her hands on some paperwork but Carter hasn't put anything down. And Marie is still over at the Bishops' house with Nolan. She'll likely be there all day."

Gertie nodded. "Marie won't leave until she's certain Nolan is in decent shape."

"Does he have any family?" I asked.

"I've never heard him mention any," Gertie said. "Of course, I assume Gail's parents have been notified and are on their way, but given that their only child was murdered, I don't know that they'll be much help to anyone."

"I imagine not," I said. "So...we finish lunch, then try to convince Florence to give up her source?"

Ida Belle reached for the whiskey bottle. "I think we'll all have that double now."

HALF A BOTTLE of whiskey and two-thirds of a casserole later, we were all in the living room, stretched out like cats sunning, except there was no sun, and none of us had the flexibility of a cat.

"I shouldn't have had that third helping," I said.

"Or the fourth," Ida Belle pointed out.

"No fair counting," I said.

"Then I won't comment on the five pieces of bread you had," Ida Belle said.

"Hey, I ran five miles this morning," I argued. "What exercise did you have?"

"I cleaned out my pantry," Gertie said. "Then I cooked."

"I lifted up that bottle of whiskey and walked out to the street to get into Gertie's car," Ida Belle said. "I'll exercise tonight. I'm just getting my muscles warmed up right now."

"Your stomach muscles, maybe," I said.

"The worst part is that even after all that whiskey, I'm still completely sober," Gertie complained.

"The casserole and bread soaked it all up," Ida Belle said.

I sat up a bit, trying to work up the desire to get completely upright. "We have to go talk to Florence." Then an idea hit me. "Or maybe you two should go. She doesn't really know me, but I'm going to guess she wouldn't like me. She'll probably be more willing to talk without me there."

"She doesn't like me, either," Ida Belle said.

"You told her she looked like Grumpy Cat," Gertie said.

"She does."

I grinned. "Maybe Gertie should call her...ask a question about knitting. Give her some compliment on her work and then eventually get around to talking about Gail. That would be standard operating procedure here, right?"

Ida Belle looked over at Gertie. "She's getting good at this."

"You two just want to push this off on me," Gertie said.

"So my idea isn't a good one?" I asked.

"Hand me my phone," Gertie grumbled.

I grabbed her phone off the coffee table and tossed it to her. She made the call and we proceeded to listen to one side of the conversation.

"Hi, Florence, this is Gertie. How are you doing...Yes, the humidity has been bothering my dry skin as well. Look, the reason I called was to ask about the pattern you used for the cap you made for the Spencer baby...Yes, the orange one. A cousin of mine who lives up north is expecting...I don't know how people live in that cold, either... Maybe you're right. They might all be a bit touched."

Gertie rolled her eyes.

"I see. From the pattern website you used for the shawl. That's excellent. I'll print it out. Thank you so much. I really loved the way that cap turned out, and although I don't approve of where my cousin lives, naturally, I figure her baby shouldn't have to suffer with a cold head just because of his mother's foolish choices."

I looked over at Ida Belle and grinned. Gertie was really laying it on thick.

All of a sudden, Gertie's eyes widened and she gave us a thumbs-up.

"Yes, of course. I'll be happy to make a blanket for the charity drive. I'm surprised no one has contacted me already. Usually Gail did that...I suppose you've heard. Simply horrible. I can't imagine...even with good locks and an alarm, I worry about such things. I don't suppose the police have any idea who would want to hurt her. I haven't a clue. Such a nice woman and a spotless reputation. So rare these days."

There was a longer than usual pause as Gertie listened. I could hear Florence's voice pick up in volume and speed but couldn't make out what she was saying.

"Really? That's most incredible. I would never have thought. No, of course things like this didn't happen in our day. I suppose whoever told you was quite certain? And someone who gets things right—not like old Mrs. Wainwright who confuses everyone with brown hair. Oh! Yes, that makes all the difference. How distressing. I'll pray for him, of course. Yes, thank you so much, Florence. You've been a lifesaver with the pattern."

Gertie hung up the phone and looked at us, frowning.

"Well?" Ida Belle said. "Don't drag it out, woman. Who told that old gasbag that Gail was having an affair?"

"Nolan," Gertie said.

I sat upright. "What?"

Even Ida Belle looked surprised by that announcement.

Gertie nodded. "The same day Fortune met them at the general store, Florence said she overheard Nolan on his cell phone. He was behind the Catholic church during one of the clothes drives that Gail was assisting with. Florence went out to get some air and before she realized the conversation was private, she heard him say he feared his wife was having an affair."

"Bull," Ida Belle said. "She probably saw him outside on the phone and deliberately went out there to see what he was saying."

"Probably," Gertie agreed. "But that point aside, do we think she's telling the truth?"

"I think so," Ida Belle said. "Florence loves gossip, but she's always careful to not be the one starting it. She wouldn't stick her neck out as the creator unless she was sure of what she'd heard."

"So we take as fact that Nolan thought his wife was having an affair," I said. "Do we think that is true, or could Nolan have been misreading something?"

Ida Belle shook her head. "That's certainly a possibility from our perspective because we don't know why Nolan came to that conclusion. He could have made a mistake. Given even a small dependence on Gail, I imagine he would have been scared by the thought of their marriage dissolving."

"Not to mention, he might actually love her," Gertie said drily.

Ida Belle waved a hand in dismissal. "Love is a secondary consideration when one can't live independently. An important one, of course, but probably not the biggest worry Nolan had if Gail were to leave him for another man."

"So where do we go from here?" I asked. "Trying to figure out who she was having an affair with seems premature since we don't know for certain that was the case."

"But if she wasn't having an affair," Ida Belle said, "then we're back to having no motive."

"If she were having an affair, what would be the motive?" I asked. "Assuming the man she was having the affair with wanted to be with her, why would he kill her? There's no monetary benefit for him."

"Maybe she broke it off with him," Ida Belle said.

"And he figured if he couldn't have her then no one would?" I asked. "I suppose that's possible. I've been watching those forensics shows and people commit the dumbest crimes over affairs."

"What if it was someone who hated Nolan?" Gertie asked.

"What do you mean?" Ida Belle asked. "If Nolan was the target, why not kill him?"

"Because taking Gail from him might be worse than death," Gertie said. "Now he's alone again, unable to completely support himself, financially or physically."

"You think someone killed her to make Nolan's life miserable?" I asked. "It's possible but it's so..."

"Evil?" Gertie finished.

I nodded. Beulah had used the word first. I agreed with her then and I agreed with Gertie now. So far, everything that had happened since I'd been in Sinful had a solid motive behind it. And even though some of the motives wound around a bit, they always came back to money. I couldn't think of a single thing that could be called an emotional crime. Certainly emotions were involved in so many instances, but never as the primary motivator. In fact, I'd never had a case in my work for the CIA that was emotionally motivated. Everything always came back to power and money.

Evil.

It was an old-fashioned word, but maybe this was an old-fashioned crime.

CHAPTER TEN

I CLIMBED out of the backseat of Gertie's car and reached back for the casserole dish. Ida Belle snagged a bowl of creamed corn and a basket of rolls, and the three of us walked up the sidewalk to Nolan's house. Gertie must have broken some sort of casserole-making record. That was four that I knew of in a matter of days. And who knew if she had a spare lurking in her refrigerator.

I glanced over at Carter's truck, parked in Nolan's driveway. "Are you sure this is a good idea?"

"Marie needs a break," Ida Belle said. "If Gail had died of a heart attack, we'd be doing exactly this, and Carter knows that. He might not like it, but he can't argue with facts. When people die, we bring food and sit with the family. Doesn't matter how they go."

It sounded reasonable, probably because it was. But I doubted Carter would want to see it that way. He would jump right to the conclusion that we were there to interfere with his investigation. He was right, of course, which was going to make it harder to take offense at his aggravation, but if Marie sent for us and Nolan needed the help, then Carter would have to take it at face value.

We knocked on the door and a couple seconds later, Marie opened it up. She stepped back to allow us in, and I couldn't help but notice how worried she looked.

"I'm afraid it's still messy in here," Marie said. "The police searched the entire house and they managed to rumple everything. They sealed off the master bedroom. I have no idea what they were looking for."

"It's standard procedure," I said. "They are looking for anything that might give them an idea who killed Gail and why."

"Well, they could have been a little tidier tidy with it," Marie said. "I've been straightening things up for hours."

"How is Nolan?" Ida Belle asked.

Marie shook her head. "Not good. The only thing I've been able to get him to eat was a piece of toast and that was this morning. His strength is going fast."

"Is he talking much?" Gertie asked.

"He'll answer if I ask him something," Marie said, "but sometimes I have to touch him before he realizes I'm speaking to him at all. I've never seen someone so devastated. It's a bit overwhelming, not knowing what to say. His situation..."

Ida Belle nodded. "It's different from our usual fare. I'm sure you've done everything you could. Taking care of people has always been your gift."

Marie gave her a grateful smile. "Thank you, but this time, I don't feel I've lived up to my calling. I appreciate you guys filling in for me. I sat a chicken out to thaw this morning before I heard and I need to do something with it or it will ruin. And I ran out without a shower."

"And you need a break," Gertie said. "It's rough on the

heart to sit in a house of mourning, especially without company."

"Yes," Marie agreed. "Myrtle is coming this evening when she gets off from work. We'll probably stay the night, just in case."

"I'm surprised he's allowed to stay here at all," I said, "with it being a crime scene."

Marie flushed. "There was a bit of a row over that. Carter wanted Nolan to leave, but I cut him right off. Where is Nolan supposed to go? No one else's home is set up to handle Nolan's needs. I suppose one of those hotel rooms with the proper equipment is possible, but why should the man leave a place that can accommodate all his needs and move to a place that can only accommodate some?"

"Not to mention that it would hardly be appropriate for people to sit with Nolan in a hotel room," Gertie said. "I'm glad you were here to talk some sense into Carter."

"I know he's just doing his job," Marie said, "and I appreciate that it's not optimum for people to be here while they're trying to look for clues and take fingerprints, or whatever, but Nolan's situation isn't optimum either, and I didn't want him to have even one more thing to worry about."

Ida Belle patted her on the back. "You did fine. The master bedroom is the biggest concern and that still leaves the entire downstairs to live in. Go on home and get refreshed. Nothing will happen to Nolan on our watch."

Marie gave us all quick hugs, then headed out. We heard voices drifting down the hall and I assumed Carter and Nolan were at the back of the house, which probably contained the kitchen. Ida Belle set out down the hall, and we found Carter sitting at a kitchen table, talking to Nolan. He looked up as we walked in, first a bit surprised, then I saw a flash of irritation that he quickly tried to mask.

Nolan's expression was almost blank, like his entire face had gone slack. He looked toward the doorway when we entered, but I don't think he really saw us. It looked as if he was acting on instinct but actually staring right through us. His face was pale and he had dark circles beneath his eyes. I noticed his hands shook slightly. He didn't resemble at all the cheerful man I'd met the day before.

Gertie went over and squeezed Nolan's shoulder. "We're so sorry," she said. "Marie needed to run home and see to some things before she comes back this evening. We're here to help until she returns. We've brought you a casserole and some fixin's. We'll be in the living room when you're done in here."

Nolan managed a slight nod but didn't speak or even look up at her.

"Don't go upstairs," Carter said.

Ida Belle gave him a dirty look. "Of course not."

We sat the food on the counter and headed back into the living room.

"Does he think we're idiots?" Gertie asked.

"No," I said. "He thinks we're interfering. I figured he would."

"Of course we're interfering," Ida Belle said. "But that's neither here nor there."

She walked to the center of the living room and looked up the stairs. "I wonder," she said.

"About what?" I asked.

The stairs were positioned at the back wall of the living room, across from the front door, and went straight up where they connected with a hallway. There wasn't a balcony, so you wouldn't be able to see someone on the second floor of the house unless they were at the landing.

"I wonder why he didn't go back out the window," Ida Belle said.

"It was faster to leave by the front door," Gertie said. "Running downstairs has to be quicker than scaling down that trellis. Not to mention the risk of the trellis breaking."

"I suppose so," Ida Belle said, "and I guess we have to assume he had a car parked somewhere nearby. Coming around from the backyard would take up more time. But still, what if Nolan had been armed?"

"Watching television in his own living room?" I asked.

Ida Belle raised one eyebrow. "When you're home alone watching television, where is your gun?"

"If I'm alone, it's next to me on the couch," I said. "If I've got company, then it's on my body. But you can't compare Nolan to someone like me. I'm hardly the norm. Neither are you and Gertie. I know she has a rifle under her couch cushions. It puts my butt to sleep if I spend more than ten minutes on it."

"You're right about the differences," Ida Belle said, "but how could the killer know that for certain?"

"I guess he couldn't," I said. "Unless he knew Nolan as well as he knew Gail. I mean, not that well, if we take Florence's story for the truth. You know what I mean."

"I think," Ida Belle said, "we need to have more details. For example, we know the lights went out, but why? Myrtle didn't have that information but it's important. If the time between when the lights went out and when Nolan heard the scream and the shot was only seconds, as it seemed when it was relayed to me, then assuming the killer tripped the power at the meter, how did he get from the meter, up the trellis, jimmy the window, and get inside to shoot Gail in a matter of seconds?"

"All good questions," I said. "My guess is the lapsed time was greater than our assumptions. Maybe once Carter is gone, we can find out some of the details from Nolan."

Gertie shook her head. "It didn't sound as if he was overly chatty. And he looks awful."

"He doesn't look well," I agreed, "but he's talking to Carter, right? So he's capable."

"Maybe we'll get lucky and he'll decide he needs to talk it through while we're here," Gertie said.

"I wouldn't count on it," Ida Belle said. "I've seen that blank look before. He's barely present. I bet Carter has to ask him every question three or more times before he gets any response, and then it's probably not a very detailed one."

"If he doesn't talk," I said, "I don't know how this is going to do any good."

"I want a look upstairs," Ida Belle said.

"I doubt you're going to get it," I said. "It wouldn't surprise me if Carter plans to sit right here until Marie returns and the three of us leave. Even if he leaves the house, I'd bet odds he sits in his truck and watches. Does the bedroom only have windows on the back of the house?"

Ida Belle sighed. "No. It runs the width of the house and has windows on the front side and back."

"So if anyone went upstairs, he'd see light," I said, "and I promise you, he'll be looking for it."

"She's right," Gertie said. "We're under a bigger microscope now than we would have been if we'd never come at all."

Ida Belle pulled out her phone and started tapping on the screen. "Then we just have to be smarter than Carter." She paused and I heard a text come in. She tapped again, then smiled. "It's taken care of. Just give her a few minutes to get the ball rolling."

"Who?" I asked.

"Myrtle, of course," Ida Belle said. She walked around to the couch, grabbed a car magazine, and plopped down. Figuring that was all the explanation I was getting at the moment, I sat in the recliner and turned on the television. Gertie took a seat on the other end of the couch and clapped.

"Oh, look," Gertie said. "There's a magic show on. I love magic shows. Hey, we should take a trip to Las Vegas and see one. I've always wanted to do that."

"As soon as people aren't trying to kill me," I said, "I'd be happy to take a trip with you to Vegas."

"Ha!" Ida Belle let out a single laugh. "You wouldn't be so quick to say that if you knew what happened that time we went to the riverboat casino in New Orleans."

"I don't think it's necessary to go into all that," Gertie said.

"What happened?" I asked.

Ida Belle pointed at Gertie. "Someone thought it would be a good idea to have a drink every time those girls came by with a tray."

"It was dollar drink night for seniors," Gertie said.

"Uh-oh," I said.

"They're watered down quite a bit, of course," Ida Belle said, "but ten of them will do you in, even if they're not a full serving of liquor."

"I did not have ten drinks," Gertie argued.

"It was probably more, but ten is all I counted. The slot machines I played the first thirty minutes didn't give me a clear view of you. God only knows what you managed to throw back during that time."

"So ten drinks, at least," I said.

"Which means she had to go to the bathroom," Ida Belle said. "So she goes walking toward the back of the casino, all willy-nilly, and I figure I better follow her in case she runs into problems. She ran into problems all right. At the end of the hallway, instead of turning left into the ladies' room, she pushes open the emergency exit, walks outside onto the deck, straight into the railing, and flips right over."

I looked over at Gertie. "You fell overboard?"

"It's not a big deal," Gertie said. "The boat doesn't actually leave the dock."

"So she's down there thrashing around," Ida Belle said, "and the alarm from the emergency door is going off like a siren. Two security guards rush me and I'm pointing over the side and yelling that someone needs to fish Gertie out of the bayou."

I put my hand over my mouth. "Oh no."

"So one of the guards pulls out a walkie-talkie and tells someone they've got a passenger overboard, then we all go running around the side of the boat and down to the dock."

"And they fished Gertie out?" I asked.

"Nope," Ida Belle said. "A drunk fisherman docked behind the casino heard the splash and thought fish were jumping. He threw a cast net over her and was trying to drag it in when the security guards got there. I've never seen a man so disappointed. He thought he'd snagged a hundred-and-forty-pound bass."

"A hundred and ten pounds," Gertie said.

"Maybe in 1953," Ida Belle said.

"Why doesn't that story surprise me?" Carter's voice sounded behind me, and we turned to look at him. "I'm done for now. I have no problem with you guys staying here. I think he needs someone to watch him, but I don't want anyone upstairs or in the backyard."

"How is he?" Gertie asked.

"Completely broken up," Carter said. "I can't begin to imagine...anyway, my mom said to let her know if Marie can't stay tonight and she'll be happy to do it."

"Tell her thank you," Gertie said. "And we'll let her know if we need her."

He nodded, then glanced at me before heading out. I rose

from the recliner and looked out the front window. "He's driving away. Unbelievable." Then I remembered Ida Belle's phone call to Myrtle. "What did you do?"

"I asked Myrtle to get him out of here for a bit," Ida Belle said.

"And how did she do that?" I asked.

Ida Belle shook her head. "I assume she told him there was police business that needed handling and no one else was available."

Ida Belle's phone signaled that she'd received a text and she looked down at it. "Oh no."

"What?" I asked. Based on her expression, it was nothing good.

"She sent him to the hotel. It seems the state police have turned over the case of the night desk clerk who accused the maintenance man of attempting to sexually assault a nun in the hotel lobby."

IT TOOK SOME DOING, but Gertie finally coaxed Nolan into eating some casserole. He was slow to take the first bite, but once he did, he seemed to realize he was hungry. He ate a smaller portion than what a man his size would probably have consumed under normal circumstances, but it was enough to keep him from passing out. Gertie urged him to taste one of the cookies she'd brought but he'd given them a glance and said "maybe later."

He'd eaten the entire meal in silence and we hadn't tried to get him talking, but once the dishes were cleared, Ida Belle gave us a nod, signaling that she was going to see if he was up to a chat.

"Is there anything else we can do for you?" Gertie asked.

"No, thank you," Nolan said. "You've all been quite kind. Everyone has been so kind."

"We're all very sad and upset," Gertie said. "I can't imagine how hard this is for you."

Nolan nodded. "She was everything. No other woman was like Gail."

"She was an incredible person," Ida Belle agreed. "I think that's why it's all so shocking..."

I watched Nolan's face closely as Ida Belle let that sentence linger. We all knew what she'd left unspoken. Nolan's jaw tightened so briefly that if I hadn't been paying attention so well, I might have thought I'd imagined it.

"I can't imagine," he said, "who would do such a thing. Everyone loved Gail."

I felt a tingle at the back of my neck. He was lying, but about which statement? Either he had an idea who might have killed his wife, or he knew someone or more than one person who didn't think Gail was as great as the rest of us did.

"I suppose," Ida Belle said, "with her work there is the possibility of unpleasantness. Someone who didn't qualify for help, or that sort of thing."

"A good percentage of the homeless are mentally ill," I said. "It's possible someone imagined a slight or misunderstood what could be done to help. It's such a difficult problem."

Ida Belle nodded. "So many layers." She looked at Nolan. "Gail never mentioned a client that she was frightened of, did she? Fortune makes a good point. If mental illness were involved, that would explain a lot."

Nolan frowned. "She never said anything. Lately, she'd look more worried than usual. I could see the strain on her face, but when I asked about it, she said it was concerns over an upcoming grant renewal."

"Yes," Ida Belle said. "Maintaining funding for such

endeavors is a constant worry. When I served on a charity board years ago, it seemed we were always busy trying to find more money and struggling to keep from losing what we had. It's unfortunate that there's so much more need than we can find the funds for."

"She was dedicated to her work," Nolan said. "Lately, she had to spend so much time on it, sometimes working so late into the night that she didn't even have the energy to make the drive back to Sinful. She'd get a room in New Orleans."

"That's sensible," Gertie said. "One's eyes simply aren't the same when they're overly tired, and the highway is not particularly well lit. And with no shoulders to speak of, it only takes a second for things to go wrong."

"She was sensible," Nolan said. "Which is what makes it all the more confusing. Sensible women don't go around getting themselves killed." His eyes filled with tears. "I can't believe this happened. I can't believe she's gone. Every time I doze off, I wake up thinking I've had a nightmare, and then I remember the nightmare is real."

He collapsed into tears and I looked over at Ida Belle and Gertie, completely at a loss. This was well outside of my skill set. Gertie reached over and put her hand on Nolan's arm. "Everything will be all right," she said. "Carter is a very smart young man. He'll figure out what happened and the person who did this will pay. It won't change the way things are, but it should bring you a small amount of peace."

He looked over at her and nodded. "I hope you're right. If you don't mind, I think I'll lie down for a bit. Marie rearranged the downstairs guest room to accommodate my chair. If one of you wouldn't mind pushing me in there. I'm still a bit weak."

"Of course," Gertie said and jumped up from her chair. "Do you need to use the uh...facilities, first?"

"Not right now," he said. "But you needn't worry about

that. All the bathrooms in the house are equipped for such a thing. Again, I appreciate the meal and the company. I don't think I'd like being alone right now."

Gertie pushed him out of the kitchen. Ida Belle waited until they were out of hearing, then looked over at me.

"What do you think?" she asked.

"I think he's distraught," I said, "and I think he lied."

She gave me an approving nod. "You caught that too, huh?"

"It was subtle, but it was there. I don't think he knows anything or he would have told Carter. When Carter walked out of the kitchen earlier, he looked perplexed, and not at all like a man who had an angle to pursue."

"So it's merely suspicion," Ida Belle said. "I'd agree with that, but still, why not offer it up anyway? It's not like Carter would go arrest someone over a hunch."

"Maybe because his suspicion is wrapped up in something he didn't want others to know."

"The affair angle. Yes, I could see that. No use sullying the woman's reputation right at the start."

I nodded. "He'll wait a bit and see if any other explanation is forthcoming. If not, then he'll volunteer his idea."

We both sat staring at each other, focused on our thoughts, so when the telephone rang, we both jumped. Ida Belle rose from her chair and answered.

"Bishop residence," she said. "I'm sorry, but Mr. Bishop is resting at the moment. This is Ida Belle, a friend of his. Can I take a message and have Mr. Bishop return your call when he awakens?"

Ida Belle picked up a pen from the message rack next to the phone and wrote a name and telephone number on the pad of paper hanging there. When she finished taking down the phone number, her eyes widened. "I understand. I'll have Mr. Bishop contact you as soon as he's available."

She hung up the phone and looked over at me. "That was a man with an insurance company in New Orleans. He needs to talk to Nolan about the life insurance policy Gail had. Apparently, he feels that Nolan could benefit from talking to an investment adviser rather than putting the entire amount in a regular bank account."

"I wonder how much?" I asked.

Ida Belle shook her head. "He didn't say, but it has to be a good amount. I mean, if it were only a hundred thousand or so, one wouldn't need an investment counselor."

"I wouldn't think so. Well, that's good news, right? Maybe Nolan will have enough to pay for the in-home care he needs. That way he won't have to move into one of those homes."

"That would be ideal," Ida Belle said. "I can't imagine living in one of those places. Oh, don't get me wrong, the care is often top-notch and so many of the facilities are quite new and comfortable, but all the same...people."

I nodded, understanding exactly what she was saying. I wouldn't do well with people around me all the time. It would feel claustrophobic. Perhaps Nolan didn't feel like Ida Belle and me and would be quite content in such a situation, but if he had some money coming, then hopefully, he'd have a choice.

As much as choice could sometimes be a burden, not having one was far worse.

"We need a look at that bedroom," Ida Belle said, "and the trellis."

"I don't see how we're going to get it. We can't go upstairs without Nolan hearing us. If we go outside, the neighbors behind can see into the yard, and I'll bet money half of them have binoculars trained over here right now."

Ida Belle's eyes widened. "You're a genius."

"I'll take the compliment, but what's it for?"

"Guess who lives in the house directly behind this one?"

I shook my head.

"Your new friend, Peaches."

"So you think I should knock on her door and ask to look out her back window with binoculars? I can't imagine any scenario where that would sound appropriate, not to mention what trouble we'd get Peaches into if Carter found out."

"No, of course. We don't want to get the poor girl in trouble. She's a nice sort, and her mother would have a heart attack at any whisper of impropriety where that girl is concerned. Quite frankly, I don't want that one on *my* conscience. But if we were to pay her a visit, then one might find a need to see the upstairs or perhaps use an upstairs restroom."

"Don't most of these houses have a downstairs restroom for guests?"

Ida Belle grinned. "You of all people should know. All sorts of things can happen to disable a restroom."

CHAPTER ELEVEN

It was almost six o'clock before Marie returned to take another shift. She fluttered in with a million apologies for the late hour. Apparently, she'd sat in the recliner for a minute to rest and awakened a good two hours later, much to her dismay. We assured her that everything had been fine in her absence and we were happy she'd gotten some sleep. Nolan was still resting.

Once Gertie had returned from getting Nolan settled, we'd filled her in on Ida Belle's plot to get a look at the trellis. Gertie said she had a pattern for the cutest baby shawl ever and some lavender yarn that Peaches would love. Gertie said she could whip out the shawl that evening, and we'd pay Peaches a visit late the next morning. Apparently, young people had a different opinion of what constituted a reasonable hour for visiting. Anything before 10:00 a.m. was considered quite rude.

We told Marie about the message from the insurance man, then headed out. Myrtle had checked in earlier but didn't have any news, as Carter had yet to return to the sheriff's department, much less file a report. We were at loose ends as we climbed into the car, all feeling like there was something we should do but having zero idea what it could possibly be.

"Maybe we should all head home and do some thinking," Ida Belle said. "I think best when I'm out in my garage. Gertie thinks best when she's knitting and that's what she'll be doing."

They both looked at me.

"Uh, I sorta think best when I'm shooting guns," I said, "but I figure that's probably not a good idea."

"Certainly not at your house," Gertie said. "But there are places you can go let off several rounds."

I perked up. "Sinful has a shooting range? And you never told me?"

"It's not exactly a range," Ida Belle said. "Old Man Calhoun retired about ten years ago and sold off his dairy cows. He's got over a hundred acres, a lot of it marsh, so he lets people do some target practice back there. Has some boards set up to hold cans and the like. You give him a twenty and shoot as long as you want."

I glanced up at the sky. I still had over two hours of daylight, and shooting guns always beat sitting around bored. Besides, it wasn't a lie. I did think best when I was using a firearm. "Where is Old Man Calhoun's place?" I asked.

Thirty minutes later, I was bumping along in my Jeep on a narrow dirt road that appeared to lead directly into the center of the marsh. According to Gertie, more and more of Calhoun's farmland had succumbed to the bayou each year, making it harder for him to find places for his cows to graze. Each year, he'd cut the size of the herd to account for the loss of land but eventually, age and hassle won out and he retired from the business altogether.

As I rounded a corner, completely blocked by a line of oak trees, I almost hit an oncoming truck. The truck swerved to the left and I swerved to the right, my Jeep sliding off the side of the road and a little into the ditch. The all-wheel drive saved me from going all the way into the ditch of water, and I pulled back onto the road and stopped. The truck, a black Dodge with off-roading tires, didn't even pause. I gave it the finger as it disappeared on the other side of the trees.

Now, completely aggravated and needing a shooting round more than ever, I put the Jeep back in gear and continued my journey into nowhere. A couple minutes later, I spotted a house out in the middle of the marsh. The log cabin didn't look remotely like the farmhouses you saw in movies, but it was an impressive structure, all the logs notched and fitted perfectly together. As I pulled up to the house, an old man wearing overalls, a T-shirt, and rubber boots stepped out onto the porch and squinted at me.

Somewhere between eighty and death. Five foot eleven. A hundred fifty pounds soaking wet. Bad vision. Too many medical ailments to list. Threat level zero unless armed.

"Mr. Calhoun?" I asked as I climbed out of the Jeep and approached the house.

"I ain't buying nothing from you," he said. "Don't vote and I already found Jesus."

I grinned. "Lucky for me, I'm not here for any of that. Ida Belle and Gertie told me you have a target practice area on your farm."

"Ida Belle and Gertie, huh? Didn't know those two old broads was still alive and kicking."

"They're alive and kicking quite well."

"Good. They're intelligent women. Not many like them around. Most are silly and a mass of nerves. What about you, girl?"

"Me? I'm neither silly nor nervous. I just like guns and wanted to get in some practice."

He gave me a once-over. "Got good muscle tone. A little too skinny for my taste, but you look fit enough to handle a gun." He pointed at a barn about a hundred yards from the house. "The practice area is behind the barn. Got some boards with nails for you to put cans on. Did you bring some with you?"

"Yes. Ida Belle told me to. I have a whole garbage bag."

"Hmmpppfff. Wasn't kidding about wanting to practice, was you? Hand me twenty bucks and you're welcome to shoot them cans as long as you got daylight."

I pulled out a twenty and handed it to him. "Thank you."

"Enjoy yourself. If you decide you need a rest, I got a bottle of moonshine...best batch I made so far. It's been a long time since I had a pretty young thing out this way. Got some money to leave and no kids. You think about that."

He turned around and headed back inside. I stared after him for a minute, not sure if that had been a proposition or a proposal.

I climbed back in the Jeep and drove out behind the barn. It took a couple minutes to set up a row of cans, and then I unloaded my guns on a makeshift table. I looked down at the collection and smiled. Marge had certainly known her weapons, and loved collecting them. And this was just the pistols. I hadn't dared pull out the barely-legal and not-even-legal parts of her collection. I didn't want people to know what she'd hidden behind that secret panel in her bedroom closet. I pulled on safety glasses got down to business.

I loaded the nine-millimeter I usually carried and let off sixty rounds, pausing only to change out the empty magazine with a loaded one. Then I switched things up a bit and did a couple rounds with a revolver. The 1911 kept calling to me, so I pulled .45 rounds out of my bag and got to shooting. The 1911 was one of my favorite weapons, and this one was an excellent pistol. The trigger was smooth as butter and with hardly any recoil, it wasn't any more difficult than firing the nine-millimeter. By the time I was done, only shards of aluminum remained, the tiny pieces wrapped around the nails that held them in place.

I loaded another magazine in the nine-millimeter and leveled the pistol at one of the nails. A second later, I squeezed and the bullet cut the nail in half. I smiled and lowered the gun. I better stop at one. It wouldn't do to tear up Mr. Calhoun's shooting area. I put the pistol down on the table and pulled off the glasses.

"Impressive." Carter's voice sounded behind me.

I whipped around, startled that I hadn't heard him walk up and already bracing myself for whatever accusation was likely forthcoming.

"I figured you were really good," he continued, "but that nail...that's fifty yards at least. I wonder can you handle farther."

"Yes. The distance depends on carry, of course."

He nodded.

"Are you here to arrest me?"

He raised his eyebrows. "Am I supposed to be?"

"Well, it's become a common occurrence. Maybe not arresting me, but questioning me about my movements to make sure I'm not some notorious criminal hiding out in Sinful and single-handedly destroying the town."

He looked over at the table. "Did you get that stash from Harrison?"

"No. It belonged to Marge."

"I searched her house after she died to make sure there were no weapons. The house was going to sit empty for a while and it's never a good idea to have guns lying around unattended."

"You missed a spot."

"But you found it, and didn't tell me."

"It's not your inheritance. I'll let Sandy-Sue know where to find them when she eventually gets here to handle this for real."

"I don't suppose that's all of it," he said, looking a bit pained.

"Not even close," I said while simultaneously admonishing myself for enjoying his discomfort as much as I did. "Anything else you can pin on me besides borrowing weapons?"

"I don't know. Do you know any nuns?"

"Not the last time I checked," I said, holding in a smile.

"Bummer."

"So if you're not here to harass me, then what are you here for?"

He pointed to a duffel bag sitting on a stack of wood that I hadn't noticed before. "I came to shoot. I didn't know you'd be here. Didn't even know you knew about this place."

"Just heard about it today. Ida Belle told me."

He looked at the row of shredded cans again and frowned. "Are you dusting off the cobwebs before you head back to DC?"

Given his stance on our ill-fated relationship due to my profession, I couldn't imagine why he cared, but the edge in his voice was unmistakable.

"No," I said finally. "After New Orleans, Ahmad disappeared into the shadows again. My freedom is no closer today than it was the day I arrived."

"I'm sorry," he said.

I was momentarily surprised that he sounded as if he meant it, but then I wondered if he was sorry for me because I was still in limbo or sorry for himself because I had to remain in Sinful.

"Hazard of the job, I guess," I said.

He nodded and looked out across the marsh. Several uncomfortable seconds of silence ensued and I was about to pack up my pistols and head home when he said quietly, "I've missed you."

I stared at him, no idea what to say. My pulse rate jumped and my heart pounded in my temples. "I've missed you, too," I said finally.

"I...I wasn't fair to you," he said. "I didn't explain my reasons, and I owe you better than that."

"You don't owe me anything. I'm the one who lied. I'm sure your reasons are important to you, but since I can't change who or what I am, they really don't matter, do they?"

"Maybe not," he said, "but I'd still like to tell you. That is, if you're willing to listen."

Was I willing? I wasn't sure. Part of me wanted to know simply because that part still had feelings for Carter and wanted to know more about him. But the piece of me that belonged in DC knew that no matter what he said, it wouldn't change anything. I didn't need closure. I needed a miracle.

"Okay," I said, going against all good judgment. This conversation couldn't serve to do anything but hurt me more —pointing out all my flaws and all the reasons why I would never be good enough for Carter LeBlanc. And yet I couldn't bring myself to say no.

"Not now," Carter said. "I only had an hour break and I've got to be back to work in fifteen minutes. Your place? Tomorrow night?"

"Yeah. What time?"

"With everything going on, I'm not sure. I'll let you know. Is that all right?"

I nodded and he picked up his duffel bag. "I'll see you tomorrow then."

I watched until he disappeared around the barn, then wondered how long he'd been standing there. He'd said he had fifteen minutes left on his hour break. It took about ten minutes to drive out here from downtown Sinful. Had he been watching me for that long and I'd never noticed? He'd looked almost sad when he'd complimented me on my shooting ability. Was he starting to realize what I already knew—that someone like me wasn't made to live a regular life?

I started packing the pistols into the bag. Speculating was a waste of time. If Carter was serious about explaining himself, then tomorrow night, I'd have all the answers I needed.

And they wouldn't make a bit of difference.

GERTIE PULLED the tiny purple shawl out of a paper bag and showed it to me. "Isn't it cute?"

Even though I had a slight to moderate aversion to babies, shawls, and the color purple, I had to admit, it was kinda cute. I had no earthly idea under what circumstances a baby needed a shawl, but I didn't figure it was information I'd ever need, so no point in asking.

"It's fantastic," Ida Belle said. "Now can you put it down and watch the road?"

Gertie looked out the windshield and yanked the steering wheel to the right just in time to keep her car from launching over pink flamingos and into someone's front lawn.

"Peaches will love it," I said. "You're sure she's at home?"

Gertie nodded. "Yesterday evening, at the General Store, I heard Brandi Monroe say Peaches was watching her son, Barclay, this morning at eight-thirty for an hour so she could get her hair done."

"Barclay?" I asked.

"Brandi fancies herself highfalutin," Ida Belle said, "so she picked an English name."

"Isn't it Scottish?" I asked.

"Not according to Brandi," Ida Belle said.

I checked my watch. Nine forty. Hopefully, Highfalutin Brandi and Barclay would be long gone by the time we got there. Baby shawls and chitchat were already outside my comfort zone. I didn't want to add more pieces to the morning puzzle.

"What time are we relieving Marie?" I asked.

"Whenever we can get there," Gertie said. "She doesn't have an appointment or anything. She just wanted to get home for a shower and change of clothes and to get some things done around her house."

Gertie pulled into the drive of a pleasant two-story house with light gray siding and bright white shutters. No other vehicles were parked in the driveway or on the street near the house, so it looked like we were in the clear. We made our way up the driveway and Ida Belle rang the doorbell.

A minute later, a somewhat harried-looking Peaches opened the door and peered out. When she saw the three of us, she looked a little surprised, then smiled. "Good morning, you guys," she said and pushed open the screen door. "Come on in. This is a nice surprise."

"I hope we're not intruding," Gertie said. "We're on our way to the Bishop house to take over for Marie but I had this shawl I made for your daughter and thought we'd drop it off on the way."

"Are you all right?" Ida Belle asked. "You look a little out of sorts."

"Oh, I'll be fine," Peaches said. "I just got done watching Barclay Monroe. If it wasn't so early in the day, I might toss back a shot of whiskey."

"He's a bit of a stinker," Gertie said.

"That's putting it nicely," Peaches said. "I tried to tell Brandi that everything she thinks is cute when he's three isn't going to be so amusing when he's fifteen, but you can't tell that girl anything."

"Never could," Gertie agreed.

Peaches grinned. "You had your hands full trying to corral all us youngsters, didn't you? I've only got the one and she's a really good baby, but when I think about the job teachers have, it makes me itch just a little."

"Me too," Gertie said.

"You guys come in and have a seat," Peaches said. "You've got time for a short visit, don't you? Ever since I had the baby, I don't get to chat with people as often as I'd like. And with Brandon working so much, I start to crave conversation that includes two-syllable words."

Peaches shoved a set of plastic toys off the couch and grabbed a box of Cheerios from a chair. "Does anyone want coffee or tea? I can make up a pot."

"I would love some water," Gertie said. "Tap is fine. I've had this scratchy throat. Probably allergies."

Ida Belle and I declined a drink, and Peaches went down the hall and returned with the baby and a bottled water. She handed the water to Gertie and stuck the baby in a swing set in the corner.

"That thing is a lifesaver," Peaches said as she flopped onto the love seat, then reached underneath her rear and pulled out a rag doll and tossed it to the side. "Unless she's hungry or wet, she's always happy in the swing. Gives me a bit of a break, if there is such a thing when you're trying to keep up a house and take care of a baby."

"She seems to like it," Gertie said. "Does she sleep in it too?"

"Only if she's dead tired," Peaches said. "She can't stand light when she's sleeping. It took us forever to figure it out, but if even a sliver of light gets into her room at night, she pops right up and starts crying."

"You said Brandon has been working a lot?" Gertie asked, then chugged back some of the water.

Peaches nodded. "Jumbo shrimp have been running strong this summer. Not everywhere, but Brandon's been finding good patches of them almost every day. The extra money comes in handy, but it sure is tough being here alone all the time. Makes for long days and even longer nights."

"I guess you gotta make it while it's there to be made," Ida Belle said.

"That's what Brandon always says," Peaches agreed. "You said you were going to relieve Marie? How is Nolan doing? Have you heard anything?"

Ida Belle nodded. "We stayed with him some yesterday as well. He's shocked and overwhelmed, but is managing about as well as one could expect."

"It's so sad," Peaches said, "and so wrong. I don't know how anyone could do that to Gail, especially with it leaving Nolan in the situation he's in. I know I complain about having to do everything alone, but then I think about Nolan and figure I should shut up. I have a whole lot to be grateful for."

"We all do," Ida Belle agreed, "but sometimes it takes a thing like this to remind us."

"Did you hear anything?" Gertie asked. "I mean, that night?"

"Nothing at all," Peaches said, "but then, I sleep like the dead, especially since I don't get as much as I used to. Unless the baby cries. Then I pop out of bed like I'm spring-loaded, but otherwise, a bomb could go off in here and I probably wouldn't even stir."

"Quite normal, I would think," Ida Belle said.

Gertie downed more of the water, then squirmed a bit. "I wonder if I could use your restroom," she said, and got up from the couch. "The downside of all that water for my throat is the constant trips to the ladies' room."

"Of course," Peaches said. "It's down the hall. First door on the left."

Gertie headed down the hallway, giant purse in tow, and I braced myself for whatever she had planned. I knew she was going to disable the toilet somehow, but neither Ida Belle nor I had been able to get her plan out of her. She said she wanted us to be as surprised as Peaches. None of that sounded particularly good.

Ida Belle asked Peaches about her mother, and about that time, Gertie came back into the living room, looking a little sheepish. "I'm afraid there's a problem with your toilet, dear, and I couldn't reach the shutoff valve..."

Peaches jumped up from the love seat and ran into the bathroom. She came out a couple seconds later, her shoes leaving wet footprints everywhere she stepped. "What happened?" she asked Gertie.

Gertie held up a sponge ball. "I fished this out of the bowl when I got in there. Then I thought I'd better make sure it was working properly before I used it, but I'm afraid this ball might have a friend that got lodged down there."

Peaches sighed. "Barclay. I try not to let him out of my sight, but he's like a tornado. He probably sneaked in there when I was cleaning fruit punch off the living room rug. I need to grab a mop, if you ladies will excuse me for a minute."

"Um, if it's not too much trouble," Gertie said. "Is there another restroom I could use?"

"Oh!" Peaches said. "Of course. There's one in the hallway upstairs."

"Fortune," Gertie said, "if you wouldn't mind helping me up the stairs. My knee's been giving me heck lately."

"No problem," I said, and jumped up from the chair. I grabbed Gertie's arm and headed upstairs with her.

At the top of the stairs, there was a large game room with a hallway beyond it. The game room had an enormous television hanging on the wall. Below the television was a nice ornate entertainment center with an expensive stereo and two gaming consoles. A leather reclining sofa sat against the far wall facing the television. We headed past the television and couch and straight for the windows in the game room, but a large oak tree in Peaches' backyard completely blocked the view. The next room on the back wall of the house was the bathroom, and it only had one small frosted window. The room after that was the master bedroom. Instead of windows, French doors led out onto a deck.

Gertie handed me her purse and I almost dropped it from the weight. "What the heck do you have in here?" I asked.

"Necessary stuff," she said as she unzipped it and pulled a camera with a huge, zoom lens out. The purse got lighter, but not as light as I thought it should have. I didn't even want to think about what kind of firepower was weighing it down.

"Go close the bathroom door," Gertie said, "then head back to the landing and make sure Peaches doesn't come up here."

I wasn't sure how I was supposed to keep Peaches from coming upstairs in her own house if she wanted to, but I figured there was no use worrying about it until it happened. Hopefully, the flooded bathroom floor would keep her occupied long enough for Gertie to get some pictures.

I closed the door to the hallway bathroom and headed back into the game room. I peered downstairs where I had a clear view of Ida Belle and gave her a thumbs-up. I headed over to the window in the game room and looked out again, trying to peer through the foliage and get a peek at the back of Nolan's house, but the oak tree was simply too large and full to see through it. I glanced over to the left and spotted Gertie on the far end of the deck.

She lifted the camera, then lowered it and cursed. She squeezed as much as possible into the corner of the deck and leaned out over the railing, then lifted the camera again. Once again, she lowered it and cursed. Because of the big oak tree, I couldn't see what was going on, but assumed something else between the lawns was impeding the view from the deck. It had been a good idea, but we might have to give the whole thing up.

I figured Gertie would head back inside and we'd find another avenue to investigate, but I should have known better. Not about to be deterred, she pulled a deck chair over, climbed up it and slung one leg over the railing. I grabbed the drapes and clenched, probably putting a set of wrinkles in them that would need an iron to remove it. No way was this going to end well.

I took off for the master bedroom, walking as fast as I could because running would echo downstairs. When I got to the bedroom, I hurried out the patio door, just in time to see Gertie lose her balance and fall off the railing.

CHAPTER TWELVE

I RAN ACROSS THE DECK, but the *thud* I'd expected never happened. I looked over the railing and saw Gertie lying in a thick shrub.

She held up the camera. "Didn't even break it."

"I'm more worried about you than the camera." Camera lenses were a lot easier to repair than a broken bone.

"Is everything all right up there?" Peaches' voice sounded from downstairs.

Holy crap!

I dashed out of the bedroom and hurried to the landing and looked down at Peaches, who was standing at the bottom of the stairs. "Everything's fine," I said. "I'm afraid we took some time admiring your oak tree from the game room window, so it's taking a bit longer than it should."

Ida Belle's eyes widened and I could tell she knew things had gone horribly wrong.

"Okay," Peaches said, but still looked a bit confused. "I thought I heard a noise like something falling, but maybe it was outside. I just need to dry the bathroom floor and I'll be right back."

Right back. Downstairs. Holy crap part two!

Gertie couldn't exactly stroll in the front door, and Peaches had a clear view of the downstairs entry from the hallway the bathroom was situated on. I hurried back out onto the deck and looked down. Gertie was upright now and appeared to be mobile, although I bet she'd be sore as heck the next day.

"I think I can climb back up," Gertie said. "If I could find something to stand on."

"No way. Duck down and get to the front of the house."

"What about Peaches?"

"I'll figure something out."

I hurried back into the bedroom, grabbed Gertie's purse from the bed, and headed to the landing, pulling out my cell phone as I went. Just as I hit the top of the stairwell, I heard Peaches come back into the living room and speak to Ida Belle.

Ida Belle glanced up at me, and I waved my phone in the air, then sent a text.

Get Peaches out of the room. Way out!

She pulled out her phone and glanced at it. I saw her jaw flex, but otherwise, she managed to keep her expression blank.

"One of those text reminders," Ida Belle said as she slipped the phone back into her pocket. "I need to take blood pressure medicine at the same time every day. If I didn't set up these alerts, I'd never remember. Could I take you up on that offer for something to drink? I'm sorry for the inconvenience."

"Oh, it's no inconvenience at all. I didn't realize you had high blood pressure."

"It's a fairly recent occurrence," Ida Belle said drily.

"I'm sorry to hear that," Peaches said. "What would you like to drink?"

"I don't suppose you have any sweet tea? The pills have an

awful chalky taste. I can never get them down very well with plain water."

"I only have unsweetened. I've been trying to watch my diet to get off the last of this baby fat. But I can add some sugar for you."

"That would be great. Thank you so much."

I heard footsteps leading away from the living room and Ida Belle motioned to me. I hurried down the stairs, tossed Gertie's purse on the couch where she'd been sitting before, and hustled to the front door. Ida Belle followed my every movement but didn't say a word. Gertie was standing at the side of the front porch, just out of sight. I glanced back to make sure the coast was clear, then waved her in.

Gertie came inside the house, shuffling as fast as she could to get to the couch. I yanked two sprigs of bush from her hair as she passed by and tucked them in my pocket before jumping over the chair and landing in place. Gertie shoved the camera into her purse just as Peaches reentered the room with Ida Belle's tea.

Ida Belle put her hand up to her mouth and pretended to swallow a pill. She even grimaced a bit before downing a big gulp of tea. I had to give her props. She was good. The silence was uncomfortable, so I looked over at Gertie, hoping she'd get a topic started, but one look at her flushed face and slightly heaving chest and I knew she was breathless. Since Ida Belle was chugging tea like a prizefighter with a jug of water, I figured it was left up to me.

"That's a pretty vase on the bookcase," I said. "I really love that shade of blue."

Peaches perked right up. "Isn't it? I got it from one of those ridiculously expensive antiques shops in New Orleans. I've been admiring it for a year now but never thought I'd be able to afford it. But with the big shrimp running, we had some extra money. Brandon wanted to buy me a wedding ring with a larger diamond, but I'm perfectly happy with the one we got engaged with. I told him if he was dead set on spending some money on me, then what I really wanted was that vase. Every time I walk into this room, it makes me smile."

"I can see why," I said. I didn't have a domestic bone in my body, but it really was a pretty decoration.

Ida Belle checked her watch and cleared her throat. "I'm afraid we need to get going," she said as she rose from the couch. "I'm sure Marie is dying to have a shower and change clothes."

"She's such an angel," Peaches said. "I really hope this election audit puts her in charge. I can't imagine why people voted for Celia Arceneaux. She's so, well, mean."

"I think more people are starting to figure that out," Ida Belle said.

"It's a shame they didn't come to their senses before we voted," Peaches said.

Gertie started to get up and lifted about an inch off the couch before falling back down. "Darn this knee," she said.

I walked over and helped her up, checking out her gait as we headed for the front door.

"Thanks so much for the baby shawl," Peaches said to Gertie. "You always make the prettiest things."

"You're welcome, dear," Gertie said, "and I'm so sorry about the downstairs toilet."

Peaches waved a hand in dismissal. "That wasn't even your fault. I swear, I'm going to start charging Brandi a damage fee to babysit. Although I suppose mine will be walking soon enough. I should go ahead and get those lock things for the toilets."

We headed down the sidewalk to the car.

"Let me know if I can do anything to help with Nolan," Peaches called.

We gave her a wave, climbed into the car, and headed down the street. As soon as we rounded the corner, Gertie stopped the car. "Would you mind driving?" she asked Ida Belle.

Ida Belle narrowed her eyes. "Less than a block?"

"My guess is she's sprained her right ankle," I said. She'd tried to disguise it, but I had noticed the limp when we left and given that the right foot was the driving foot, I figured that's where the problem was.

"What the heck did you do to yourself?" Ida Belle asked.

"Well, she walked upstairs," I said, "then reentered the house through the front door, so that should give you an idea."

"You fell out of a window, didn't you?" Ida Belle asked.

"I did not," Gertie protested.

"Well, you didn't fly down from the second story," Ida Belle said.

"She fell off the deck," I said. "A giant shrub broke her fall, which is why we didn't have to call 911."

Ida Belle shook her head. "If that shrub hadn't been there, more likely we'd have been calling the coroner."

"Hey, at least I saved the camera," Gertie said.

"Wonderful," Ida Belle said. "Please tell me you got a picture before you went deck diving?"

I sucked in a breath. I hadn't even considered that all that might have been for nothing.

"Of course I did," Gertie said. "I had it on that rapid thing, you know, where I get a bunch of pictures at one time."

Ida Belle shook her head. "Why in the world did you bring that fancy camera with you? It's too complicated."

"We needed the zoom lens," Gertie said. "The phone camera wouldn't have taken as good a picture."

"Uh-huh," Ida belle said. "I suppose if the pictures are in focus, we might be in business."

"I had the camera on the autofocus setting," Gertie said.

A ray of hope beamed in. If we weren't relying on Gertie's sketchy vision for focus, then the pictures might be usable.

"Great," Ida Belle said as she climbed out of the car. "If you had your glasses on when you selected the autofocus feature, we might be in business."

Crap.

Marie looked tired, but happy to see us. She said Nolan was taking a shower—the downstairs bathroom was equipped for him to manage by himself—and should be out soon. A lady from the insurance company, whose associate had left a message the day before, would be there in fifteen minutes for an appointment. Marie had managed to get Nolan to eat eggs and toast around 10:00 a.m. but suggested we start pushing lunch on him after the insurance lady left. Half of Gertie's casserole from the day before remained, and the ladies of Sinful had dropped off a collection of other items.

"It's like a buffet exploded in there," Marie said. "You should be able to entice him with something. I apologize that I haven't had time to organize it all. As soon as I got one woman out the door, it seemed another showed up."

"Don't worry about it," Gertie said. "We'll get it all organized and make sure he eats."

"And don't rush back," Ida Belle said. "You're exhausted and need some rest yourself. Take a hot soak in the tub and a long nap. We've got all day."

"You're sure?" Marie asked. "I don't want to interfere with your schedules."

I held in a laugh. Since our "schedules" only included figuring out who killed Gail and why, and Nolan and this house were the only leads we had, the only thing interfering with our schedules at the moment was Marie and police tape.

"We don't have anything scheduled," Ida Belle insisted. "Please take your time."

"Thanks," Marie said, looking relieved. "Emmaline is going to come by tonight after I return. I feel guilty and hate admitting it but I'll like having the company. It's hard to know what to say. I don't usually have trouble with grief, but..."

"This situation is hardly an ordinary one," Ida Belle said.

"Get going," Gertie said. "We'll go organize the kitchen. If we run out of things to do, we'll find some trouble to get into."

Marie laughed. "If only that weren't true. I'll see you guys later."

She headed out the front door and we trailed into the kitchen. I stopped in the doorway and stared. Marie hadn't been joking. The countertops and kitchen table were covered with dishes, plates, and pans, all filled with yummy food. At least, all the scents hitting my nose smelled yummy.

"Wow," I said. "Is this normal?"

"Of course," Gertie said. "You never want grieving people to worry about things like food. And if it's all sitting here in front of them, they'll remember to eat and have plenty of choices."

"How long does this go on?" I asked.

"Everyone usually makes sure the family has a weeks' worth of food," Ida Belle said. "In Nolan's case, people will probably drop stuff by for a bit longer."

"Because he's disabled?" I asked.

Gertie shook her head. "Because he's a man."

"That's a disability," Ida Belle pointed out.

I grinned. "Well, I think it's a very nice thing for people to do. So how do we arrange it?"

"First," Gertie said, "we need to sort it by refrigeration required and not. Then we can group by entrées versus sides and desserts. You take the kitchen table and Ida Belle and I will start on each end of the cabinets. Set anything that goes in the refrigerator to one side."

I stepped over to the kitchen table and started lifting lids and foil, dividing the offerings up. My mouth began watering about two dishes into the task. The food was way better-looking than any buffet I'd ever seen, and every time I opened something up, the rich aroma of Southern cooking wafted up. At least we didn't have to worry about Nolan getting in enough calories. A couple bites of any of this should get him a meal count's worth easily.

We were shifting the last of the desserts to the far end of the counter when Nolan wheeled into the kitchen. His color looked a little better than the day before but the dark circles under his eyes hadn't diminished. He gave us a weak hello and we all said good morning.

"Would you like anything to eat?" Gertie asked.

"No, thanks," Nolan said. "Marie made me breakfast."

"What about something to drink?" Gertie said. "There's a container of fresh-squeezed pineapple juice in the refrigerator."

"That sounds nice," he said. "Thank you for coming to check on me. I'm worried that Marie is wearing herself out."

"We told her to take as long as she needs," Ida Belle said.

"Good," Nolan said. "I don't want her to collapse before she gets that mayor position." He forced a small smile and Gertie placed a glass of pineapple juice in front of him on the now-cleared table.

As he picked up the glass, the doorbell rang and he started

a bit, sloshing some of the juice onto his hand. Ida Belle reached for a paper towel and I headed for the front door, hoping it was the insurance lady and not someone else bearing food that required refrigeration. The fridge was overflowing a bit. I opened the door and gave the woman a once-over.

Forty-ish. Five foot six. A hundred thirty pounds. Good general muscle tone. Corrective vision and boring suit. No threat and definitely the insurance lady.

"Please come in," I said and stepped back so that she could come inside. I pointed to the hallway. "Nolan is in the kitchen."

"Thank you," she said and repositioned a folder under her arm as she headed down the hallway for the kitchen. I trailed behind her.

"I'm Francesca Rossi with Southern Life and Property," she said and extended her hand to Nolan. He shook it, all the time giving her a curious look. I checked her out again, thinking maybe I'd missed something, but didn't see anything odd the second time around either.

"Let's give them some privacy," Ida Belle said.

"Actually," Nolan said, "I'd like for you to stay, if you don't mind. My concentration isn't what it used to be, so it would help having someone else to remember things."

Francesca nodded. "It's always a good idea, when things are...difficult, to have someone you trust assist you with things. That being said, what I'm here to tell you is very straightforward and shouldn't take much of your time. Shall we get started?"

Nolan nodded and waved his hand at the table. We all took seats and Francesca pulled a set of papers out of the folder she'd been carrying.

"This is a copy of the life insurance policy Gail had with our company, and here is my business card. All I need from you is a copy of the death certificate, when you receive it, and I can process the claim."

Nolan picked up the papers and frowned. "I don't understand. I never signed anything for life insurance."

"Gail took out the policy on herself," Francesca explained, "and your signature wasn't necessary as the beneficiary." She pursed her lips, then continued, "I'd hoped Gail would tell you about the policy, but I guess that's not the case."

Nolan shook his head, still staring at the document. "She never said anything."

"I apologize for my associate who telephoned yesterday," Francesca said, looking slightly annoyed. "He should have consulted with me before calling you. I wanted to convey the information in person, in case Gail had decided against telling you."

"That's okay," Nolan said, then his eyes widened and he stiffened. "A million dollars! Good Lord! That can't be right."

"That's the amount of the policy," Francesca said, "and I assure you, it's correct. I talked with Gail and processed the application myself. She was adamant that if something happened to her, you wouldn't have to worry about the future."

Nolan's eyes reddened and he sniffed. "She wanted me to be able to live independently."

Francesca nodded. "Although so many of the facilities designed to assist people in your situation are extraordinarily nice, Gail knew that you preferred your own space. She wanted to make sure that if anything happened, your independence wasn't jeopardized."

"I don't know what to say," Nolan said. "It's so overwhelming. I had no idea that she'd done this, but then it doesn't surprise me, either. Gail always put my needs before her own. She was a wonderful woman."

He teared up again and Francesca put her hand on his arm.

"She was indeed a wonderful woman, and she'll be missed in New Orleans. Unless you have any more questions for me, I'm going to get out of your way."

"I don't think I have any questions," Nolan said. "Can you guys think of anything?" He looked at the three of us.

"It seems very straightforward," Ida Belle said.

Francesca rose from the table. "If you think of anything later on, please don't hesitate to call me."

Nolan nodded. "Thank you."

As Francesca started out of the kitchen, I jumped up and headed out behind her, figuring I'd see her to the front door. That was a Southern hospitality thing, right? That was my excuse, anyway. The real reason I wanted out of the kitchen is because crying made me uncomfortable, especially now that I'd discovered it myself.

When she stepped out onto the porch, Francesca turned and shook my hand. "I didn't get your name..."

"Everyone calls me Fortune," I said.

She smiled. "That's a nice nickname. I didn't want to say this to Nolan as he seemed a bit ragged, but if he needs any assistance finding a medical aide or would like to transfer to a facility while he's thinking over his options, I am happy to assist with that. I have a lot of connections and can recommend the best of just about anything in that field."

"Thanks," I said. "When he's a little more settled, I'll let him know."

"Great. Call me if you need anything." She headed down the steps and hopped into a silver Honda Accord.

I went back inside, hoping that Nolan had processed this new set of information and was feeling better.

Apparently, Gertie had persuaded Nolan to eat something, because she was placing a pan in the oven and had a glass bowl in the microwave. I noticed she had a dishrag tied around her ankle. Nolan sat staring at the insurance documents, still looking a bit stunned.

Ida Belle sat at the table, looking at Nolan and wearing a slight frown. I wondered what she was thinking.

"Well," I said, eager to break the silence in the kitchen, "that was unexpected good news, right?"

"Very good news," Gertie said.

Nolan shook his head. "I'm still trying to take it all in. So much has happened..."

"Don't worry about trying to process it all," Gertie said. "Just take one day and one task at a time. That's the easiest way to get through difficult times."

"I know you're right," Nolan said, still staring down at the table. "After my accident, I tried to rush everything—tried to do too much with too little—and ended up setting myself back both physically and mentally instead of moving forward. It was a hard lesson to learn, especially when it meant admitting that I couldn't take care of myself without help and might never be able to."

He looked up at us. "My first wife left me after the accident. She tried, but my future was nothing like the life we had planned. We were outdoors people from California. Camping, hiking, white-water rafting, rock climbing...anything that was outside and required a lot of physical exertion, we were up for it. If she'd remained with me, all of that would have been sacrificed."

"That may be true," Gertie said, "but you were her husband. Her partner in life."

Nolan nodded. "Oh, I resented her at first. The whole 'in sickness and in health' thing, but I eventually came to realize it was for the best. If someone stays for any reason other than they want to be there, it will only lead to resentment. And then what do you have?"

"Two miserable people," Ida Belle said.

"Exactly," Nolan agreed. "I was very depressed at first, but as I learned how to do things and my upper body strength improved, I started to realize how lucky I was to still be alive. And then one day, I woke up and I didn't think about how much easier things would be if I could walk. I think it was that day that I began to feel content. Not quite happy, at least not yet, but content."

Nolan's words resonated with me. The comment about sacrificing one's desire leading to resentment hit home when it came to Carter. He'd returned to Sinful to get away from the very thing I made a living doing. But the contentment comment registered even more. When I'd first come to Sinful, I was definitely miserable, but as I slowly adapted to my new environment and all the new experiences that came along with it, I realized that not only was it not so bad, but that I actually immensely enjoyed parts of it. Without Sinful, I'd have never met Ida Belle and Gertie, and now I couldn't imagine my life without them in it.

"I think what keeps us mired in the past," I said, "is the constant dwelling on what we can no longer do, especially if those things that are now unavailable to us were important. Even more so if our livelihood depended on it. Finances are never a small concern, and then so many people's identity is firmly wrapped up in what they do."

Nolan's eyes widened. "I think you've made an excellent summation of the problem. Have you known someone who dealt with these type of issues?"

"Oh, well." I scrambled for a cover story, then finally decided that a version of the truth was probably the easiest. "I'm a librarian back home and a couple of our regular clients were men who had been injured during their military service. When they first returned home and were adjusting to the life they would now have to live, I could see their anger and frustration. I felt bad for them because if someone took away everything that made me who I am, I would feel the same way."

"But eventually they adjusted?" Nolan asked.

I nodded. "Some quicker than others, but eventually, they all found their new niche. I daresay that in some ways it will never be as good as their old one, but in other ways, it might be even better."

"At first," Nolan said, "my biggest fear was that I'd spend the rest of my life alone, but I think that was mostly wrapped up in the fear of being unable to manage by myself. Once I realized how much I was capable of, and that with a little assistance, I could still have an independent life, that fear went away. I was often lonely, but I was no longer scared."

"And then you met Gail," I said.

He nodded. "I had given up the thought of a romantic relationship. Who would want to take on the limitations and difficulties I came with?"

"Someone who could see what you had to offer," Gertie said.

"I think Gail saw in me things I didn't see in myself," Nolan said. "I couldn't believe my good fortune." His expression shifted from longing to sad. "I think I always knew it couldn't last."

I looked over at Ida Belle, who was studying Nolan. She'd been oddly silent during the entire exchange, but now she cleared her throat. "That seems a strange thing to say," Ida Belle said. "Since I can't imagine that you were expecting her to pass away, I assume you had other reasons for thinking things might end?"

I stiffened. So that's what she'd been waiting for—the lead-in to see if Nolan would discuss the affair that may or may not have happened. Gertie put down the bowl she'd been stirring and looked at Nolan. I realized I was holding my breath.

Nolan looked down at the table again, then slowly back up at Ida Belle. "You're very perceptive. I'd heard that about you. I suppose I could make up some story to pass off but you probably wouldn't buy it, or I could simply tell you it was none of your business, which would be true. But the reality is, I spoke to Carter about it this morning, so I figure it's all going to come out eventually."

"What's going to come out?" Ida Belle asked.

"Gail was having an affair," Nolan said simply.

"Not Gail," Gertie said, doing her best dramatic shocked look. "I can't believe it."

"I wish it weren't true," Nolan said.

"Do you know..." Gertie asked. "I mean..."

"Who it was?" Nolan asked. "Yes and no. It wasn't the normal sort of affair. It was all online."

I looked over at Ida Belle and could see she was as surprised as I was. We were both doing an excellent job holding it in. Gertie didn't even try. Her jaw dropped and she stared at Nolan, clearly shocked. His announcement was the last thing we'd expected to hear.

"Facebook, I suppose," Ida Belle said. "I read an article about how social media was breaking up marriages. People were locating their high school flames and leaving their spouses for them. The entire thing is rather depressing."

Nolan nodded. "I hadn't realized that kind of thing was going on. I'm afraid I'm not well versed on popular culture. But one night she left her laptop open and I was going to check the weather before going to bed. I saw the messages between the two of them."

"Was it someone from her past?" Ida Belle asked.

Nolan frowned. "I don't think so. At least, none of the

messages reflected on the past. The man was, uh, a bit younger than Gail, and was in the military, currently serving overseas. So you see why I say it wasn't a traditional sort of affair. I would have never believed that a person could develop feelings by simply talking online, but apparently I was wrong. The messages were quite explicit about the way they felt."

"I don't suppose she sent him money?" Ida Belle asked. "I've heard some of these situations are more about getting money out of the deal than having an actual relationship."

"I'm sure you're right," Nolan said. "And one of his messages did suggest that she forward funds so that he could visit her on leave, but she replied that she couldn't work that out because she had a joint bank account with her husband." Nolan flushed. "He knew she was a married woman. What kind of excuse for a man is he?"

"A sorry one," Gertie said. "What did he have to say when she couldn't send the funds?"

"He got a little testy about it," Nolan said, "but he couldn't exactly force her. He was an ocean away, and if what you're saying is true, he probably just moved on to the next target. Or maybe he's always working several women at one time."

"I think that's probably the case," Ida Belle said. "Was she still corresponding with him up until..."

"I don't know," Nolan said, looking miserable. "I think she realized that I might have seen the messages. She changed her password and never left her laptop signed in again."

"You said you told Carter about it?" Gertie asked.

"Yes. And he took Gail's laptop," he said. "I didn't want to tell him. It's so embarrassing, but Carter asked me specifically who Gail had been in touch with recently. I didn't want to lie. I know it's probably not relevant, but I felt guilty keeping it from him."

"I think you made the right decision," I said. "Even if it

turns out to be nothing, it's better that you told him than not doing so and then worrying that you should have."

"That's what I thought," Nolan said.

Ida Belle shook her head. "Well, I am so sorry you had to find that out. It certainly doesn't help your mind, adding more clutter."

"No," Nolan said, looking incredibly sad. "I think, if you guys don't mind, I'm going to lie down for a bit. I'm sorry about the lunch, Gertie. I promise I'll eat something when I wake up. Please help yourself to anything you'd like. There's more food here than I could eat in a month. It will go bad if someone doesn't eat it."

"Don't you worry about lunch," Gertie said. "Let me help you into the bedroom. You're exhausted and need to reserve your strength for the things you don't want help with."

Nolan nodded and Gertie turned his wheelchair around and limped out of the kitchen. I waited until they had been gone for at least a minute and looked over at Ida Belle.

"I never saw that one coming," I said. "I figured if she was having an affair, it was with someone in New Orleans."

"That's what I thought, too," Ida Belle agreed. "That would have been the most efficient route given that she was there most of the week and Nolan was ensconced in Sinful."

"Nolan did say she'd been spending nights in New Orleans recently," I pointed out. "So maybe there was someone else locally."

Ida Belle frowned. "I don't know. It's hard for me to imagine a woman of Gail's character having one affair, much less two."

"So what are you thinking?"

"I wonder if Gail's relationship with the catfish continued after Nolan could no longer access her computer. What if the reason she was spending so much time in New Orleans was so she could talk to the other man?"

"The simplest explanation is usually the right one?" I nodded. "It would fit, except for the part where she was murdered."

"What if Gail found out that he was a fraud and threatened to expose him?"

My eyes widened and I stared at Ida Belle. "Because we think he's someone living in or with close ties to Sinful."

Ida Belle nodded. "Which means Gail might have guessed who he really was."

"Holy crap."

CHAPTER THIRTEEN

By the time Gertie got back from getting Nolan settled, Ida Belle and I were serving the lasagna, meat sauce, and French bread Gertie had heated up. It smelled incredible and I could hardly wait to dig in. Italian food wasn't standard fare for Sinful, so I was determined not to get my hopes up. Lasagna was one of the few things I missed about DC.

"This looks great," I said as I sat down with a piled-high plate of pasta.

"It is great," Gertie said. "The woman who made that is an Italian from New York. She's been here forty years or better so no one considers her a Yankee anymore, but her mother doesn't speak a lick of English, only Italian."

Ida Belle nodded and cut off a bite of the lasagna. "Best Italian food you'll find in the South, that's for sure."

Feeling hopeful, I took a bite and sighed. They were right. It was just as good as anything I'd ever eaten up north and better than most. I followed it up with a bite of crunchy garlic bread and almost felt guilty for enjoying it so much, given the circumstances by which I'd come by the meal.

"She should charge for this," I said. "I'd pay."

"A lot of people would," Gertie said, "and I've pointed that out to her, but she has no desire to be a cottage industry. Said she spent enough time at the stove when her kids were little, and now she only does it when the mood strikes her."

"She has seven kids," Ida Belle explained.

"Jeez," I said. "Between cooking, cleaning, and the laundry, she must have never gotten a break unless she was sleeping."

Gertie nodded. "And probably did very little of that."

I looked over at Ida Belle and she asked Gertie, "Is Nolan asleep?"

"He was starting to doze off when I left. The television is on, so as long as we keep our voices low, he won't be able to hear us. Fortune can keep an eye down the hallway and let us know if she sees him coming this way."

"Good," Ida Belle said and filled Gertie in on our thoughts from earlier. I could tell Gertie hadn't had time to process the information like we had, but the gravity of the situation hit her before Ida Belle finished with our conclusion.

"The whole thing is so troubling," Gertie said. "I mean, I always have a problem with truly horrific crimes, but this entire thing has a feeling of...malevolence to it that I haven't felt before. At least not in Sinful."

Ida Belle nodded. "I'm not often prone to fanciful thoughts, but I have to agree with you. My mind is usually very logical and structured but now, I have this feeling like a dark cloud is hanging over us. I don't like it. We've seen some pretty bad things recently. For this to bother us this way means something is so very wrong."

Although I didn't feel as strongly about the situation as Ida Belle and Gertie, I had to admit that this crime left me feeling more uneasy than I had before. Maybe it was because I'd met Gail and liked her, or because I felt sorry for Nolan, but I didn't think that was it. Not entirely. It was something else, something elusive and dark.

"So we're back to figuring out who the catfish was," Gertie said. "Assuming we think it's the same man."

"I think it would be a huge coincidence if it wasn't," Ida Belle said.

"But where do we start?" I asked. "And before you answer, consider that this man has already killed once to protect his identity. I don't think he'd hesitate to kill again."

"And he's made a good job of it," Ida Belle said. "According to Myrtle, no one heard a thing."

I nodded. "I find that interesting as well. I know Peaches says she sleeps like the dead, but a pistol shot coming from the house directly behind her should have jogged her out of sleep. And Myrtle overheard Carter saying Nolan heard a pop, which doesn't jibe either."

"You're thinking suppressor?" Ida Belle asked.

"Has to be. All those people in all those surrounding houses and no one heard anything? It's not possible."

"I agree," Ida Belle said. "So we have a killer who's well equipped and prepared. Where do we go from there?"

We all sat in silence for a while, then Gertie perked up. "What about the photos? It may not be anything but it's something to check."

"It's worth a look," Ida Belle said, "especially after you crippled yourself to get them."

"And made Peaches mop her bathroom," I reminded her.

"It was for a good cause," Gertie said. "Let me go get the camera."

"No," I said and jumped up from the table. "You stay put. You'll be lucky if you're walking on that ankle at all tomorrow."

I grabbed Gertie's purse from the back doorknob where it

was hanging and pulled out the camera. I sat down and started scrolling through the photos. The first couple contained only a partial view of the backyard and not even a sliver of the trellis. The next set was taken from the balcony railing and I was relieved to find several well-focused shots of the trellis, in varying degrees of distance.

I scrolled back, then went to stand in between Ida Belle and Gertie to show them the pictures. "These are good shots of the trellis," I said, "but I don't see that it tells us anything."

Ida Belle studied the photos as I flipped through them. "We need a larger screen. Then we might be able to see some detail that we'd otherwise miss."

I nodded. "There are also some close-ups of the ground below. I think I can make out footprints, but I agree, we need to download these to a computer to get a better look."

I flipped through a couple more close-ups of the ground, then the next photo was a blurred canvas of blue and white. It took me a minute to figure out what it was, then I realized Gertie still had her finger on the button when she fell. That was a rather confusing picture of the sky. The next was a blur of green with spots of blue and I assumed that one had been taken from her vantage point inside the shrub.

Ida Belle shook her head. "You should have that ankle looked at," she said.

"Why?" Gertie asked. "Doctors can't do anything for a sprain. They'll make me wait forever, charge me a mint, then send me home with instructions to rest."

"What if it's fractured?" Ida Belle asked.

"Then they'll send me home with one of those funky boots to wear and instructions to relax," Gertie said. "Amounts to the same thing."

"I'm afraid Gertie's assessment is correct," I said. "There's not much they can do for a sprain or a hairline fracture. And honestly, if it was broken, I don't think she'd be walking on it at all."

"You're probably right," Ida Belle said. "But one of these days, Gertie's aversion to medical treatment is going to send her straight to the coroner."

"So what now?" I asked.

"I wish we could get a peek at Gail's laptop," Gertie said.

I shook my head. "Oh, no. That laptop is locked up in the sheriff's department. We already had an almost-fiasco at the hotel, and if those security cameras hadn't been broken, we'd all be sitting in a jail cell about now."

"I didn't say we should do anything," Gertie complained. "I was just commenting that it would be nice to see it so we knew what Gail and the catfish were talking about after she changed her password."

"Well, it's not going to happen," Ida Belle said, "so put the thought right out of your mind."

Gertie pursed her lips and slumped back in her chair. I knew if she had her way, we'd be formulating a plan to blow open the back door on the sheriff's department and make off with the laptop, but no way was I getting dragged into something that crazy. I was already on thin ice with Carter and my boss at the CIA. If I kept drawing attention to myself, Director Morrow would pull me out of Sinful and stick me someplace far worse.

"We'll think of something," I said.

But I had no idea what.

MARIE RETURNED at 6:00 p.m. and we briefed her on the meeting with the insurance agent.

"That's great news!" Marie exclaimed. "I wonder how she managed it? She didn't think she could."

"She talked to you about it?" Ida Belle asked.

"Not so much talk as mentioned that she'd inquired about a policy but was a bit shocked at the cost. Being an insulin-dependent diabetic drove the cost up, even though her diabetes has always been controlled."

"Ah," Ida Belle said. "I'd forgotten she was diabetic. Yeah, I imagine it took a pretty penny to get that much coverage."

Marie nodded. "Did you get him to eat anything?"

Gertie nodded. "Lasagna, bread, and half a piece of pie."

As happy as Marie had been about the money, she seemed even more excited to hear about the food. She thanked us again for helping out, and I hurried Ida Belle and Gertie out of the house as quickly as I could.

Ida Belle drove again, and as soon as we closed the car doors, she turned around and narrowed her eyes at me. "What was that about?" she asked. "You were practically pushing us out the door."

I felt a flush creep up my neck. "I, uh, didn't want to see Emmaline."

I hadn't seen Carter's mother since the breakup and wasn't prepared to answer the questions I was certain she'd have for me. Emmaline was a straightforward, no-nonsense lady, and I liked her a lot. I didn't like that I had to keep lying to her, and felt even more guilty for putting Carter in a position of having to do so.

"I see," Ida Belle said. "I guess I can't blame you. That would be uncomfortable."

I nodded. To say the very least.

"Do you guys mind if we swing by Mary Esther's place before we go to Fortune's?" Gertie asked.

"Swing by?" Ida Belle asked. "She lives a good five miles up the highway."

"Okay, so we'll drive there," Gertie said. "I promised her I'd drop off some knitting plans two days ago and with all that's going on, I keep forgetting. She's starting to stalk me on Facebook."

Ida Belle shook her head and turned the next corner, directing the car to Main Street.

"Who's Mary Esther?" I asked. That was a name I hadn't heard before.

"She's an old widow who lives in one of those old bayou houses," Gertie said. "Her family was one of the first to settle in Sinful."

"Her family, my butt," Ida Belle said. "That woman looks at least two hundred years old. She was probably original to the town."

"Well, she's got good eyesight for a two-hundred-year-old woman," Gertie said. "She still knits and is online."

"So?" Ida Belle retorted. "You do both of those and your glasses needed updating back when disco was cool."

I grinned. That argument never got old.

"I'll have you know," Gertie said, "that I have an appointment to get that handled."

Ida Belle and I both stared at her.

"Seriously?" I asked. "You're going to get new glasses?"

"No," Gertie said. "I've decided I'm too young and hip to wear glasses all the time, plus they get in the way of some of our more active pursuits. I'm going to have LASIK surgery."

"God save us all," Ida Belle said. "Don't they have an age limit on that?"

"They do not," Gertie retorted. "I'm not diabetic and don't have cataracts, so I'm well within the scope of qualifying for surgery."

"A doctor told you this?" Ida Belle asked.

"Well, not exactly," Gertie said, "but I looked it up on the Internet."

"Uh-huh," Ida Belle said. "Maybe you should wait and see if a real doctor concurs with that idiocy on the Internet before you donate your old glasses."

Gertie frowned. "Why do you always have to be Debbie Downer?"

Ida Belle shook her head. "I'm Reality Rita."

"You know," I said, "LASIK can fix distance vision but you'll still have to wear reading glasses."

Gertie waved a hand in dismissal. "I'm not running or getting shot at when reading glasses would be needed."

I nodded. Seemed like perfectly reasonable criteria to me.

Ida Belle merged onto the highway on the outside of downtown and I watched as the weeds and trees rolled by. A mile or so farther, she turned onto a dirt road and headed into a wooded area of the swamp. As we rounded a corner, she yanked the steering wheel to the side, narrowly missing an oncoming truck that was in the middle of the road.

"Watch where you're driving!" Gertie yelled, not that it mattered. The truck was long gone.

"I saw that same truck the other day when I went to shoot," I said. "He wasn't any better at staying in his lane then, either."

Ida Belle slowed until the car came to a stop. She looked at Gertie and me. "That truck belongs to Brandon Dugas."

"Peaches's husband?" I asked.

Gertie frowned. "Then what is he doing roaming around the back roads of Sinful when he's supposed to be catching big shrimp?"

"That's a good question," Ida Belle said.

"Maybe he's lying to Peaches," Gertie said, "and goofing off instead."

"Then where is the money coming from?" I asked. "That vase that Peaches wanted couldn't have been cheap, and the stereo and television setup in the game room was top-of-the-line. I know. It's the only thing I spend money on besides weapons."

Ida Belle pulled out her cell phone and dialed. "I'll call the shrimp house and clear up part of this right now."

"Hello," Ida Bell said. "I'm preparing a dinner for a large number of visiting family and they really want butterflied shrimp. They're usually priced at a premium that I can't afford, but I heard that lately, there's an abundance, so I thought the cost might be a bit better."

She paused, then said, "I understand. Thank you for your help."

She hung up the phone. "Big shrimp haven't been running for six months or better. In fact, there's more of a shortage right now than usual."

"Why did he lie?" Gertie asked.

"More importantly," I said, "what is he really doing?"

Gertie bit her lower lip. "I don't like this at all. Peaches is such a nice girl—a girl with manners and class. If Brandon is up to no good..."

"Whatever he's doing is making money," I said, "and since he's lying to his wife, I'm going to have to vote for the 'up to no good' option."

"I have to agree," Ida Belle said. "Well, one thing at a time. Let's worry about Brandon when this situation with Gail and the catfish is resolved."

She put the car into gear and headed back down the road. Gertie cast a worried glance at me before turning around. I didn't blame her. I was worried as well. Peaches was a nice girl.

She didn't deserve the kind of problems Brandon might bring down on them.

A minute later, we turned onto an even narrower road and after a half mile or so, pulled up in front of a tiny, run-down house that was completely surrounded by cypress trees.

"I suppose if the walls of the house ever come loose," I said, "the trees will hold them in place. It's like the creepy cousin of the Keebler factory."

"Her son tried to get her to move into an apartment in New Orleans," Gertie said, "but he could never get her to leave."

"So he just stopped trying?" I asked.

"Sort of," Gertie said. "He died."

"I suppose that gets him a pass," I said.

"I'll just run this in so we don't all get tied up in there," Gertie said.

"Good," Ida Belle said, looking relieved.

Gertie climbed out and limped up the stairs and onto the porch. She knocked on the door and someone must have yelled, because a couple seconds later, she pushed the door open and walked inside.

"That woman makes me crazy," Ida Belle said.

"Which one?" I asked.

"Ha! Both of them, but Mary Esther is the worst. She does nothing but complain. It's too hot or too cold or the wind's blowing too much or not enough. That's probably why God's let her live this long. He doesn't want to hear about all the mistakes he made when building heaven."

I smiled, then remembered Brandon and the smile faded. "What could Brandon be doing out in the swamp that makes money?"

"Poaching is the most likely answer. He has a cover on the bed of his truck, so he could have anything in the back of it."

"I always thought most people poached for their own benefit—I mean, to stock their own refrigerator."

"I'd say the majority do," Ida Belle said, "but there's a black market for things like alligator, dove, and deer. Some of the butcher shops are less than ethical about things. Not the one in Sinful, mind you. Shorty's always been aboveboard, but others are less particular about things like the law, especially when it comes to extra dollars in their pocket."

"Don't ask, don't tell?"

"Yep. If the police question them, they say they had the meat in the freezer from last season and are bringing out a little at a time so they don't run out completely."

"And without a search warrant, the police can't look at their freezers and see what's actually there."

"You got it."

"Do you really think that's it?" I asked. Poaching was illegal and very uncool, but in the list of things Brandon could be doing, it was one of the lesser offenses. Other locals hiding out in the swamp had been running drugs, brewing up crystal meth, and arms dealing. A little poaching would probably only get Brandon a slap on the hand if he got caught. A little crystal meth brewing would get him serious time.

The front door popped open and Gertie hobbled back out to the car. "I had to tell her I hurt my ankle and you're taking me to the hospital," she said. "Otherwise, I would never have gotten out of there."

"We should be taking you to the hospital," Ida Belle said.

"Stop your grousing. Fortune can take a look when we get to her house," Gertie said. "If she thinks I need to see a doctor, then I will."

Ida Belle seemed satisfied with that and we headed back to Sinful. Ten minutes later, we pulled into my driveway. As soon as we got inside, I pointed to the recliner and told Gertie to sit, then I opened the shades on the front windows, allowing evening sun to flood the room with light. I raised the footrest on the recliner and proceeded to unwrap the dishrag from Gertie's ankle.

It was already swollen and purple, but not as bad as I'd been expecting. I touched the side with one finger. "Does that hurt?" I asked.

"Some, but not too bad," Gertie said.

"Will you grab some cough syrup?" I asked Ida Belle. "There's two bottles in the pantry."

Sinful Ladies Cough Syrup would stop a cough and cure a host of other things. It was the Sinful Ladies Society's special brew of moonshine, but as long as it was packaged and sold as an herbal medicine, everyone in Sinful was happy to look the other way...and purchase a bottle or two.

Ida Belle returned with the bottle and handed it to Gertie.

"Take a big swig of that," I said.

Gertie tossed back a big shot of the moonshine, then handed the bottle back to Ida Belle. "Take that back to the kitchen. If I drink any more, I'll be asleep in this chair instead of looking at photos."

"Do you feel it yet?" I asked.

"Got that tingling warm feeling," Gertie said. "Do your thing."

I reached over with both hands and began gently pressing on Gertie's ankle, locating the bones and ensuring they were all where they belonged and weren't protruding. Gertie grimaced a couple of times, but otherwise, said nothing.

"Well?" she asked when I finished.

"Nothing's broken," I said. "It could be a hairline fracture but I think you'd have a harder time walking on it if it was. My best guess is that it's a sprain."

Gertie looked up at Ida Belle. "Is that good enough for you?"

Ida Belle nodded. "Let's get it wrapped up good and get some ice on it for the swelling. You can take an aspirin and I'll put a pillow under your foot to keep it propped up."

"But the photos," Gertie protested.

"I'll grab my laptop and load them," I said. "We can go through everything right here in the living room."

I spent some time getting Gertie's ankle wrapped well, then Ida Belle propped it up on a pillow and secured the ice pack around it. I snagged my laptop from the kitchen, hooked up the camera, and downloaded the pictures. It took me fifteen minutes to delete all the duplicates and unusable shots, but eventually, I had it down to fifteen good shots that we could review. I perched on one arm of the recliner, Ida Belle on the other, and started the show.

"Here's the ground," I said. "From a distance and then close up."

We all peered at the shot. "If you look here," I said and pointed to the loose dirt directly in front of the trellis, "you can make out footprints."

"I see them," Gertie said, getting excited. "That's a big foot, isn't it?"

Ida Belle nodded. "Definitely made by a man."

"Or Beulah," I said.

"True," Ida Belle agreed, "but I don't like her for this."

"Me either," I said and flipped to the next shots. "Here is a shot of the trellis and you can see where it leads from the ground right up to the bedroom window. Here's a close-up of the bottom part."

Ida Belle and Gertie leaned in and studied the picture. "Do you see that?" Ida Belle asked and pointed to a section of leaves that were starting to curl on the ends.

Gertie nodded. "That's where he went up. He damaged some of the vine and it's dying."

I took a closer look. "Isn't that more on the other side?"

"Looks like it," Gertie said. "Maybe when he came down?"

"But he didn't come down the trellis," Ida Belle said. "He ran down the stairs, remember?"

I moved to the next photo, which showed a close-up of the other side of the trellis. "This side looks more curled than the other," I said, "and it's already a shade or two lighter." I frowned and switched back to the close-up of the ground.

"What are you thinking?" Ida Belle asked.

"There are several impressions on the ground," I said, "but this one appears to be a tiny bit deeper, although it's hard to tell from this angle."

"What would that mean?" Gertie asked.

"Either it was made by someone heavier wearing the same brand of shoes, or he made it by jumping off the trellis when he got close to the ground, creating a deeper impression than if he had stepped off."

"But he didn't come down that way," Ida Belle repeated.

"That time," I said, "but what if that wasn't his first time up the trellis?"

Gertie's eyes widened. "You think he was spying on her? A Peeping Tom thing?"

I shook my head. "I think it's far more simple than that. I think he was scouting the area to ensure that when opportunity arose, the situation was conducive to his plan. Basically, he was doing reconnaissance."

Ida Belle nodded. "So he tested the trellis to make sure it would hold his weight and that there weren't any weak spots on it."

"Exactly," I said.

Gertie's eyes widened. "But that means he's been watching

her for some time. He knew which window was the master bedroom, and he must have been somewhere nearby waiting for Gail to be at home and go to bed before Nolan." She shuddered. "That's creepy."

"And very premeditated," I said.

"He certainly won't be able to claim the 'fit of passion' defense," Ida Belle said.

"How old do you think that first bit of damage to the vines is?" I asked.

"I wouldn't put it at more than two or three days older at the most," Gertie said, "or it would be a lot more obvious."

Ida Belle agreed. "Marie told me Gail was out of town two nights before the murder."

"Then that's probably when he did his scouting," I said. "Less chance of being seen or heard with only Nolan in the house."

Ida Belle frowned. "This is what I don't understand. If we assume Gail figured out who the catfish was, why didn't she go to the police as soon as she got back to Sinful?"

"Maybe she didn't know for sure," I said. "It might have only been suspicion at that point. Or maybe she thought she knew but had no proof."

"And remember," Gertie said, "if she went to the police, then she'd have to admit that she'd been having an affair." She sighed. "It's all so sordid, using people's emotions to steal from them. Drugs, gunrunning, and the like I kind of understand because for the middleman, it's impersonal. But what kind of person can do this over and over again?"

"A sociopath," Ida Belle said. "Someone without a conscience."

I nodded. "And unfortunately, it's not as easy to spot them as one might think."

Ida Belle and Gertie fell silent, and I knew their minds

were rolling through the citizens of Sinful, trying to figure out which one of them had been hiding a dark side from the entire town.

"Hey," I said, "did either of you look at Gail's Facebook page?"

They both shook their heads.

"It didn't even occur to me," Ida Belle said. "Surely she wouldn't have corresponded openly with the man or even been friends with him."

"Let's check," I said, and brought up Gail's page. I scrolled down to her wall. Another dead end. She hadn't posted in six months.

"If she's never on her page," I said, "how would she know if someone sent her a private message?"

"If she had notifications set up," Gertie said, "she would have gotten an email at whatever address she indicated."

I closed my laptop. "Then I guess that's how he did it. But we still don't know why he would have zeroed in on Gail in the first place. The other women were single and a bit older."

"Maybe because Nolan is disabled?" Ida Belle suggested. "He might have thought she found her life less than what she wanted, which was apparently true."

"And she ran a charity," Gertie said, "so he might have figured she'd be a soft touch for cash."

My cell phone went off and I started, then pulled it from my pocket. It was Carter.

I can be there in 15. Does that work?

"What's wrong?" Gertie asked. "Your face got that pinched look like when I make you wear that push-up bra."

I didn't want to go into it all. Not now. But I didn't see any way to get them out of my house without telling them the truth.

"I ran into Carter at the shooting range yesterday. He wanted to come by tonight and talk with me."

Gertie perked up. "Maybe he's come to his senses."

"I don't think so," I said. "He said he felt he owed me a better explanation of why he couldn't be with me."

Ida Belle scowled. "I agree with that much, but in the big scheme of things, what difference does it make?"

"It doesn't," I said.

"But you want to know," Gertie said.

"Damn it, I do." I blew out a breath. "Why can't I just let this go?"

"Because you care for him," Gertie said simply. "When is he coming over?"

"Fifteen minutes," I said, "assuming I give him the go-ahead."

Ida Belle rose from the chair arm. "Do it. Maybe whatever he has to say will help you let go. Maybe it won't. But he does owe you better than what you got. We'll get out of here. Call us if you need anything."

I nodded and replied to his text.

Sure.

Then wondered what I'd just opened myself up to.

CHAPTER FOURTEEN

CARTER PULLED up in my driveway exactly fifteen minutes after his first text. Gertie had insisted I have a shot of cough syrup to steady my nerves, but I didn't think it had done much good. It confused me how a simple conversation with someone who wasn't a physical threat had me more nervous than being undercover and talking to a target.

He's an emotional threat.

I sighed and went to open the door. That was the only threat I wasn't trained to deal with.

He walked in quietly, almost hesitant, and it hit me that he was nervous too. That was something, at least, and it did make me feel a tiny bit better.

I headed back for the kitchen. I thought whatever he had to say would be easier with a table in between us, and it gave my arms somewhere to rest instead of hanging limp at my sides. Even better would be if I had something to drink, so I went straight for the refrigerator.

"Do you want a beer?" I asked.

"That would be great," he said, and gave me a grateful look as he took a seat at the table.

I opened two beers and sat across from him. He looked tired and something else, sad maybe? I wondered if that was because of me or because of the case.

"You look beat," I said, breaking the unbearable silence.

"I am," he said. "I would never admit this to Mom, but I don't think I'm a hundred percent."

"A concussion can take a long time to completely heal. And you haven't really given it a good rest."

"I know, but lately, there doesn't seem to be time for rest. It's like this entire town has turned upside down." He looked down at his beer bottle and tapped his finger against it. "This is exactly the sort of thing I was trying to avoid by coming back here...things like this murder."

I nodded. Carter had told me the reason he came back to Sinful when he left the Marine Corps was because he thought it would be as far removed from the things he'd seen in Iraq as he could get. Unfortunately, it wasn't working out that way.

"But surely," I said, "crime happens everywhere."

"Of course. But crime in Sinful used to be limited to poaching and drunks and the occasional assault charge. Even the deaths were garden-variety—natural causes or accidental drownings and the like."

"That's not exactly correct," I said. "Marie's husband was murdered years ago. You just didn't know about it until this summer. And that's not the only crime that went back in time. Maybe Sinful isn't as peaceful as you believed."

He stared at the wall behind me for a bit, then nodded. "That's probably true, and crime has gotten worse overall everywhere. I guess it was foolish to think it wouldn't escalate here as well. Still, this situation with Gail is one I didn't expect. A domestic dispute gone bad, I could see, but this?"

"I think everyone is surprised and shocked. You're not in the minority."

"I don't suppose I am." He looked directly at me. "Anyway, it looks like my reasons for returning to Sinful have been rendered useless. I'm right in the thick of the kind of tragedies I'd hoped to avoid."

"A big city would be worse."

"Yeah, but it probably wouldn't be personal."

I nodded, completely understanding his viewpoint. Until I came to Sinful, none of my missions had been personal, which made them easy from a mental standpoint. Get in. Do the job. Get out. But in Sinful, I'd made friends. There were people who mattered, and when they'd been at risk, I had been unprepared for the overwhelming emotions that came over me. I couldn't imagine how much harder it was for Carter, having known most of the people here all of his life.

"I can appreciate that," I said. "My work is, well, my work, but the things I've gotten mixed up with here were because the people mattered to me. Not because it was the next assignment."

He gave me a small smile. "You've certainly done your share of getting mixed up in things. I think back about how worried I was that you were going to get yourself hurt or killed. I should have been worried about everyone else you came in contact with."

The smile remained in place so I knew he meant it to be funny and a compliment. But it was still a harsh reminder of the position I'd put him in, and I still felt guilty for all the worry Carter had endured over my safety.

"I'm sorry you worried about me," I said before I could change my mind. "I mean, I'm not going to say it wasn't nice to have someone worrying about me—that's sort of a new thing in my life—but I wish I could have informed you better so that you wouldn't have worried quite as much."

"I appreciate the apology, but honestly, I don't think it

would have mattered if I'd known, not if I'd already developed feelings for you. In fact, I worry about you more now that I know why you're here and the risks you're willing to take because of who you are."

I frowned. I hadn't thought about it that way, but perhaps he was right. An amateur poking their nose into police business could get caught in the cross fire, but after so many years with the CIA, the very nature of my existence was risky. Ahmad was the biggest threat, but I'd made more than one enemy.

"That's part of what I wanted to explain," he said. "I've never told anyone what I'm about to share with you, not even my mother, so I'd appreciate it if you kept it between the two of us."

"Of course," I said, a bit surprised by his admission. What in the world could be so horrible that he hadn't shared it with a single other person until now?

"You know I served in Iraq with the Marine Corps," he said. "What you don't know is that I was Force Recon."

My eyes widened a little. I figured Carter had done his time in a special unit—he had the demeanor of someone with advanced training and experience—but Force Recon was an elite group of reconnaissance marines. In short, they were the most badass of the badasses. The few times I'd worked with a unit, I'd been blown away by their efficiency and reaction time.

"Wow," I said. "That explains why you desperately needed some downtime after you got out."

He nodded. "I saw my share of things, that's for sure. But the one that did me in happened right before my time was up. It's the main reason I didn't reenlist."

He looked down at the table, took a deep breath, then blew it out. "We were on a joint mission with three Mossad agents. I can't tell you the details, of course, but we'd been working with them for six months collecting intelligence for a strike. One of the agents was a young woman—your age and just as deadly."

He looked back up when he delivered the last sentence and without even hearing the rest of the story, I knew where it was going. He'd fallen for the woman. I could see it all in his sad and wistful expression. And she'd died. I was sure of it.

"You fell in love with her," I said simply.

"Yes, maybe. Given the emotional high of our situation, it's hard for me to know for sure, but I cared for her. I cared for her more than I ever had anyone else before."

"What happened? If you can say."

"Something went wrong, as they do sometimes with that type of work. You can gather mountains of intelligence, but that one tiny thing you don't know could be the thing that makes everything fall apart."

I nodded. I had firsthand knowledge of that.

"She died," I said.

Carter nodded, clearly miserable. "And there was nothing I could do to prevent it. Even worse, we had to leave her there or we would all have died with her and the mission would have been a complete failure."

My stomach rolled and my breath caught in my throat. It was a soldier's worst nightmare...to leave a member of their unit behind. Losing a member was bad enough, and almost always left the others with horrible guilt, even when there was nothing they could have done to change things. But in Carter's case, all that was amplified by his feelings for the woman. It was a million times more devastating. A million times more painful. And in that instant, I understood why he couldn't have a relationship with me. He couldn't take that loss again. And someone like me had a high risk of repeating the very horror he'd been trying to avoid. Every day, he'd be looking over *my* shoulder, worried that someone was gunning for me.

"I'm so sorry," I said. "I won't say I understand how you feel because I don't. I've never lost anyone under those circumstances, not anyone I had deep feelings for. And I understand why you can't be involved with me. I don't blame you. If I were in your place, I wouldn't want to either."

"But that's the problem. I know I don't want the things you bring into my life, but it doesn't stop me from still wanting you. I just don't see any way to resolve it..."

"As long as I'm still with the CIA," I finished.

He nodded. "And you're sure that's where you want to be?"

The tiny bit of hopefulness in his voice almost did me in. But how could I answer? Right now, I was uncertain of almost every aspect of my life from my past to my future. I was drowning and in desperate need of a life preserver.

"That answer used to be easy," I said finally, "but now, I'm not so sure. I've spent all my time and energy dedicated to my job without ever asking myself why. It wasn't until I came here that I even realized I should be."

"Harrison told me your mother died when you were young. Maybe if she hadn't, you would have had more than one path to consider."

I nodded, just now realizing that although Carter knew who and what I was, the only things he knew about my past were what Harrison had told him.

"I'm sure you're right," I said. "My mother was nothing like my father. Looking back, I have no idea why they ever got together, and if she'd lived, I wonder if she would have stayed with him for the long term."

"But he didn't have a long term either."

"No. He was killed on a mission when I was fifteen."

"What happened to you after? Did you go to family?"

I shook my head. "Both sets of grandparents died when I was a baby and my parents were only children. I think I have some distant cousins, but I've never met them. You can't exactly drop a teenager in on strangers. That's not a good situation for anyone."

"Foster care?"

"God no! Morrow made sure I avoided that horror. My father had made provisions that Morrow be in charge of my care in the event that something happened to him. Morrow is the closest thing to family that I've got. He and his wife took me in until I finished high school, which I managed to do a year sooner than scheduled, so I was only with them a little over a year. I had insurance money from both parents, so college wasn't an economic issue. I graduated and went straight to the CIA."

Carter shook his head. "Wow. That's a whole lot for you to handle at such a young age. So you went from living with your father, who was CIA agent extraordinaire, to living with his boss, who has his own reputation for his accomplishments back in the day. It's no wonder you had a one-track mind. You'd never known anything else."

"That's true, but it's the easy way out as far as explanations go." I leaned across the table and looked him directly in the eyes. "See, if it was just a matter of doing things because of other people, I could walk away without a qualm, but the truth is that what I do is part of me. Coming to Sinful has taught me so many things about myself, but one of the big ones is that what I do is part of who I am. If it wasn't, I would never have let Gertie and Ida Belle involve me in things I should have kept well out of."

I could tell he wasn't overly happy with what I said, but at the same time, he understood it. After all, he hadn't returned to Sinful and taken up shrimping. He'd gone into law enforcement. I truly believed that some people are called to that type of work and are unable to do anything else.

"So you've made up your mind," he said. "When Ahmad is out of play, you'll return to DC and the CIA?"

I sighed. "If only it were that simple, but I don't think it would be. Being here has changed me...not in a bad way for me, personally, but probably not in a good way for my future with the agency. I've been thinking about that day ever since I arrived here and my thinking from that first day when you caught me throwing my shoes into the bayou is not at all the same as my thinking now."

Carter nodded. "You can never go home again."

"That's exactly it. I'm starting to see my previous life as very narrow, and I think going back and attempting to slip into my old life would be impossible. In order to do my job well, nothing can be even remotely as important as the job. Now that I've met people I care for, and experienced actually having a life outside of my work, I don't think I want to let that go. Not completely."

"But you don't want to let the work go completely, either."

"I don't think I can. I think what I have to do is create a new life that gives me both options. Neither at one hundred percent, but neither at zero."

He was quiet for several seconds, studying me, and I could tell he wanted to ask something but wasn't sure about it. Finally, he asked, "So you've never had anyone you cared about enough to make you question things before now?"

"No." And that was the God's honest truth.

"What about Harrison?"

"It never once crossed my mind. Don't get me wrong—I like Harrison and I have huge respect for him. But I don't think either of us has ever viewed the other outside of our abilities and our obligation to keep each other safe. I guess if I thought hard about it, I'd have to admit that I do care about him, but it's not something I think about because it might interfere with my work."

"And you think Harrison feels the same way?"

"I'd bet money on it. Harrison is a great partner and a damned fine agent. I wouldn't trust my life to anyone else at the agency, but that's where it begins and ends. Besides, Harrison has a girl that he's been seeing casually. In fact, I just spoke with him about it. When all this is over, he's leaving the agency. Apparently, my crisis has made him question things as well."

"Well, I would tell you police work has fewer risks, but lately, it doesn't seem that way. And then there's the personal element if you set up shop where you know everyone." He shook his head. "This murder has really hit me hard. Gail Bishop is one of the nicest women I've ever known, and she made a real difference with her work. It's a huge loss for Sinful, New Orleans, and so many people who will never be helped because she's no longer here."

"And Nolan," I said. "I can't imagine how he must feel. The only silver lining is that he doesn't have to worry about going into a facility. With the insurance money, he'll be able to afford in-home assistance as he needs it."

"What insurance?" Carter asked. "I asked Nolan about insurance the other day...I knew he'd need a death certificate."

I told him about the insurance agent's visit and the policy Gail had taken out in secret. "Isn't that great? I mean, considering."

He nodded. "It takes away one worry, at least."

"I think Ida Belle was going to handle the paperwork for him when the death certificate is ready."

"I'll let her know when it's available."

An awkward silence ensued and I wiggled a bit in my seat,

feeling like a five-year-old in church—or my adult self in church. My only saving grace was that a quick glance at Carter let me know he was feeling as uncomfortable as I was. Or maybe it was something more. He was staring out my kitchen window and frowning.

"Is everything okay?" I asked.

He came back into focus and looked at me. "Yeah. I mean, no, but it's as good as it's getting for now. I guess I better get going. I've got a mountain of paperwork to do."

I'm sure that was true, but at the same time, I felt like it was more of an excuse to leave than a reason to leave. I rose from my chair and followed him to the front door, not sure what I thought about our conversation. Did I feel better? Had I gotten closure? I so hated that word. It was too pop psychology.

Carter stepped outside and turned back to face me. Before I could change my mind, I blurted out, "Are you still mad at the three of us for lying to you?"

He sighed. "It would be a lot easier if I were. But then I'd be a hypocrite. The three of you were doing what you were supposed to do—protecting secrets you'd been entrusted to protect. I appreciate that necessity because it's part of my life as well. But I'd be lying if I said I liked it. For any of us."

I nodded and felt a wave of guilt wash over me all over again. Carter was such an honorable man, and he was trying so hard to be fair even though I knew it was killing him to be.

He turned to walk away and I touched his arm. As he stopped and turned back to look at me, I said, "Be careful. Someone murdered Gail for a reason. I don't think another would be a big deal to him."

"Neither do I."

CHAPTER FIFTEEN

I WAS JUST ABOUT to head upstairs for a shower when my phone rang. It was Ida Belle, and she was in a twist.

"Is Carter gone?" she asked.

"He just left," I said. "Is something wrong?"

"Yes. Emergency meeting at Gertie's. That way she doesn't have to get up. I've got to change clothes and I'll be there in ten."

She disconnected the call and I looked at my phone and frowned. Ida Belle was always the calm, efficient one, but she was clearly stressed. Whatever was going on, Gertie must not know about it yet since Ida Belle wasn't over there. Which told me exactly nothing except that something had happened between when Ida Belle took Gertie home and now. Something that had her normally calm demeanor thrown completely off.

I grabbed my keys and headed out. Gertie's house wasn't far away, but there was a killer on the loose somewhere in Sinful. I had no idea how long this would take, and wandering around after dark probably wasn't the best idea. Not right now. Not even for me. Bullets beat martial arts every time.

I had a key to Gertie's house, but I knocked and yelled my name before opening the door. I was fairly sure Gertie was armed when she showered. No way was she sitting in the recliner, at a disadvantage with her injured ankle, and not armed up to the gills. I stuck my head in and she waved from her chair. I closed the door and locked it behind me.

"I assume you heard from Ida Belle?" I asked.

Gertie nodded. "She called a couple minutes ago. What's going on?"

"I have no idea. Carter had left my house just a bit before when I got her call to hurry over here. I'm going to grab a soda. Do you need anything to drink?"

"A soda would be great, and don't think I'm letting that comment about Carter slide just because Ida Belle has her panties in a bunch. I want to know what happened."

I grabbed three bottles of soda from the refrigerator and headed back into the living room. With any luck, Ida Belle would arrive before Gertie started grilling me. I really didn't want to have the conversation more than once, so she was going to have to wait until we were all together. And I had a feeling that whatever had upset Ida Belle's chi was going to take priority over my sadly-interrupted love life.

As I handed Gertie the soda, I heard Ida Belle's motorcycle pull up in the drive. I went to the door and opened it for her to enter. She pulled off her helmet and I could see the strain on her face. Her hair contained tiny bits of foliage clinging to the strands and she had a couple scratches on her left cheek. I had brought an extra soda for her and passed it to her before taking a seat on the coffee table. Ida Belle sat on the couch and took a big swig of the drink.

I looked over at Gertie, who gave me an anxious glance. "You might as well tell us what's wrong," Gertie said. "It's written all over your face and we already know it's not good."

"Got that right," Ida Belle said.

"Tell us," I urged.

"After I got Gertie settled, I was feeling restless so I took my motorcycle out for a ride," Ida Belle said. "I cruised out to the highway, figuring I'd get some wind under my helmet, and that's when I saw Brandon's truck pulling off the highway and onto a road that I knew dead-ended in the swamp. I couldn't imagine what business he had back there, but I knew it wasn't shrimping. And after that run-in we had with him today and Fortune's yesterday, I figured I'd follow him and see what he was up to."

I felt my back tighten. I hadn't known Peaches for long, but I liked her. If her husband was up to something bad, it would be devastating for her.

"And?" Gertie asked. I could see her fingers digging into the armrest. Her jaw was clenched and I could tell she was already processing the worst possible scenarios just like I was.

"I kept a ways back," Ida Belle said. "There's nothing down that road but a couple of falling-down shacks, so I didn't figure I would lose him. When I got close to the end of the road, I pulled off behind some bushes and left my bike, then cut through the woods so he wouldn't see me coming."

That explained the foliage and the scratches, anyway, but no matter how hard I tried, I couldn't come up with something Brandon had been doing on a road that dead-ended into a swamp. If people had been disappearing, I'd say he was disposing of bodies, but no one was missing that I was aware of.

Ida Belle took another drink of soda, then continued. "When I got close to the end of the road, I could see his truck through the brush. He was parked in a bit of a clearing that looked like it had been made from people turning their vehicles around. He was still sitting in the truck, but I couldn't get any closer without him seeing me approach, so I climbed a tree, figuring it would give me a vantage point to see what he did."

"What if he'd seen you?" Gertie asked.

Ida Belle shrugged. "I figured he wouldn't be likely to look up without a reason. It was a calculated risk. Part of me yelled that I needed to turn around and get out of there, but the other part of me couldn't leave without knowing what Peaches was in for."

Gertie frowned but she didn't belabor her point. The reality was, if she'd been there, she wouldn't have hesitated to scale a tree either.

"What did you see?" I asked.

"He was using a laptop," Ida Belle said. "I couldn't see what was on the screen, but his cell phone was sitting on the dash and he had it attached."

"Oh no," I said as my shoulders slumped.

"What does that mean?" Gertie asked.

"He probably had his laptop tethered to his phone," I said. "So that he could get an Internet connection."

Gertie looked confused. "But why would he drive out into the middle of nowhere to get on the..." Her eyes widened. "You don't think...he's not..."

"He's the catfish," I said. "Damn it."

"Maybe there's another explanation," Gertie said.

Ida Belle shook her head. "If there is, I can't think of it. Why else would he be on his laptop in the middle of the swamp when he's supposed to be on his boat? Where is all that money coming from? We know he lied about big shrimp running."

"He'd be in a position to know everyone in Sinful," I said, "and make a good guess as to their financial positions."

Gertie paled. "But—"

"He was in the perfect position to know about the trellis, too," I said. "And Gail's comings and goings."

"I can't believe it," Gertie said. "I've known Brandon his entire life. He sometimes shoots off his mouth without thinking and he had the normal scraps in school that boys do with each other, but I can't believe he'd murder someone."

"Believe me," Ida Belle said, "I don't like it any better than you do."

"There has to be something we're missing," Gertie said.

I didn't blame her for being upset. I barely knew Peaches and didn't know Brandon at all, but the entire thing made me feel ill.

Ida Belle's phone rang and she pulled it out. "It's Myrtle."

She answered the call and a couple seconds later, her eyes widened. "You're kidding," she said. "Are you sure? Yes, of course. Okay."

The conversation went on for several minutes as Gertie and I sat there anxiously waiting for her to get off the call and fill us in. Myrtle was on night shift at the sheriff's department, so that meant that whatever she was telling was police business.

Finally, Ida Belle hung up and looked at us. "Carter just apprehended the catfish, and it's not Brandon Dugas."

"What?"

"Who is it?"

Gertie and I both sounded off at once.

"Derrick Miller," Ida Belle said.

"Really?" Gertie said. "Are you sure?"

"Who's Derrick Miller?" I asked.

"He's a local," Ida Belle said. "Works construction and inherited the land next to Beulah. He's always been trouble, but the usual sort. Apparently, Beulah made some fuss with him over property lines and dogs and he was out a good bit of money before it was over. He saw the show and thought he'd mess with her. He claims he never thought she'd really send him the money."

"So he has the money?" Gertie asked.

Ida Belle nodded. "He transferred it from PayPal to his bank account."

"And the underwear?" Gertie asked.

Ida Belle frowned. "Myrtle didn't say and I didn't ask."

"How did Carter find him?" I asked.

"Derrick was bragging at the Swamp Bar," Ida Belle said, "and someone called in the tip hoping for some reward money."

"So he got easy money out of Beulah and he couldn't stop?" Gertie asked. "Did Gail figure out it was him?"

Ida Belle shook her head. "That's just it. He swears Beulah is the only person he catfished. When Carter accused him of Gail's murder, he started yelling at Carter that he wasn't going to be railroaded for murder just so Carter could look good."

"So what do you think?" I asked. "Is this Derrick capable of killing someone?"

"Given the right circumstances," Ida Belle said, "we're all capable, but he's always short on cash. If he figured out that he could scam women out of money, I don't think he'd stop with one."

"And if someone found him out?" I asked.

"I just don't know," Ida Belle said. "He's drunk a lot of the time, and there are rumors of a drug habit."

I considered this. "A drunk would have a hard time negotiating that trellis. It would be risky."

"But high on something else, it might be possible," Gertie said.

I nodded. "It's possible. And if you think he has questionable character..."

"Oh, there's no question about his character," Ida Belle said. "It's not good."

"So it's over?" Gertie asked.

She looked like a child whose balloon had just deflated.

"Maybe that part is," I said, "but we still don't know what Brandon Dugas is doing when he should be shrimping, and I know it's none of our business, but I'd still like to find out. For Peaches."

What I didn't say was that until Carter had concrete proof that this Derrick had killed Gail, or unless he confessed, I wasn't ready to put the lid on that line of investigation. It was clear that Derrick had catfished Beulah, but that was all we knew for certain.

"Oh!" Gertie said. "I'd completely pushed that out of my mind, but you're right. Brandon is up to something and he's lying to his wife about it."

"Agreed," Ida Belle said. "I say we keep watch on Brandon and follow Carter's case against Derrick as it develops. As far as I'm concerned, this isn't over until it's over."

I smiled. I never had to worry about missing a trick in this town. If I didn't suspect someone, Ida Belle was always there to pick up the slack. She appeared to have as high an opinion of most people as I did. But then, maybe that came from living among them for decades and knowing all their dirty secrets.

"Maybe he's having an online affair himself," Gertie suggested.

"Everyone in Sinful can't be having an affair," I said.

"It does seem to be spreading like a virus," Ida Belle said.

I shrugged. "I suppose anything is possible."

"So what do we do now?" Gertie asked.

"Nothing," Ida Belle said.

Gertie looked confused. "But you just said..."

"I meant nothing tonight," Ida Belle clarified. "It's already nine forty-five and you need to rest that ankle."

"I agree," I said. "Let's all sleep on it. We can meet here tomorrow morning to see how Gertie's ankle is doing and formulate a plan for the day."

"What if Brandon has already left by the time we get done planning?" Gertie asked.

"Don't worry about that right now," Ida Belle said. "Everything doesn't have to happen tomorrow. We'll get it handled, but we need to make sure you can walk first."

"Oh no!" Gertie said. "Tomorrow's Sunday."

"I am not doing a banana pudding dash," I said. "Celia would probably have me arrested for running on Main Street."

"I don't think the church will collapse if we skip a day," Ida Belle said. "We've got Gertie's ankle and Nolan to deal with. No one will think anything of it if we're not there."

I rose from the coffee table. "Well, if you don't need me for anything, I'm going to head out. I need a shower."

"Me too," Ida Belle said. "I'm itchy all over from climbing that tree."

"I'm good," Gertie said. "You guys get going."

"Call if you need anything," Ida Belle said.

We headed out and I gave Ida Belle a wave as I drove off in my Jeep. I pulled into my garage but didn't close the door. Instead, I went straight into the pantry to retrieve a box of goodies Harrison had sent me. I opened the box and checked the contents, pleased at both the quality and quantity of surveillance equipment contained inside. Harrison had meant for me to use it to secure my residence, but at the moment, I had different plans.

I hefted the entire box up and carried it out to my Jeep. Storm clouds were rolling in overhead, and I heard thunder in the distance. Hoping the rain would hold off until I was done,

I drove the couple blocks to Peaches' street and parked several houses down from theirs. I pulled a GPS tracker from the box and headed up the sidewalk. Brandon's truck was in the driveway but there were no lights on in the house. They were probably already in bed.

It only took me ten seconds to attach the tracker to Brandon's truck. I was just about to turn around and hightail it down the sidewalk when I saw a small light come on inside the house. I froze. It was too small to be a lamp, and besides, lamps didn't usually move. It was definitely a flashlight. I glanced around the neighborhood, but there didn't appear to be a power outage. I saw the light come down the stairs and move through the living room and down the hallway toward the kitchen. The silhouette was too large to be Peaches. It must be Brandon.

It was such an incredibly odd behavior that I couldn't let it go. I slipped around the truck, then down the side of the house to the back fence. I peered between the slats in time to see the light move across the backyard. What the hell!

A million thoughts ran through my mind, and none of them good. I needed to find out what Brandon was doing in his backyard. There was a night-vision scope in that box of supplies. I'd grab it and find a better position to see into the backyard. I whirled around, ready to dash to the Jeep and grab the goggles, and ran smack into Ida Belle.

"What are you doing sneaking up behind me?" I whispered. "I could have shot you."

"You're not that reckless. Why are you looking through the fence?"

"Come with me," I said and hurried for the Jeep. I didn't know what was going on in that backyard, but if I didn't get to that scope soon, there was a good chance I was going to miss it.

"Where's your motorcycle?" I asked as I opened the box.

"Your house. I was going to follow you from Gertie's but she sent me a text before I could leave asking me to get something upstairs. You had that look, so I knew you were up to something besides a hot shower and bed. By the time I got to your house you were pulling away, but I saw where you turned and had a good guess where you were going."

"So you walked over here?" I asked as I moved the equipment around, looking for the scope.

"I jogged. I'm in good shape. Are you going to tell me what the hell you're looking for in that box, and why?"

"Aha!" I grabbed the scope out of the box and headed back for the house, Ida Belle trotting beside me. I told her about the light and held up the scope. She nodded and pointed to the house next door.

"No dogs," she whispered and indicated a large oak tree near the side of the house.

I nodded. She wanted me to go into the neighbors' yard and scale the tree for a better view. We crept up to the fence and I was just getting ready to jump for the top when Ida Belle grabbed my arm and pointed above the fence. I looked up and saw a flashlight moving in the master bedroom of Nolan's house.

CHAPTER SIXTEEN

I TOOK off at a dead run for my Jeep. I could hear Ida Belle's footsteps pounding behind mine. She jumped in as I put it in gear and tore off down the street. "Call Marie and warn her," I said.

"She's not there," Ida Belle said. "She called me earlier. Nolan insisted that he could manage the night on his own and that she needed some real rest."

"Then call Nolan. I don't know what is going on, but we need to get him out of that house."

I wheeled around the corner and practically jumped the curb into Nolan's driveway.

"He's not answering," Ida Belle said as she leaped out of the Jeep and we ran to the front door. I pressed the doorbell, then banged on the door.

"Call Carter," I said.

Ida Belle started dialing and I banged on the door again, yelled Nolan's name, then started banging again. I heard Ida Belle telling Carter to get to Nolan's house now.

It felt like it took forever, but it was probably less than a minute when the door opened and Nolan peered out, looking confused and slightly out of breath. "Sorry, I was in the restroom," he said. "Is something wrong?"

"Someone is upstairs in your house," I said.

Nolan's eyes widened. "What?" He backed up his wheelchair, allowing us to enter. "I don't understand."

"We were driving by and saw a small light moving in the master bedroom," I explained. "Is anyone here with you?"

"No! I told Marie I'd be fine. She was so tired...we should call the police."

"I already have," Ida Belle said. "They'll be here any minute."

"I'm going upstairs to check," I said.

"Should you do that?" Nolan asked. "What if he has a gun? I don't want..."

"Don't worry," I said and pulled my pistol from my waistband. "I'm armed."

I took two strides toward the stairs when a huge boom of thunder ripped through the night air and the house went dark.

"Power's out," Ida Belle said.

I pulled out my cell phone and turned on the flashlight, refusing to be deterred by a little thing like no light.

"Be careful," Nolan said as I continued up the stairs. "Shouldn't we do something?" I heard him ask Ida Belle.

I bounded up the stairs and hurried down the hallway. Crime scene tape was still draped across the doorway to the master bedroom and the door was pulled shut. A new dead bolt had been installed on the outside so that the door could be secured from the hallway. That way, they could delay repair of the breached window in case they needed to review it again, but prevent entry into the rest of the house. I unlocked the dead bolt and turned the doorknob, then pushed the door open a crack and peered inside. I didn't see the flashlight moving around, but he could have extinguished it and been hiding in a corner just waiting for me to step inside.

Carter would probably pitch a fit, but that's exactly what I did. I pushed the door open wide, then bent under one set of crime scene tape while stepping over the other. I turned on my cell phone flashlight and shone it around the room. No one was lurking in the corners, but that didn't mean there weren't hiding places. I pulled open the closet doors and moved the clothes around, making sure no one lurked behind them, then dropped down and peered under the bed. It was one of those with an adjustable base, so no place to hide there.

I stood back up and walked over to the window. The latch was closed, but I knew from what Marie had told us that if you jiggled it a bit, you could get the window open with little problem. I didn't want to touch anything, so I turned around to head back downstairs and Carter stepped into the bedroom, carrying a flashlight.

"Trying to do my job?" he asked.

"No. Just making sure the room was clear. I touched the dead bolt, doorknob to the room, the closet doors, and the clothes. Nothing else."

He nodded and glanced around the room. I could tell he wasn't happy.

"What the hell is going on?" I asked. "It makes no sense for someone to return to a crime scene."

"No, it doesn't."

I wondered if Derrick Miller was still in police custody, but then I supposed it didn't matter. I'd seen Brandon Dugas leave his house with a flashlight. Ida Belle had seen him in the swamp using his computer. He was lying to his wife. The evidence was circumstantial but it all pointed in the same horrible direction.

"Let's get out of here," Carter said. "I'll have a team work the window again, but I don't expect they'll find anything this time either."

"I, uh, I need to tell you something else," I said. "But I don't want to do it in front of Nolan because I could be wrong."

Carter frowned. "Okay. Let me get the situation on-site handled and then we'll talk."

We headed back downstairs to find an anxious Nolan and Ida Belle waiting at the bottom of the stairs.

"It's clear," I said. "There was no one up there."

"Was the window open?" Nolan asked.

"No," I said, "but that doesn't mean it wasn't used. I'm sure he heard us pounding on the door. He had plenty of time to leave before I got up there to check."

"I don't understand," Nolan said. "Why would he come back here? What possible reason could he have?"

"I don't know," Carter said. "But I don't like it. I'm sorry, Nolan, but I'm going to have to insist on removing you from the house tonight, for your own safety. You're already at a disadvantage, and with the power out, it makes it worse."

"But that's not possible," Nolan protested. "I can't just pop over to a friend's house and stay."

"I know you need special accommodations," Carter said. "The sheriff's department will gladly pay for a room at the hotel just up the highway. It won't be fancy, but you'll be able to function and it will be safe."

"Wow," Nolan said, apparently still trying to process everything and coming up short. "If you think it's best. I just need to pack a few things from the guest room. Ida Belle, if you wouldn't mind, I think there's a small duffel bag on the top shelf of the closet in there. If you could get it down for me."

"Of course," Ida Belle said. "And I'll help you put some things together."

Carter called Deputy Breaux and told him to get over to Nolan's house now, then called the hotel and made a reservation. Deputy Breaux had just stepped inside when Ida Belle and Nolan returned with a packed bag. Carter instructed the deputy to take Nolan to the hotel and see that he was comfortable.

"That's not necessary," Nolan said. "I'd prefer to drive my own car. Besides, I need to return here tomorrow, assuming it's all right."

Carter nodded. "Then I'll have Deputy Breaux follow you."

"Do I wait on your call tomorrow?" Nolan asked. "To know when I can return home?"

Carter shook his head. "Hopefully, they'll get the power back on sometime tonight. I'll have my team work the window first thing tomorrow morning. It won't take long. If you want to return sometime midmorning, you should be in the clear. I'll probably go ahead and release the master bedroom back to you as well. That way you can have that window fixed."

"Oh, that's a relief," Nolan said. "My upper back is killing me sleeping in the guest bed. The adjustable one is much better for me." He flushed a bit. "I know it sounds morbid, sleeping in there, but I ordered new mattresses. They should arrive in a day or two."

"It's not morbid," Ida Belle said, and patted his shoulder. "You do what you need to do."

He gave her a grateful look. "Thank you, all of you, for looking out for me. I don't know what I would do without you."

"Get to the hotel," Carter said, "and try to get some rest. I'll come by tomorrow to bring you up to date on everything."

"Thank you," Nolan said again and headed to the kitchen for the garage.

Deputy Breaux went outside and hopped in his truck,

ready to follow Nolan to the hotel. We trailed outside onto the porch and Carter locked the front door.

"Do you want to come down to the sheriff's department?" he asked.

Ida Belle looked over at me, eyebrows raised.

"I told Carter we had some information for him," I said.

Ida Belle nodded. "If it's all the same, I'd prefer to do it at Gertie's house. She's laid up with a bad ankle, but she was there for part of it, too."

"Okay," Carter said. "I'll follow you over there."

We jumped in the Jeep and Ida Belle called Gertie to inform her that things had happened and we were on our way to her house, Carter in tow. I could hear her excited voice asking Ida Belle what had happened, but Ida Belle said we only wanted to tell it once and would be there in less than a minute.

The drizzle that had been coming down turned into giant sheets of rain by the time we pulled into Gertie's driveway. Her power was off as well, but I could see light behind the living room blinds. We ran to the door and let ourselves in, Carter only steps behind us. Gertie was still in her recliner, but she'd retrieved two gas lamps and had them sitting on the end table and coffee table in the living room. They illuminated the room fairly well.

"I'm going to grab some towels," Ida Belle said and headed into the guest bedroom, using her phone as a flashlight. She returned with three towels and we all did our best to dry ourselves.

"It's really coming down out there," I said. "No surprise that the power is gone."

"Yes, yes," Gertie said, "it's raining cats and dogs, but what happened?"

Ida Belle looked over at me and I knew she was waiting on me to take the lead, especially as she still didn't know exactly what I was doing at Peaches's house in the first place and didn't want to say the wrong thing.

"Ida Belle and I were here at Gertie's tonight," I said, "making sure her ankle was wrapped well and that she had everything she needed downstairs."

"What happened to your ankle?" Carter asked.

Gertie waved a hand in dismissal. "I fell off the back deck. It's just a sprain."

I held in a smile. She didn't say whose back deck she'd fallen from, nor did she add that it was on the second story, but then we couldn't exactly hand out that information, either.

"Anyway," I continued, "Ida Belle and I left and I had a book on guns that I was going to lend her so she followed me to my house. We chatted for a bit and noticed the weather getting bad. I offered to take her home and store her bike in my garage, so we took off in my Jeep, trying to beat the storm. When we passed by Brandon Dugas's house, we saw someone walking through the living room with a flashlight. The shape was too big to be Peaches, so we assumed it was Brandon."

Carter's eyes narrowed. "You saw Brandon Dugas with a flashlight?"

"Unless there was another larger person in their house," I said, "there's no other explanation. The power wasn't out yet so it looked strange. I stopped the Jeep and we saw the light go down the hallway to the kitchen. We sat there a couple of minutes, wondering what could be going on when Ida Belle saw a light moving in the master bedroom of Nolan's house."

Ida Belle nodded. "Fortune hauled butt around the block. I tried to call Nolan, but he didn't answer. When we got there, we ran for the front door and Fortune started yelling and pounding while I called you."

Gertie's hand flew up over her mouth. "Oh my God. Is Nolan all right?"

"He's fine," Ida Belle said. "I think we startled him more than anything, but it startled us as well."

Carter, who'd been silently taking all this in, frowned. "Back up to the part about Brandon. Do you actually think it was him in Nolan's bedroom?"

Gertie, Ida Belle, and I looked at one another, and I could tell none of us were thrilled about the things we were about to say. But we also knew we had no choice.

"The Brandon part of things is what I didn't want to say in front of Nolan," I said. "We've discovered some things about Brandon that don't add up."

"I think you better explain," Carter said.

We took turns telling what we had seen until Carter knew everything about Brandon that we did, except I left out the part about putting a tracker on Brandon's truck. It was bad enough I went into Nolan's master bedroom, and quite frankly, I was surprised he hadn't complained about that yet. But I was certain the tracker thing would send him right into the stratosphere.

Carter blew out a breath. "Why didn't you tell me this information before now?"

"For what purpose?" I asked. "We didn't know what he was up to."

"I thought it might be an affair," Gertie said. "We didn't want to say anything unless we knew for sure because of Peaches."

"And you think it was Brandon who was inside Nolan's house?" Carter asked.

"We can't be sure," I said. "It certainly looks that way, but we didn't actually see him go there. Everything we've told you is circumstantial."

"Yeah," Carter agreed, "but damning." He cursed and rose from his chair. "What the hell is Brandon thinking? He's got a great wife and baby and makes a good living. Why would he want to go screw all that up?"

The three of us shook our heads.

"We don't know," Ida Belle said. "But if Brandon is the one who killed Gail..."

Carter nodded. "Yeah, I get it." He ran one hand through his hair. "I need to get back to the sheriff's department and process all of this. I appreciate the information, but from this point forward, I need you to steer clear of Brandon and Peaches. At least until I get this figured out."

We all nodded. The general mood in the room was beyond gloom. No one seemed to have any fight left in them.

"Are you going to question Brandon?" Gertie asked.

"Not yet," Carter said. "Not until I have a plan." He headed for the front door, then turned as he was about to exit. "I know I don't have to say this, but watch your backs."

He closed the door and Ida Belle went immediately to lock it.

Gertie looked up at us. "I assume that wasn't everything?"

"Of course not," Ida Belle said.

Gertie grinned. "Then what are you waiting for?"

I explained to Gertie that I'd gone home but decided I wanted to check out Brandon's truck and see if there were any clues inside as to what he had been up to. I didn't want to tell either of them about the tracker. Not yet. Maybe not at all. If Brandon had killed Gail, he wouldn't hesitate to kill any of us as well. Ida Belle had seen the box of equipment in my Jeep, but when she'd arrived at Brandon's house, I was at the back fence, so she didn't know I'd had time to put anything in place.

We told Gertie exactly what we saw from the time Ida Belle accosted me at the fence up until when we arrived at Nolan's front door. Gertie looked slightly disappointed that we didn't have more to tell, but she agreed that we'd definitely gone the right route, leaving out my intended search of Brandon's truck and hedging a bit on how we saw the flashlights.

"What could he possibly want in that room?" Gertie asked.

"I have no clue," I said. "It's a desperate move, and I can only see making it if you know for sure that something in there exposes you."

"But surely Brandon would know that the house was already worked by a forensics team," Ida Belle said. "They always take laptops, and that's the only place I can imagine proof might be."

I shrugged. "When it comes to criminals, I've learned there's no telling what they might think."

"That's true enough," Ida Belle said.

Gertie sighed. "If only we knew for sure what he was doing in his truck. No matter how hard I try, I can't wrap my mind around Brandon as a killer."

"I'm a killer," I pointed out. "Most people who've met me would have a hard time believing that, but it's true."

"But you're a professional," Ida Belle said. "You're trained to play the role you're dealt. Granted, this cover has been a bit of a reach, but I don't think anyone would ever come close to guessing your true identity. You immersed yourself in the role, or at least, gave it your best attempt—extensions, nail polish, wearing a dress—all of it goes to creating the persona that you wanted people to believe."

Gertie nodded. "And since this is a small town made up of mostly nice people, no one thinks twice about it. No one assumes you're anything but what you claim to be. But Brandon has lived here his entire life. How could he hide something that disturbing for so long?"

I frowned. It was a damned good question. Granted, sociopaths were capable of the most extraordinary things, but surely there would have been a crack in Brandon's armor before now.

"I wish I had an answer for you," I said, "but I'm afraid we're just going to have to wait and see what happens. Maybe we're wrong. Maybe there's some perfectly logical explanation that doesn't include Brandon as the villain."

Ida Belle and Gertie glanced at each other, and I could tell they'd like to believe that was possible, but neither of them could come up with a good explanation for everything we'd seen either.

"I'm going to get out of here," I said. "I need some dry clothes, and then I'm going to hop in bed and sleep until we have power again. You ready, Ida Belle?"

"I think I'll just stay here tonight," Ida Belle said. "I'll get my motorcycle tomorrow."

"Sounds good," I said. "Make sure everything is locked down here."

I headed out and heard the dead bolt slide into place as soon as I stepped off the porch and the beep of the security system. The rain was still pouring down as I drove home. I parked in the garage, then retrieved Ida Belle's motorcycle and moved it inside the garage. I reached for the garage door opener before realizing it wouldn't work while the power was out, so instead of pressing it, I stood staring out into the stormy weather.

If only we knew for sure what he was doing in his truck.

No one assumes you're anything but what you claim to be.

How could he hide something that disturbing for so long?

Gertie's words echoed in my mind and the longer I thought about them the more frustrated I became. And then suddenly it hit me—the one answer that made sense. The only way all the pieces fit together.

I turned on the flashlight on my phone, opened my Jeep,

and dug around in the box of equipment. Somewhere in there was a camera. It was tiny, but it had a chip that could record at least a day of footage. It would fit easily into an air vent and unless someone was looking for it, they'd never know it was there.

Aha!

I pulled the tiny black camera out of the box and smiled. Now I just had to get it in place and somehow manage to avoid Carter seeing me do it. Despite his claim that he would wait to question Brandon until he had a plan, I had no doubt that action would take priority over the paperwork he claimed he needed to complete. Which meant he'd be lurking around to see if anything odd happened.

Carter would spot my Jeep blocks away, so I couldn't risk taking it. Instead, I grabbed a black rain jacket from a hook in the garage and pulled it on, then slipped the camera in my pocket and set out down the street. Twenty-four hours of camera footage. With any luck I'd get what I needed the first round.

CHAPTER SEVENTEEN

IT WAS STILL RAINING the next morning, but the power was back on. I took my time stretching before I got out of bed, pretty sure I broke some kind of record by sleeping until 8:00 a.m. No pounding on my door or emergency phone calls. No creepy critters of the four- or two-legged variety disrupting my slumber. And best of all, I didn't have to put on a dress. If it hadn't been for the whole murder thing, it might have been an almost-perfect day.

I headed downstairs to fix breakfast and grabbed my cell phone. A quick check of the GPS tracker showed that Brandon's truck was still parked in his driveway. Given that it was Sunday in Sinful, I wasn't sure he'd go anywhere, but if he did, I intended to know about it. I stuck a Pop-Tart in the toaster and gave Gertie a call to check on her ankle.

She said she thought it was a tiny bit better than yesterday, but Ida Belle had made her breakfast and insisted she stay put. Gail's parents were due in town sometime that afternoon. They were staying with Marie, but Ida Belle and Gertie wanted to be on hand to pay their condolences as they'd known them all their lives. Gertie was still fussing over following Brandon, but Ida Belle said Carter would be all over him and we needed to steer clear, at least for a little while. They planned on having a *Gunsmoke* marathon until Gail's parents arrived, and told me to come over and join in.

I declined the invitation. One, because despite the fact that it had guns, the television show didn't appeal to me. Two, because I wanted to be available to track Brandon if needed. Ida Belle assumed Carter would be watching him, but I figured Carter would want to work Nolan's house with the forensics team, and he couldn't do both. If Brandon took off this morning, Carter would probably still be at Nolan's house. By the time I got off the phone, my Pop-Tart was singed around the edges and the coffee was done brewing. I poured a cup and headed into the living room with my breakfast and turned on the television. I flipped through the channels and located a *Jurassic Park* marathon. I'd seen the first movie and liked it, so I figured what the heck. Maybe prehistoric killers could take my mind off the more contemporary kind.

I had just started the fourth installment when I realized that I couldn't recall what had happened in the previous two. I sighed. I'd tried to get into the movies, but I couldn't focus. I was antsy about the camera. Was it working properly? I hadn't tested it before I put it in. I was sure the equipment Harrison sent me was top-notch but you never knew when something might be flawed. Until it didn't work when you needed it. And even if it worked, would I get the footage I needed to prove my theory? Granted, if the first set of footage didn't yield anything it wasn't like I could put the camera back and try again. But in the meantime, a murderer was running loose in Sinful.

My cell phone dinged and I picked it up, then bolted off the couch and ran for my keys. Brandon was on the move! I was in my Jeep and on the road in a matter of minutes, but the dot on my screen showed that Brandon had already left town and was on the highway driving toward New Orleans. I headed that direction, watching the dot to see if it turned off.

When I reached the highway, it was empty as far as I could see, but there was a bend in the road a good mile ahead and then it disappeared around a line of trees. I rounded the corner and checked the phone again, but the dot had disappeared. A couple taps on the screen didn't yield any change. I pulled over on the side of the road and checked the signal, but I had plenty of strength. Moving to the next option in my box of tricks, I shut off the phone, then turned it back on to reboot the app, but the dot didn't reappear. When I accessed the tracker, it came back with a message that said Unavailable.

I tossed my phone on the passenger's seat and cursed. Something had happened to the tracker. Quite possibly, Brandon had gone barreling down one of those narrow bumpy roads like he usually did and it had disengaged. Then maybe he'd run it over. Or perhaps he'd gone through a muddy area and the tracker was so coated it stopped performing.

Whatever the case, I'd reached a dead end. The number of roads and trails that spun off the highway was practically unlimited. It would take a month to cover them all. Disgusted with the cold trail and frustrated that there was nothing I could do but sit and wait until tonight when I could retrieve the camera, I turned the Jeep around and headed back to Sinful.

My cell phone rang on the way back home. It was Ida Belle. Gail's parents had arrived and they were going to visit them at Marie's house. They wanted me to come. I couldn't think of a good reason why I needed to meet Gail's parents, but I also couldn't think of a good reason to refuse. I assumed Ida Belle and Gertie didn't want me sitting in my house alone and this was their way of forcing me into socializing. I wasn't sure grieving parents were the best people to expose to someone like me, but I figured at this point, I couldn't make things worse, either.

I told her I needed to shower and get presentable, then I'd stop by for a bit but probably wouldn't stay very long. This sort of thing wasn't within my skill set.

I took a quick shower, blow-dried my hair, and put on a dash of lip gloss. I know it was the South and Sunday, but I still balked at putting on a dress. I'd been given the day off and I intended to take it. Instead I pulled on jeans and a polo shirt and headed for Marie's house.

Gail's parents were an older couple and I could immediately tell where Gail got her nice gene. They were clearly overwrought but couldn't stop thanking everyone for their kindness. Marie for letting them stay with her. Ida Belle, Gertie, and me for giving Marie a much-needed break and sitting with Nolan. The entire town for bringing food and for the many phone calls and emails from residents sending their thoughts and prayers.

Nolan showed up about twenty minutes after I did. He looked like he hadn't slept in days and that was probably true, more or less. Dozing for ten or even thirty minutes didn't give your body the rest it needed. I'd played the sleepless game enough times to know that eventually it caught up with you.

He approached Gail's parents and immediately apologized that they couldn't stay in their prior home.

"I don't want you to feel that you're not welcome," Nolan said. "It's still your home as well. But I've had to move to the guest room because of the police—" His voice cracked and he coughed and looked down for a bit.

Gail's mother put her hand on Nolan's shoulder. "We understand. It's probably for the best anyway. I'm not sure..."

Her voice trailed off but we all knew what she was thinking

—that being in the same house where her daughter had been murdered might not be the most comfortable place to be. Assuming that there was any comfortable place to be given the circumstances.

Ida Belle cleared her throat and looked down at Nolan. "Did the police, uh, finish?"

Nolan nodded. "I haven't been there yet, but I spoke with Carter earlier. He said I'm free to return home. I have some paperwork and a few other things I need to handle, but I think I'll pack some more clothes and stay at the hotel again. The soonest someone can get out to fix the upstairs window will be tomorrow, and I need to hire someone to clear the room, uh... anyway, the hotel wasn't too bad and at least it's secure."

We all shifted uncomfortably at the thought of someone hauling the bed that Gail had died on out of the room, and that wasn't the end of the things that would need to be addressed. Murder wasn't a tidy business.

"Do you need any help today?" Ida Belle asked.

"No, thank you," Nolan answered. "I don't have that much to do, really. I guess I mostly just need some time to think."

"And to rest," Gertie said. "If you can manage it."

He nodded. "I'm certainly going to try."

Gail's father stepped forward and I could tell he'd spent a good amount of time crying. "Would you like us to help with the, er, arrangements?"

Nolan gave them a sad smile. "You know Gail. Everything was prearranged and paid for. She always said that if something happened she didn't want us dealing with such things."

My eyes misted up a bit and I moved away from the discussion and went to stand at the back window, looking out over Marie's well-manicured backyard. Bones, the old hound dog I'd inherited with the house and rehomed with Marie, was lying in the backyard, stretched out in the sun and enjoying the afternoon. He was completely oblivious to all the sadness and turmoil around him.

If only everyone could view life from the perspective of an aging hound dog.

JUST AFTER MIDNIGHT, I peered over a hedge and checked out the house. The front porch light was on but that was it. Looked like no one was home. Perfect. I could retrieve the camera, and hopefully, Sinful's latest nightmare would be over by tomorrow morning. I'd driven through downtown and spotted Carter's truck at the sheriff's department, then went back home and pulled on a black hoodie before setting out. I took a circuitous route to the house, making sure that Carter wasn't lurking somewhere on foot, as he sometimes did, but all appeared to be clear. All I needed was ten uninterrupted minutes. Then I'd have the camera secured and would be back in my kitchen watching the footage that hopefully would nail a murderer.

I slipped down the side of the house and pushed up the window I'd left unlocked the night before when I'd placed the camera in an air vent in Nolan's living room. I lifted myself over the window ledge and rolled silently onto the carpeted floor, pausing for a moment to listen. The house was completely silent, and I moved quickly to the couch and climbed on the back directly below the air vent. I pulled a screwdriver out of my pocket and removed the vent from the wall. I flipped the vent over, expecting to see the camera on the back of a vent slat, where I'd attached it, but it was gone.

"Looking for something?" Nolan's voice sounded behind me and I turned around, still balanced on the back of the couch. He stood in the hallway that led to the guest room, a pistol with suppressor leveled at me. The camera dangling in his other hand.

"I set up my own little televised network days ago," he continued. "I was afraid if I couldn't get out of Sinful soon enough, something like this might be in the cards."

"I see you've had a miraculous recovery," I said, and pointed to his legs.

"I think we both know that's not the case. You know, I wondered which of you it was. Carter couldn't do it without a court order, and he needed a good reason and time to get one. Marie was out because, well, she would never have made the leap you did. But the three of you...you've managed to be in the middle of everything that happens in Sinful. I knew you wouldn't be able to keep your nose out of this. I just didn't expect you to hit on the answer so soon."

"I'm so sorry I interrupted your murder-and-insurance-grab timeline."

"No interruption. Merely a small delay that caused another shift in plans, like the one created by that idiot Derrick. If he hadn't catfished that Latour woman and brought attention to all of this, Gail might have had another six months or a year of life."

"You're despicable."

He smiled. "I'm clever. Derrick did it all wrong and got caught. Greed is the problem with the short game. If Derrick hadn't asked for such a large amount, she probably wouldn't have reported him. None of my victims came trotting forward until Beulah started braying like an injured donkey."

"So you figured you'd make Gail another victim of the catfish, except this time, you'd escalate it."

"It did seem to be the easiest solution for a speedy exit. By tomorrow, I'll have a death certificate in hand and the insurance company is already prepared to expedite my check."

"I'm sure your partner Francesca is only too happy to see to it that it happens. What's her cut—twenty percent? Half? Or maybe she's your partner in more than just crime."

He narrowed his eyes at me. "You're even more clever than I realized. Perhaps I'm not the only person in Sinful who isn't what they seem. It's almost a shame to kill you. You would have made a great criminal."

"And how do you propose to explain shooting me?" I asked.

"I don't propose to explain it at all. I'll simply return here tomorrow morning with Gail's parents and gasp at the shocking discovery of a dead woman in my living room. Ballistics will match the weapon used to kill Gail and everyone will think you were in on it with him or snooping about again and this time, you came up short."

I felt my heart drop. He was right. Suspicion wouldn't fall on Nolan. Everyone thought he was tucked away in a hotel, not to mention the fact that no one else knew he could walk. That was exactly what I'd been hoping to capture with the camera. It would have blown Nolan's entire alibi out of the water.

"I told the others," I said, trying to come up with a way to delay the inevitable. Time produced options.

He cocked his head to the side and studied me. "You're a convincing liar, but nonetheless a liar, I think. And even if you told them your suspicions, they have no proof. By the time those two busybodies convince anyone to check their story, I'll be long gone."

He lifted the gun and I looked down and saw the red line move up my chest. I knew it stopped on my forehead. "Goodbye, Sandy-Sue Morrow. You were too smart for your own good."

I dived off the couch as a shot rang out. I hit the ground and rolled, expecting the shock to hit me at any moment.

Instead, I instinctively popped back up, gun drawn, and looked over to see Nolan lying on the floor, a single bullet through his forehead.

I whirled around and spotted Carter standing at the window I'd used to climb in.

He shook his head. "I keep having to kill people when I'm around you."

Crap. Nolan was dead and I was breaking and entering. There was no good way to arrange that story.

"What do you want me to do?" I asked.

"Get out of here before someone reports that shot," he said.

"But what about Nolan?"

"I heard everything. I'll handle it, but I can't do that if you're in the middle of it, so go."

He didn't have to tell me twice. I headed to the window and bailed out. When I landed on the ground, I threw my arms around Carter, momentarily startling him.

"Thank you for...everything," I said, then dashed off through the hedges.

CHAPTER EIGHTEEN

I'D BARELY MADE it home when my cell phone started ringing. It was Ida Belle.

"Shots fired at Nolan's house," Ida Belle said. "Peaches heard it this time and called the police, then Marie, because she was afraid she was still staying there."

"Yeah. I kinda have inside knowledge on that."

"I knew you were up to something! What the hell have you done? Do we need to raise bail money? Get Harrison in gear to find you a safe house?"

"Nothing that dire. Carter's covering for me. Again. It's no wonder he doesn't want me as a girlfriend. I present enough trouble as a resident."

"Well, don't just stand there lamenting. Get your butt over to Gertie's house and fill us in."

She disconnected the phone call and I smiled. They were going to be pissed that I'd left them out, but it wasn't a mission that required two, so why run the risk?

Until the end. If not for backup, you'd be dead.

I shook my head, refusing to dwell on the facts. They were too inconvenient.

I grabbed my Jeep keys and headed for Gertie's house. They were going to have a stroke when I told them who the real villain was.

When I walked through the doorway to Gertie's house, they were ready for me. Ida Belle stood in the middle of the room, hands on her hips and a disapproving look on her face. Gertie was sitting, so the hands-on-hips thing wasn't a good option. Instead, she wagged her finger at me, looking totally disappointed.

I held my hands up in the air. "I'm sorry I didn't tell you. But I wasn't sure and if I was right, I didn't want you implicated in what I was doing. The worst Carter could do to me is have the CIA move me to a farm in Idaho, but the two of you would be left here to deal with Celia hounding him to arrest you."

Ida Belle looked over at Gertie. "Should we forgive her?"

"Hell yeah," Gertie said. "Now get those lips to flapping. Start with who's dead. We heard the paramedics carried out a body bag."

"Nolan is dead," I said.

"What?"

"Oh no!"

Their expressions reflected shock and horror.

"Before you start feeling bad," I said, "Nolan killed Gail."

For the first time since I'd met them, Ida Belle and Gertie were absolutely speechless. If they'd been required to utter even one word at that moment, I don't think they would have been capable. They both stared at me, eyes wide, jaws dropped, waiting for the punch line. When it finally dawned on them that none was forthcoming, they looked at each other, probably ensuring they'd heard me correctly, then Ida Belle sank onto the coffee table and they both looked back at me.

I sat on the couch and started telling them what I knew and what had happened. When I got to the part about Nolan standing, Ida Belle jumped up from the coffee table and both of them shouted an impressive number of expletives. It took several seconds for them to calm down, but finally Ida Belle sat on the coffee table again and gestured for me to continue. When I told them about Carter saving me from being the one in that body bag, they both sobered.

"That was a close call," Ida Belle said.

"Too close," Gertie said. "You shouldn't have taken such a risk."

"Probably not," I said, "but what could I have done? I only had suspicion. No proof. And on the surface, it was a wild idea. Who would have believed it?"

"How did you put all of it together?" Ida Belle asked.

I frowned. "I don't know exactly, and there's parts that I still don't have answers for, but I'm sure Carter will get it all sorted out. I think the biggest part of it centered around people not being who others thought they were. That's been the biggest issue in my life lately, and something about all of this—the catfish, Gail's murder, and whatever Brandon is up to—kept pushing me back to that point."

"That someone wasn't what or who they were pretending to be," Gertie said. "I can see how you'd be sensitive to that, especially in your current state, but how do you fix on Nolan? It still seems such a leap."

"Not really," I said. "Think about it. Who was on site when Gail was murdered? Nolan. Who had easy access to the house and knew her schedule? Nolan. Most importantly, who benefited from her death? Again, the answer is Nolan."

Gertie nodded. "The spouse is always the first suspect."

"Exactly," I said, "but no one suspected Nolan because everyone thought he was disabled."

"And if you take away the disability," Ida Belle said, "it changes everything."

I nodded. "So I removed that from the equation and then thought about the remaining facts of the case. Who repeated the private messages between Gail and the catfish? Who did Florence Thompson overhear saying Gail was having an affair? Who said the lights went out and there was a scream? Who said someone shoved him down and ran out the front door? The answer was always Nolan."

"So the affair was all Nolan's invention," Gertie said.

"I think so," I said. "Remember when we looked at Gail's Facebook account? She hadn't posted on her wall in months. It would be easy for Nolan to claim he saw something and for Carter to assume it was deleted. It would be equally easy for him to create messages between the catfish and Gail the night she was murdered, supporting his claim about the earlier correspondence, and I bet he did."

"And the insurance?" Ida Belle asked. "I suppose Gail never took out a policy."

"No. That was all Francesca," I said. "Remember Marie said Gail had claimed the policy was too expensive to purchase. I did some checking and she was right. A luxury car would have cost less. Then there was the part where Nolan said they had a joint bank account, but claimed he didn't know about the policy. Surely he would have noticed an amount that large leaving the account."

Ida Belle shook her head. "So Francesca processed the policy and paid for it. And I bet when Carter checks, he'll find that Gail's signature was forged."

"I'm sure of it," I said.

"I still can't wrap my mind around it," Gertie said. "You're saying Nolan and that woman intended to kill Gail from the beginning? That the disability was his cover to prevent him from being accused of murder?"

"I think Nolan is a con man," I said, "and the long con is his trade. When Carter figures out who he really is, I'll bet Gail isn't the only victim. And while the disability turned out to be a great alibi for the murder, I think it was originally intended to explain the large amount of insurance purchased. That's something the police look into at great length, especially when people haven't been married for very long."

"But if you want to ensure your disabled partner is taken care of in case of your demise," Ida Belle said, "people don't think as much of it."

I nodded. "Especially when the insurance agent is claiming the benefiting spouse wasn't even aware of the policy." I frowned. "In fact, if you think about it, I bet they were hoping no one ever found out about the insurance. Remember when Ida Belle took the phone call from the insurance agency? It was a man. Then Francesca showed up and claimed her assistant jumped the gun and made the call. She seemed a little aggravated."

"They hoped the police wouldn't find out about the policy," Ida Belle said, "but just in case, Nolan set himself up in the beginning so that he wouldn't draw suspicion."

"They had a plan to back up a plan and an answer for everything," I said.

"But how could Nolan know Gail would fall for him in the first place?" Gertie asked.

"He didn't know," I said. "My guess is he went to that charity event looking for a mark, and he found Gail. A lonely, middle-aged woman who knew how to cope with the disabled and according to you guys, had a penchant for trying to rescue men."

Ida Belle shook her head. "She was practically flashing in neon."

"So how do you think Nolan actually did it?" Gertie asked. "I mean, he had so little time..."

"But did he?" I asked. "Again, no one else heard the shot because he used a suppressor. Nolan is the one who gave us the original timeline, and we know he lied. I think when he heard gossip about the catfish, he knew the gig was about to be up and he needed to form an emergency exit plan. So he tested the trellis and jimmied the window, figuring if things went further than gossip, he had a quick way out."

"Gail spent the night in New Orleans two nights before the murder," Ida Belle said. "Based on the damage to the ivy, he must have tested the trellis then."

I nodded. "Then Beulah reported the catfish to Carter, so Nolan put his emergency plan into action. Gail went up to bed. He waited for her to fall asleep, then he walked upstairs and shot her. Then he went outside to cut the power and passed off the murder weapon to Francesca, who was probably waiting nearby. Then he went back inside, flipped himself over in the wheelchair, and pressed the paramedic alarm."

Gertie shook her head. "You're right. When you remove the disability and assume that nothing Nolan said was true, what actually happened is simple to deduce. So Beulah's police report forced him to act sooner than he'd planned. I wonder what the original plan was?"

"I don't think they intended for Gail to die in Sinful," I said. "It was riskier, and because they had to move up the timeline using the catfish as the scapegoat, Nolan knew he had to get away before Carter started taking a hard look at everyone in town. My guess is they intended for it to happen in New Orleans—maybe a robbery or carjacking."

"Something that wouldn't draw any attention to Nolan." Ida Belle blew out a breath. "It's ingenious."

"It's evil," Gertie said.

"Oh, no doubt," Ida Belle said. "But all the trouble they went to...I guess I'll never understand why people don't just get a job."

"Sociopaths aren't burdened with a conscience," I said. "And most jobs don't pay a half mil a year. Two years with Gail and a million-dollar payout, plus what he made catfishing the locals."

Gertie sighed. "I understand it in theory, but I'll never be able to grasp it emotionally. So much pain inflicted and without a care for anyone who was hurt in the process."

"None of us can ever understand it," Ida Belle said. "We're simply not made that way."

"I just wish there was some way we could have saved her," I said.

"Me too," Gertie said, "but at least there won't be a next victim."

"The other good news," Ida Belle said, "is that Brandon isn't the killer. I guess it wasn't his flashlight we saw in the bedroom."

"No," I agreed. "It had to have been Nolan. Remember, when he answered the door he was out of breath. He said he'd been in the bathroom, but I bet it was from running downstairs to get into the chair and answer the door."

"I wonder what he was doing in there," Gertie said.

"I don't know," I said. "Maybe retrieving something he thought would incriminate him or something he had stored in there that he forgot to take beforehand. He told me he had cameras in the house. Maybe he was checking the footage to see what the cops did when they worked the room. We may never know."

Ida Belle frowned. "So why *was* Brandon walking around his house with a flashlight?"

"Poor Brandon," Gertie said. "We practically accused him of murder."

"Well, he still has to answer for something," I said. "Maybe once this settles down we can figure out what."

"No leaving us behind this time," Ida Belle said.

I looked down at the floor, then back at the two of them. "The truth is, I think I needed to do something on my own. In the past, I've always had a partner or a team to support me. I think I wanted to see if I could go it alone. You know, just in case I have to."

Gertie smiled. "You'll never be alone, Fortune. Not as long as we're alive."

Ida Belle shook her head. "Way to scare the girl."

THE NEXT DAY, Sinful was buzzing with the news, and a second wave of shock passed over the town as they reveled in Carter's exposure and takedown of the most diabolical criminal Sinful had ever seen. Francine's Café had people waiting outside on the sidewalk and residents were packed shoulder to shoulder in the General Store. Main Street was so crowded with people trying to get the news that Carter finally closed the street down to through traffic.

I chose to remain out of the fray. It wasn't a difficult decision. Crowds of people weren't the kind of frays that I took interest in. Gertie and Ida Belle, on the other hand, were down in the thick of it along with Marie, everyone exclaiming over how lucky they were that Nolan hadn't killed them as well. Clearly, the general population didn't understand the mechanics of the professional criminal.

I spent my morning updating a disbelieving Harrison on my latest brush with death and figuring out how to work the gas grill, in case I decided to splurge and cook a burger. I was just about to grab a book and climb into my hammock when my phone sent me a signal that the GPS tracker on Brandon's truck had activated. I picked up my phone and checked. Sure enough, the dot was moving on the screen. I had no idea what had caused the tracker to fail the day before, but it appeared to be working fine now.

I grabbed my keys and dashed out to my Jeep. Brandon was our only unresolved item, and I really felt like starting tomorrow with a clean slate. I dialed Ida Belle's number as I drove.

"Meet me at the far end of Main Street," I said when she answered. "Brandon is on the move."

They were waiting for me about a block from Main Street at the intersection where the downtown traffic was being rerouted. Ida Belle helped boost Gertie into the passenger seat, then climbed in the back. They both looked excited and confused. I handed Ida Belle my phone and told her to navigate.

"You put a tracker on his truck?" Ida Belle asked. "*That's* what you were doing that night at his house."

"Is there anything else you haven't told us?" Gertie asked.

"I think that's it," I said, then remembered that I'd never told them about my conversation with Carter and his reasons why he couldn't be with me. I made a quick decision to let my original answer stand. I wasn't sure yet what *I* thought about that conversation. I definitely wasn't ready to discuss it with anyone else.

A couple miles up the highway, Ida Belle directed me onto a narrow dirt road that led straight into the swamp. No more than a half mile in, cypress trees closed in around us, blocking out a majority of the sunlight.

"Do you know where this goes?" I asked as I slowed for a set of deep holes.

"Yeah," Ida Belle said and grabbed the roll bar to brace herself as the Jeep bounced. "There was an old fishing pier back here. But it collapsed years ago."

"Let me know when we get close to the end of the road," I said. "I don't want him to see us coming."

Ida Belle pointed to a rotted tree up ahead. "Park somewhere near that fallen tree. The road turns left and dead-ends where the pier used to be about fifty yards ahead."

The fallen tree was located in a small clearing, so I pulled off the dirt path and parked next to it. I looked over at Gertie. "Can you make a fifty-yard walk?"

"Heck yeah," she said. "If we need to run, I might be in trouble."

"I think being armed preempts having to run," I said. "I assume we're all packing."

Ida Belle patted her waist. Gertie hefted her purse up in the air. I noticed it took both hands to manage it.

Ida Belle shook her head. "Gertie's probably carrying enough to arm a small country."

"Then we're good," I said.

We climbed out of the Jeep and started down the road. My cell phone showed the dot flashing in one spot, directly ahead. Gertie was limping a bit, so Ida Belle and I put her in between us and bolstered her up a bit on our shoulders to increase pace. Otherwise, Brandon would have been filing for Social Security by the time we got there.

We got to the last bend in the road and stopped. I peered through the brush and could see Brandon sitting in the cab of his truck, windows rolled down. He was looking down and I could see the top ridge of a laptop just over the doorframe.

"What's the plan?" Gertie asked.

"Simple," I said. "We walk up to the truck and ask him what he's doing."

Ida Belle nodded. "Why the hell not."

I put my hand at my back, ready to draw if needed, but I had a feeling it wasn't going to be necessary. Brandon was so engrossed with whatever he was doing that he didn't even hear us approach. It wasn't until we stepped up to the window that I realized he had earbuds in and was listening to music.

"Hi, Brandon," Ida Belle called out.

"Holy shit!" He jumped and yanked the earbuds out as his head swiveled around to face us. "You scared the crap out of me. What are you doing?"

"We were about to ask you the same thing," I said. I held out my hand. "I'm Fortune, by the way. We haven't met, but I know your wife."

As soon as I said the word "wife," Brandon's expression shifted from slightly shocked to slightly afraid.

"Here's the thing," Ida Belle said. "We know you told Peaches that big shrimp were running and that's where you're making all the money you're spending. But we also know that's a lie, and we've seen you landlocked at least three times in the last several days rather than on your boat where you belong."

"Peaches is a nice girl and doesn't need trouble," Gertie said. "So whatever you're up to, you need to get it straightened out and be the husband and father those two deserve. You can't do that in jail."

Brandon's eyes widened. "I...I'm not doing anything illegal. I swear."

"Then what are you doing?" Ida Belle asked.

Brandon's eyes dropped down and a flush crept up his face. "I'm writing books."

I looked over at Ida Belle and Gertie, no idea what to say. If he'd said he was designing women's undergarments, I don't think I could have been more surprised.

"Come again?" Ida Belle said.

"Books," he repeated. "I read every chance I get. Always have. Miss Gertie knows that. I always had a book under my school desk, trying to read in class. Well, one night I was surfing the net and I saw this article about a lady who wrote some stories and published them herself. She bought a new car and remodeled her whole house. I figured what the heck. I love a good pirate story and can't ever find one, so I wrote my own and published it."

I leaned in the window and looked at the laptop screen. "So, Captain Cavendish, are these pirate stories making you money?"

"Yeah," he said, looking a bit surprised by the pronouncement. "At first I thought it was a fluke, but I've published three of them now and I'm making twice what I did shrimping."

"So you've been sneaking around in your truck to write pirate stories," Gertie said. "Unbelievable. Why didn't you just write them on your boat? Then no one would have suspected you of doing something nefarious with all this strange sneaking around."

"I can't work on the boat," he said, looking a bit sheepish. "It makes me sick to my stomach. Can't read there, either."

Ida Belle shook her head. "Of all the strange things we've heard this week, this one is right there at the top of the list, and that's saying a lot."

"You have to tell Peaches," Gertie said. "Before someone else notices your odd daytime behavior. If they mention it to her instead of checking with you like we did..."

"Yes, ma'am," Brandon said. "I could see where that would be a real problem. I wasn't trying to keep it from her necessarily. It's just that it was sorta embarrassing. I mean, I'm a guy's guy—fishing, hunting. You know. And I didn't really figure people would keep buying the stories."

"Surprise!" I said, tickled that the explanation had turned out to be a pleasant one. "You're an author. Tell your wife and go celebrate."

He broke out in a slow smile. "I think I'll do just that. Thanks for not ratting me out."

I looked at Ida Belle and Gertie and grinned. "Looks like our work here is done."

CHAPTER NINETEEN

I DIDN'T SEE Carter until late that night, but that was fine by me. If I'd seen him any sooner, I would have expected it to be with a set of handcuffs or even worse, that plane ticket to Idaho that I was so afraid of. It was just after 11:00 p.m. when I heard the knock on my front door. I'd been attempting a redo on the *Jurassic Park* marathon and got up to answer the door, no doubt at all who it was.

"Are you here to arrest me?" I asked.

"Do you have beer and something to eat that Ally made?" he asked.

"I think I can accommodate you."

"Then I'll leave the handcuffs in my truck."

I stepped back and let him in, then trailed behind him to the kitchen. He pulled two beers out of the refrigerator while I unwrapped a plate of cookies and set them on the table. We both sat and he took a big bite out of a cookie, then a long drink of beer. He slumped back in his chair and looked at me.

"New Orleans police have Francesca in custody," he said.

"That makes me happy," I said.

"I thought it might." He leaned forward in his chair. "I think it's time we talk turkey. What put you onto Nolan?"

I told him everything I'd explained to Gertie and Ida Belle the night before. He listened without interrupting but occasionally nodded. When I finished, he shook his head.

"I hate to say this," he said, "because the last thing I want to do is encourage you, but that's a damned fine piece of deduction."

I felt my face warm with his compliment. "Maybe I just got lucky."

"No. Everything you laid out was based on either instinct or logic. That's the basis of solid police work and how some of the biggest cases get cracked. But I won't disagree that you're lucky to be alive."

I cocked my head to the side and studied him for a moment. "You don't seem surprised by anything I said. You didn't that night, either." I narrowed my eyes at him. "You knew, didn't you?"

"I suspected, but I didn't have enough proof to take it to the DA."

"What put *you* onto Nolan?"

"Like you, I had a feeling that something didn't add up, more than the obvious. Nolan said he heard a scream, then a shot, implying that Gail saw the man shooting her, but Gail's eyes were closed as if in a deep sleep. I know eyes can close after death, regardless of what position they were in when it occurred, but in my experience, that's rarely the case with violent death. It didn't feel right."

I nodded. That had been my experience as well.

"I asked them to screen for drugs in the autopsy," he continued. "She had a large dose of Ambien in her system. I couldn't find where Gail had ever been prescribed the drug. But Nolan had."

"He drugged her. But without being able to prove that, it looks suspicious but not enough so to get a court order for a camera."

"Not to mention I didn't have a motive, until you told me about the insurance policy."

"Francesca will probably spend the rest of her life cursing that assistant for being so efficient."

Carter nodded. "If her assistant hadn't made that phone call that Ida Belle answered, we might have never known about the policy."

"I assume Nolan Bishop wasn't his real name. Have you figured anything out yet? Or can't you say."

He laughed. "Like you care whether or not I'm supposed to tell you. If you thought you could get away with it, you'd break into the sheriff's department to read my case file."

I didn't bother to argue.

"Today, I managed to track him back to his last mark, but I'm sure the more I dig, the more layers I'll uncover."

"And?"

"The man we know as Nolan Bishop was the personal assistant to an invalid named Nolan Bishop, except that man was legit. The real Nolan Bishop's wife died, leaving him with a hefty insurance policy, all aboveboard, and he took on *our* Nolan as a personal assistant. When the real Nolan died of heart failure, he left everything to our guy."

"No autopsy?"

Carter shook his head. "The real Nolan Bishop was a very sick man with a bad heart. He had no living relatives, and since he was at home alone when he died, no one suspected foul play."

"But you do."

"I'd bet my deputy's badge on it, but since the real Bishop didn't have family waiting in the wings, it doesn't matter now.

Still, I sent everything I had on our case to the police in California. If anything, maybe they can learn from it. God knows I just got an expedited education in the long con."

"The whole thing is rather sobering. I mean, I deal with people who run entire criminal organizations based on secrecy and lies but this was so..."

"Personal?"

"Yeah. It makes it harder to process."

Carter nodded.

"So our Nolan stole the man's identity and disability," I said. "Then he moved across the country where no one was likely to recognize the name and set up shop. It is all rather convenient."

"And since he observed the real Nolan collect a huge insurance policy, no questions asked, he knew what his next scam would be."

"It's still mind-boggling that someone would go to that length—play that kind of role—for so long."

"If I had to guess, I think he enjoyed the attention, and he didn't have to be in character all the time. Gail worked long hours in New Orleans. Nolan worked from home so no one bothered him during the day. He was free to pull the shades and live as an able-bodied person with no one the wiser."

"Did he create fake messages from the catfish on Gail's Facebook account?"

Carter nodded. "There was an exchange that night. He probably did it after Gail passed out from the Ambien. It was short, but enough to give us the idea that Nolan wanted us to have."

I looked down at the table, feeling a bit guilty about everything. "What did you say in your report...about shooting Nolan?"

"I said that someone had been in the house the night

before and I was keeping an eye on it—all of which is true, by the way."

"So you were already there when I climbed in the window?"

"Across the street behind the bushes. I left my truck at the sheriff's department as a decoy. Apparently it worked since you showed up." He grinned.

"Your impressive forethought aside, what made you think Nolan would return to the house that night? He'd been there all day."

"An old-fashioned hunch? I honestly don't know that I thought Nolan would return so much as I just had this feeling that I ought to keep watch for a while. Then you came along and things got interesting."

Interesting was one way to describe it. Deadly was another. "I keep waiting for you to yell at me," I said.

"Would it do any good? If you don't know how close you came to dying, then nothing I can say will convince you of it."

I sighed. "I know. If you hadn't been watching, we wouldn't be having this conversation."

"Then instead of yelling at you, I'm going to ask you a favor."

I frowned. "What favor?"

"The next time you have a hunch about something that doesn't look right, tell me."

"I figured you'd think I was crazy."

"So? Even if I think what you suggest is crazy, it doesn't mean I'd ignore it. I have too much respect for your ability to dismiss your concerns. If you think something is off, then it probably is."

"I guess I can do that."

"Good. Now, that being said, this is *not* an open invitation for you to poke around in police business. In fact, it's exactly the opposite. I want you to tell me your suspicions so that I can take care of things myself."

"Okay. Okay. I get your point."

He shook his head. "I don't doubt that you get my point. I doubt the strength of your resolve to stay out of my work."

He rose from the table and stretched his arms over his head. "I'm beat. I'm going to get out of here and head home for a shower and hopefully, a full night of sleep. It will be the first I've had in a while."

I stood up and followed him to the front door. "Thanks for covering for me. Again. And for saving my life. Again. And for not arresting me."

"Again." He smiled.

I stood at the front door, staring at him, and suddenly, a single piece of the puzzle that was my life fell into place, just like Ida Belle said it would.

"When this is over," I said, "I'm not returning to the CIA."

His eyes widened. "You're sure?"

I nodded. Even though I'd made the decision only seconds ago, I'd never been more certain of anything. "If I go back to the CIA, I have to give up everything I've gained since I came here. I don't want to let my friends go, and that's exactly what would happen if I went back to DC."

"What are you going to do instead?"

"Honestly, I don't know. I have plenty of money. Both my parents had insurance policies in my name and they had accumulated a decent amount of money before they died. Except for guns and electronics, I don't spend much, so I can afford to take some time and figure it out."

"Does that mean you're thinking about staying in Sinful?"

I shrugged. "The only thing I know for certain is that I can't go back to who I was before. Too much has changed. The rest is a blank page."

"You'll fill it in," he said.

Before I could respond, he put his arms around me and pulled my body against his, then he lowered his lips to mine and gave me a gentle kiss.

"Something to think about," he said when he released me. "While you're filling in those blank pages."

"You know that I'll never really be a librarian, right?"

He nodded. "I've been weighing the possibility of losing you now against the possibility of losing you later. If I lost you to your job, it would kill me, but the truth is, it's already killing me to lose you now. Sometimes playing it safe can be just as bad as taking risks. I don't want to live with regrets."

"I don't either."

"Tomorrow is the first day of the rest of your life, Fortune Redding."

I smiled. "It looks like it's going to be a good one."

For more adventures with Fortune and the girls read Later Gator.

For information on new releases, please sign up for my newsletter on my website janadeleon.com.

Made in the USA
Las Vegas, NV
14 September 2021

30207850R00138